I0639282

A Detour Home

By Elizabeth Bourgeret

The Bakersfield Series

DCT Publishing- St. Louis, MO

Copyright 2017 Elizabeth Bourgeret

DCT Publishing
St. Louis, MO
Printed in the United States of America

Author photo by Steve Frank
Additional artwork by Kylie Prestein

www.elizabethbourgeret.com
www.facebook.com/EBourgeret

ISBN- 13: 978-0-998286617
ISBN- 10: 0-998 286613

"For I know the plans I have for you. They are plans for good and not for disaster, to give you a future and a hope."
- Jeremiah 29:11

Other Books By Elizabeth Bourgeret

The Bakersfield Series:
Waiting for the Sun
Daddy's Girl
A Detour Home

Historical Fiction:
Captive Heart

Non- Fiction:
Pillow Talk: Connecting More Deeply
to the One You Love- One Question At
A Time
Love Begins With You- Leading With
Love Series

A Detour Home

The Bakersfield Series

Prologue

"Erin, come on. It's time to get up"

"Mother?"

"Get up now, we gotta go."

"But... but it's the middle of the night."

"Don't talk back to me. Just get up."

"Is it time for vacation?"

"Girl, don't make me tell you again. I don't have time for this," Mary Ann snapped. She tied off the top of the trash bag she was holding and took it out into the hallway with her. "You got five minutes to get to the car."

Erin rubbed her eyes and looked over the dimly lit room. The only light was coming from the glowing ballerina on her nightstand and a thin beam of light coming from the hallway where the door was open a crack. She reached over to her nightstand and slipped on her glasses to get a clearer view.

All the drawers to her dresser were pulled open and clothes were scattered about the room. Her closet door was left open but there were only a few items hanging.

She furrowed her brow trying to figure out why her room was in such disarray and then she gasped. "What if there's a fire?" Erin rolled off her bed and crouched trying to decide what to do, while panic was creeping up inside her. She put her slippers on and reached up to grab her robe off the end of her bed. She cupped her hand over her mouth relishing the fresh oxygen that she trapped under her hands. "I'm comin', Mother! I'm comin'!"

Erin ran as fast as she could, keeping her body hunched over and her eyes open only enough to see where she was going. She burst out the front door and dove to safety on the front lawn. Still guarding her mouth with her cupped hands, she looked back at the beautiful two-story house expecting the worst.

"What are you doing?" A high-pitched voice came from her left.

"She is such a retard," a male voice said.

"Carrie, Evan, get back in the house. We'll be back soon."

"No!! Don't let them go in there! They'll get burned by the fire!"

"What fire, Doofus?" Evan spat in her direction.

"There's no fire," Carrie sneered. "I'm so glad this is almost over. Things can get back to normal."

"Go on babies," Mary Ann cooed, "go get your things packed."

The two siblings made their way back inside as Mary Ann narrowed her gaze and looked at Erin. "You. Get in the car."

Erin walked toward the car and when Carrie and Evan looked back at her she said, "Bye Carrie. Bye Evan. I love you. See you when we get back."

"Get in. The car," Mary Ann said through gritted teeth. Her Southern drawl got thicker when she was angry.

Erin did as she was told and climbed into the back seat. The other side of the seat was taken up with two large, very full trash bags. Erin said nothing as Mary Ann drove the car away from her home.

The fifteen minute ride to Susan Carter's house was silent and dark. Erin brightened when she saw their destination. Mary Ann pulled in the familiar driveway and got out of the car. Before shutting the door, Mary Ann poked her head back in, "You wait here."

Erin smiled and re-buckled her seat belt. *Somethin' big is gonna happen if we're stopping to see Miss Susan in the middle of the night*, she thought. Eight year old Erin wondered at the possibilities as she smiled to herself.

Susan Carter, a woman in her forties with light brown skin and dark freckles that dotted her nose, came out of the front door as Mary Ann walked up the flat stone pathway.

"Mrs. Cavanaugh," Susan greeted her coolly.

"Susan," Mary Ann nodded. "Let's just get this over with. Are there papers or somethin' I need to sign?"

"Mrs. Cavanaugh, it doesn't have to be this way."

"I told you on the phone that this wasn't goin' to work. My mind is made up."

10

"But it's the middle of the night. She's probably scared and confused."

"She's re-tar-ded," Mary Ann enunciated each syllable as if Susan was having a hard time understanding. "She won't remember any of this by next week."

Susan drew in a deep breath to try and keep her calm. "She's not retarded."

"Really? 'Cause I have the tests that say otherwise."

"Those tests were given to her two years ago when she was in her most traumatized state. She has improved so much. If you would only..."

Mary Ann took in a deep, annoyed breath and rolled her eyes, "Besides, she's not bonding with my family."

"Now, Mrs. Cavanaugh, that is not true. She loves your son and daughter. She calls you mother..."

"You listen to me, Susan Carter. I am a professional in this school district and an upstanding member of this community. I cannot have an ugly, retarded daughter." Mary Ann turned and stalked back toward the car.

"You really should have thought about that a year ago when you brought her into your home and let her call you mother." Susan Carter was a kind and loving woman, but she could not stand the abuse of children in any way. Her job at the Bakersfield Department of Family Services kept that mission always very clear in front of her.

Mary Ann turned sharply, "I tried to help her. But it's a lost cause. My family shouldn't have to suffer because *she* can't fit in!"

Mary Ann pulled open the car door and grabbed the first trash bag and threw it on the lawn. "Come on, Erin. Get out. You're going to stay here for a little bit."

Erin questioned what her mother was saying and fingered her seat belt buckle. Mary Ann reached for the second trash bag and tossed it beside the other one.

"I said come on!"

Erin undid her seatbelt and looked up to the front porch. She tentatively climbed out of the car. She stood meekly beside the car and waved at Susan.

Susan nodded her head instructing Erin to come her direction. Susan smiled and

12

stretched her arms toward the child. Erin ran to fill her open arms and glowed in her embrace. "Hi sweetie." Susan spoke softly as she kissed the top of her head.

Mary Ann rolled her eyes in disgust. "I'll be back in a few weeks to sign whatever paperwork."

"Come on, baby, let's go inside and get some sleep." Susan wrapped her arm around Erin's shoulder and led her up the one step to the front door.

"You know," Nick Penn tapped the extra salt off his french-fry, "I'm thinking about giving up this whole television thing."

David Ripke's mouth hovered over his next bite of a juicy hamburger. He looked at his best friend momentarily then went ahead with his bite. Around his masticated mouthful of meat, lettuce, tomato, mayo and mustard he still managed to say, "You're just saying that because Christy broke up with you."

Nick stared back blankly at his childhood friend and answered as if he wasn't disgusting, "No. That's not why. I'm just done with it. Besides, that was four months ago."

"Whatever dude. She's been with you for like, twenty years."

"It's only been five, but she was right. We just weren't going anywhere. She did what I didn't have the courage to do."

"Hey Nick! I love your show!" a random stranger passed by their table and patted Nick on the back.

"Thanks, man," Nick responded as the man kept walking.

"Still, no reason to give up the best gig of your life... *our* lives! And remember, if you go, I have to go." David looked as pitiful as he could with mustard stains on the corners of his mouth. "My life is in your hands, dude."

"Spare me the pathos."

"Dude, there's other girls out there."

"I don't want other girls."

"Hey! You're that *Real People, Real Lives* guy! Awesome! I've never met a celebrity before!" The man thrust out his hand.

14

"Always glad to meet a fan," Nick smiled and shook the extended hand.

"Yeah, so... I guess I'll see you around."

Nick raised his eyebrows and nodded.

"Awesome!" The fan drifted away from their table, "Hey guys! I just met that Nick guy!"

"So," Dave continued as if they'd never been interrupted, "What are we talkin here? A little vacation? Time away from California, maybe? Or a lifestyle change? 'Cause if you're talkin about the second choice, I think we really need to discuss this."

"No... no! Not a lifestyle change..." Nick shook his head and wondered where David came up with half his thoughts. "I don't want other girls, I want the right girl. I'm never going to find her here in this world."

David shoved his mouthful of food into his cheek, "Good. You had me worried..."

Nick shrugged, not really listening and continued his thought, "I've been in this business a long time. I'm looking for something... real."

"What are you talking about? You're the *Real People, Real Lives* guy!" David Ripke mimicked their last fan. "You see real people every day."

"Exactly. I want to be a part of that, Rip. I'm tired of hotel rooms and fast food," he tossed his fry back onto the paper placemat. "... cameras following my every move..."

"A lot of people would kill for that kind of misery."

"I know," Nick said, crumbling his paper napkin and tossing it on the table. "It's not that I'm not grateful for the opportunities I've had, I am. I've enjoyed my time in the spotlight. Hell, I've even enjoyed the climb to get here, but I think it's time to move on."

"By moving on, do you mean giving up the California beach-side condo? The ski resort condo in Colorado? The horses in Kentucky? Your brand new Ford- sponsored blah, blah, blah pick-up truck?"

"I can walk away from that, yeah. It's just stuff."

"Excuse me, Mr. Penn? Can I have your autograph?"

Both Nick and Ripke looked beside the table at the bleached blonde, with big blue eyes and pouty lips and cleavage showing all the way down to there...

David bit his lip and smiled. He lifted his eyebrows and cocked his head to the left as if to say, "You gonna walk away from that?"

Nick gave her his million dollar smile but said to Dave, "I guess I can't walk away from everything... I am pretty fond of that truck." He winked at his friend and turned to the blonde, "Sure, always happy to meet a fan..."

Mark Collins came up behind his wife and wrapped his arms around her waist. He kissed the back of her neck and smiled when her body shivered. He continued nuzzling her neck until he reached her ear. When she let out a high-pitched giggle Mark laughed and added the softest bites.

"I guess you're not hungry for what I'm cooking?" Guinevere asked while her body twitched at his every touch.

"I'm hungry for what I'm cookin'..."

"But I'm not even ovulating."

"Can't we practice between times?" Mark turned her body around to face him and kissed her deeply on the mouth, and even after six years of marriage, it still touched her deep in her soul. "Practice makes perfect, you know."

"Mmmm," she unconsciously responded in his ear as he traced her jawline with kisses. "I love you, Mark Collins."

"I love you, too." He stopped kissing her to pull back and look into her eyes. He was trying to decide whether to tell her something or take her to the bedroom. He decided.

He reached behind her and turned off the stove. He slid his embrace down her arm and grabbed her hand. "Come with me," he whispered.

He led her to the living room and sat her down on their beige sofa. He got down on his knees in front of her and then kissed her right hand and then her left. "I have an idea."

"Oh, really?" She smiled sensing a conspiracy.

Mark's light short brown hair was clean cut and perfectly styled even after a full

18

day's work. He cleared a space on the coffee table. His brown eyes hinted at excitement and Gwen couldn't help but catch her breath when she looked at him.

"Okay, now just bear with me." He stretched up to kiss her again before bolting from the room. He poked his head back around the corner, "Stay right there!" and disappeared again.

Gwen bit her bottom lip in anticipation. She glanced down at the coffee table and now the clear spot in the center. *What is he up to?* she wondered. Her fertility brochures and pamphlets were all moved to one side and she was thinking about picking one up to review when Mark came back around the corner.

"Okay... close your eyes." She did as she was told and he ran back over to the coffee table and sat down beside her on the couch. "Now, open!"

She opened her eyes and saw several new brochures spread out in the center of the table.

"What are these?" She smiled at her husband.

"Options." He put his hand on her leg. "Options for our future."

Gwen reached her hand out and picked up the one closest to her. "Cancun?"

"Or…" Mark grabbed another. "Italy?" He picked up still another, "Alaska!" He looked over at her expectantly. "So? What do you think?"

"A vacation?"

"Yeah. Just the two of us. Unwind. You've been so stressed about having a baby that it's all you think about now. Maybe we just need to… set it aside for a while."

Gwen put her hand on Mark's cheek and kissed his nose. "You are the most thoughtful man. I would love to go on vacation. In a year or two we should…"

"No honey, you misunderstood. I mean now. Leave, I don't know, like next month. I have some vacation coming and you could…"

"I can't leave right now." Gwen's face had a mask of panic come across it. "I… I have too much to do! I'm the Artistic Director at the Centre! I can't just leave. I have my classes to teach, the office to run and we have a performance coming in six months; and you know how much work it is preparing for that... but most importantly, I have a new round of treatments that I'm eligible for next month. We can't miss those or it's another three months before..."

"Baby, baby... relax. This... This is exactly what I'm talking about. You need to give yourself a break."

"Honey, it's my job! I have responsibilities. You know how busy I am."

"And what about me?" Mark snapped back. "Yeah, I see how it is. Your job, then this need to have a baby and maybe if there's time left over, you can leave some space for me? What are you going to do when a baby comes along with your precious Fine Arts Centre?"

Gwen stopped short, not expecting his harsh words. He didn't understand. Nothing was more important than this baby... she'd make time when the time was right. She couldn't go gallivanting across the country.... "Mark, I can't miss this next treatment. What if it's the one?"

Mark scooted to the edge of the couch and took her hands in his. "I know how much it means to you to have a child...but... when is... enough? I mean... how will you know when..." he dropped his head down for a moment not finding the right words. "When is it... enough?"

"What are you saying?"

"I'm just saying..." Mark swallowed hard before going on, "What if we weren't meant to be parents?"

"We are, Mark," she answered him matter-of-factly. "It just hasn't been time yet." Her voice was so filled with peace that Mark almost caved.

"Baby, we've tried so many times. I can't watch you go through another miscarriage."

Gwen's face clouded over when she thought of the babies she'd lost, but she shook her head. "God is faithful. And there are other possibilities for us. We haven't tried..."

"Guinevere, we have to face reality."

"Cancun? Alaska? Is that where we'll find reality, Mark?"

"No... it was just a suggestion," Mark turned away; defeated again. He started collecting the brochures from the table.

"You still want a baby, right? A family?"

"Of course I do," he said flatly. He stood and walked back to his office and closed the door behind him.

Gwen's eyes opened abruptly. She was in her bedroom. The moon cast shadows of the big oak tree across her wall. She blinked. She reached across her bed to the empty space beside her. Mark was gone. He was really gone. A dream... A tear slipped from the corner of her eye.

Chapter One

Six Months Earlier

Guinevere counted off slowly, "...five, six, seven, and..." Her blonde hair was bound neatly in a bun. She wore the standard "uniform" of a ballet mistress: black leotard, pink tights, pink ballet slippers and a long ballet wrap-around skirt. "Tereza, arch your back, please. Erin, knees pointed to the sides, yes, thank you." The music of Chopin played softly and rhythmically in the background keeping tempo while the eleven girls of the class moved elegantly through their bar work.

Gwen placed her hands on Emily's waist to adjust her posture. "Feel the difference?"

Emily nodded. "And when you arch..." Gwen stretched her hands along Emily's arm

25

and back. "Yes... perfect. That's what I'm looking for." Gwen smiled.

Emily beamed under her words of praise.

"Sharon, you look so pretty today with that flower in your hair."

She giggled and in her quiet, tiny voice, "Thank you." And her smile lit up the room.

"And arms out to the sides... finish in plié... and... very good. Beautiful. Nice job girls. Okay, and I guess that does it for class today."

The girls shook out their arms and legs and went to gather their things.

One by one, they came by to hug Miss Gwen before they made their way to the door. "Bye sweetie." She hugged each one of them. "See you next week." Gwen looked over to see eight-year old Erin still packing up her dance bag.

"Erin, honey, how did you manage to get your stuff so spread out?"

Erin looked up and pushed her glasses back up on her nose. Her golden blonde hair was falling in her face, with curly sprigs springing out in every direction. She shrugged her shoulders in answer to her teacher's query. Gwen bent down and helped her put things back in her black and gold duffle.

"There. I think that's everything," Gwen smiled at her and pushed Erin's hair back over her ears. "We're going to have to work on that bun of yours. I can't see that pretty face when your hair is hanging in it."

Erin smiled. "I know. Sorry. My mother said we were in too big a hurry so I had to do it myself."

"Okay, well, if you need help, just ask. Fair enough?"

"Okay!" They both stood up from their crouching position. Erin wrapped her arms around Gwen's waist. "I loooove you, Miss Gwen."

"I love you too, honey. See you next week?"

"Yup!"

They walked out of the classroom together and met the last parent waiting for the last student.

"What took you so long?" Mary Ann Cavanaugh stood in the hallway with her arms crossed in front of her. Her dark brown hair was swept up in a neat twist with curls spilling over the top. She wore a cream colored pant suit with an animal print scarf and matching shoes. When she noticed Gwen's arm draped across Erin's shoulder, her voice went up a notch and sugary sweetness dripped from every word. "Now, baby-girl, didn't Mother tell you that we had to leave right after class?"

"Yes, but I couldn't…"

"Now sugar, Miss Gwen doesn't have time for this nonsense, she's got other things to do."

Erin turned to look at her ballet teacher, "Sorry, Miss Gwen."

"Honey, you're fine. I have plenty of time."

"Go on now, dumplin'. Go wait in the car so Mother can talk to Miss Gwen."

"Kay. Bye Miss Gwen!" She walked and waved. "Bye Miss Danni! Bye Miss Gillian!" Erin made her way down the hall hugging and waving to the other teachers she passed as she made her way to the door. "Bye, Ms. Betty!" Erin stuck her face in the office and straightened out her back leg in a perfect arabesque. "Goooood byyyyeeee Miss Betty!" she sang.

"Erin! I said get in the car, now!"

Gwen stifled a giggle when Erin spun around in a pirouette, "Sorry, Mother!" and flitted out the door. Gwen smiled after her.

"Erin is such a swe..."

"Mess! I know. I just don't know what to do with that girl!"

Gwen laughed, "Not exactly the word I was going for but..."

"You know she's mentally retarded, right? But for heaven's sake, I didn't know it would be this hard."

"She doesn't seem..."

"They had her tested. She is. I just don't know how they expect me to deal with that girl and raise my own two."

"Foster parenting not going so well?"

Mary Ann went into full Southern Belle mode, "You just don't know how difficult it is tryin' to raise a girl like that. I mean, she just doesn't understand things I'm tellin' her. I tell her to do somethin' and ten minutes later, it still isn't done..." she moaned in her deep Southern drawl.

"That sounds like a typical eight year old." Gwen laughed trying to make the heavy conversation a little lighter.

"Well, you say that because you don't *really* have any children, Miss Collins."

Gwen felt the slap exactly where it was intended. She straightened her posture and the levity left her voice. "You wanted to speak to me, Mary Ann?"

"Oh yes, I am in a hurry, you know. I just want you to monitor her behavior. I don't think she's adjusting well."

"Really? It's only been six months, but she's doing wonderfully in my class. She is blossoming beautifully."

Mary Ann looked away, "Well, I meant more about her relationship with the other children."

"Well," Gwen thought about her words, "she's made a lot of new friends."

"...I say it 'cause she's just not fittin' in at home."

Gwen reached out and gave her hand a squeeze. "Give it time, Mary Ann. I'm sure she's falling in love with all of you." Gwen waited until Mary Ann looked up, then she nodded and smiled at her. "Give it time," she said again. "I'm sorry to cut you off, but my next class is gathering."

Mary Ann waived her off in dismissal and shrugged while Gwen turned back to the door and greeted her teenage class.

Mark lounged on the couch with a glass of Pepsi on ice in his right hand and the remote resting on his left leg.

Guinevere breezed through the front door and saw Mark sitting with his back to her. "Hey, whatcha watchin'?"

"Hi Babe. It's a reality show called *Real People, Real Lives* with Nick Penn.

"Huh, never heard of it." She slipped up behind the couch and kissed him on his head. "I've been thinking about you all day..." She whisked away down the hall to their bedroom.

She emerged moments later wearing her satin bathrobe, brushing her hair and had a thermometer hanging from the corner of her mouth.

Mark didn't take his eyes away from the television even when she plopped down beside him. Gwen curled closer to him and swung her feet underneath her body. She picked up Mark's arm and put it around her shoulders careful not to displace the remote.

"I missed you today," she cooed in his ear, the thermometer clicking against her teeth.

"Did you?"

"Mmm, I did." She nosed him and kissed his cheek. "And just as I suspected, my temperature is just right." She pulled the thermometer from her mouth and showed him. She smiled coyly at her husband who was not giving the feedback she'd hoped for. "Do you… want to… come into the other room with me?" hoping he would catch the not-so-subtle-hint.

"Why don't you stay here with me on the couch. I can hold you, like this," he leaned forward and set his glass on the coffee table and wrapped her in both his arms. "We can watch Nick Penn and…"

"Who's Nick Penn?"

"I told you, he's on this show. He goes to various cities and towns and replaces one of the family members for three days to see how challenging their lives are. This week he

32

has to be the teenage daughter," Mark laughed in the telling. "It's pretty darn funny. He has to go to cheerleading practice after the commercial."

"But honey, my temp is *just right*..."

"I heard you," Mark sighed, "but couldn't we maybe skip this once and just spend time together?"

"I'd love to spend time with you... but... maybe when all the planets aren't aligned?" she said sarcastically.

"Baby, I do want to, but..." he sighed again, "You've taken all the passion and fun out of our love making and turned it into a job." He paused for a moment, reviewing his last sentence in his head, before adding with a droop in his shoulders, "Oh man... Jerry was right..."

"Jerry?"

"I DO sound like a girl!"

Gwen rolled her eyes and pulled away from Mark's embrace. "I don't mean to pressure you, Mark, but this is how we make babies."

"Yes." Mark leaned forward and took a sip of his drink. "I am well aware of the scientific process of baby-making, thanks to you. Sometimes, I think you'd rather have a baby than have me."

"Don't be silly. I can't have a baby without you."

"No, I suppose not."

Guinevere paused before moving back in with another approach, "Do you want me to put on the fishnet stockings?"

Mark looked at his wife as a smile spread across her face.

"I do like the fishnet stockings..."

"Meet me down the hall in five minutes," she giggled.

"If you insist..." Mark caved.

A week later, Gwen found some luxury time and relaxed in a cool bath. Her job at the Centre was both stressful but fulfilling. These times to herself were precious, but she would be willing to give them all up to hold a baby, her baby, in her arms.

"Wherever you are and when the timing is just right you'll come to us little baby. And we'll be ready for you. I might have to wait, but I'll never give up because I know I was meant to be your mommy."

Guinevere Collins smoothed out the bubbles in the bathtub and built them back up again into small mounds. She smiled to herself and used her drippy wet hands to move away the loose hairs from her face.

She furrowed her brow and doubt clouded her mind. "I'm going to be 32 years old in a few months, Lord. Are you sure there's still time for me?" She closed her eyes tightly and shook away her negative thoughts. "Some faith I have... It's YOUR timing, Lord, not mine." She rolled her eyes at her doubts and as much as she hated to get out, she pulled herself from the tub.

Mark met her in the bedroom. She was wrapped in a towel. She hummed and pulled the clip from her long blonde hair and started to brush through it. Mark handed his wife her lavender bathrobe, which she slipped on and let the towel fall.

"Nice bath?" Mark asked tentatively as he sat on the edge of the bed.

"Mmmm, it was. There's just something about a nice cool bath on a hot day. Hey, I was thinking... I know it's a last resort but I was just going to go ahead and look online about adoption."

35

"Gwen..."

"I know it's not an option you're fond of..."

"Gwen..."

"... but I've talked with a lot of people that..."

"Guinevere." Mark's voice was stern.

Gwen looked back over her shoulder and caught Mark's eyes. He immediately dropped his gaze and played with a loose thread on the bedspread. He took in a deep breath, "I'm done, Gwen."

Gwen wrapped her lavender robe tighter and cinched it. She eased herself on the bottom edge of the bed and tightened her waist knot again. "What did you say?" she asked.

Mark kept his eyes down. "I said," he sighed, "... I said 'I'm done.'"

"Done with what, exactly?" When he didn't answer, she leaned back on her elbow and tipped his chin up with her finger to draw his eyes to hers. "What's the matter, Sweetie?"

She watched, as his eyes clouded with pain. She ran her thumb across his cheekbone and looked at him with concern.

He cleared his throat and said, "I can't do this anymore."

"Honey, what's wrong? Whatever it is, we can work it out." She moved closer and reached for his hand. She brought his hand to her lips and kissed it gently. "What can't you do anymore?" She kissed his fingers.

Mark pulled his hand back from her and turned away. He took in a deep breath and turned back and did his best to look her in the eye. "Guinevere, I'm leaving you." He played with a piece of skin on his thumb only stealing a peek in her direction.

She sat up from leaning on her elbow and turned to face him. She wasn't hearing this right. He wouldn't look at her. "What?" she asked, but wasn't sure if any sound came out. He did not respond. She turned away from him on the edge of the bed and looked at nothing on her lap. She let his words and their meaning sink in.

"Gwen... Gwen. I'm sorry. I just..." He looked up to the ceiling wishing for an easier way. Does he say more? Is this where he leaves? Did she even hear him?

Mark got up and went to sit closer beside her. "Baby, say something... Did you

37

hear what I said?" She stiffened when he tried to touch her. She instead, stood up and turned to look at him. He put his head down and was rubbing his forehead when she started to cry. She backed up putting distance between them until she bumped into the dresser. She couldn't wrap her head around this moment in time. Her brain was spinning wildly looking for clues for how she is supposed to behave. She looked closely at him.

He was just sitting there. He was just having a conversation. He was in his work clothes. Tan slacks, a light blue button-down. This could be any day... but his words... Her eyes burned...

Mark wrapped his hands behind his neck, "Baby, I... I'm sorry. I just can't... I..." he clenched his fists and let out a vocal sigh. "Look, I don't know what else to say. Could you at least talk to me?"

Tears poured down Guinevere's cheeks. She covered her mouth with her hand as if she were afraid to let any sound escape her lips. Her head was spinning. Her dreams were crashing. Her heart was breaking.

"Baby, listen. I told you that…"

She locked eyes with him, cutting his thought short. Her eyes told him that she wouldn't accept excuses. He changed his tactic. "We don't want the same things for our futures."

Gwen's eyebrows pinched together and she cocked her head not understanding but still unable to bring herself to speak.

"I've changed. It's me. I… don't want the same things anymore. You get so focused on something and… " his voice drifted off. "It makes you really good at your job but… You are so focused on getting a baby that you didn't even notice. I… I don't want to be a father."

Gwen felt like she'd been stabbed and her life was spilling out through the gaping hole. Her brain was frantically searching through memories for proof of this change. Her research was interrupted with the newest data being entered in…

"I'm filing for divorce."

Was the room spinning?

"I don't want anything," he continued. "What I mean is, you can have the house…" He looked up at her but didn't cross the space that was between them. He could see how he had hurt her. She's strong. She'll get over this... it's for the best, he told himself even as she stood there silent and trembling. "Won't you say something?"

Her eyes darted to the closet and his followed.

He sighed. "Tonight. I'm leaving tonight. Well, now actually. My bags are waiting by the front door. I'll be staying at Jerry's for a few days... if... you need me."

Gwen's eyes narrowed at the mention of Mark's best friend. Instantly, she knew that he had something to do with this decision.

"Look... I'll call you later this week and we can... talk."

She closed her eyes and felt the tears soothe the burning as they spilled over. She turned her head away from him still trying to keep her sobs under control.

"Well, I guess that's it then," he shrugged his shoulders and folded his arms across his chest only to unfold them a moment later. "Baby, I'm sorry." He walked to the door. "I'm sorry I hurt you. I... I love you." He looked at her a moment more before closing the bedroom door behind him.

Gwen stood quietly, using the dresser for support. She listened for the click of the front door and then silence.

Her legs trembled and could no longer support her. She slid down the front of the walnut dresser to the floor. She filled her lungs with air and let out the most mournful of wails.

Her body shook as sobs took over shaking her thin frame.

"You don't get to say you love me!" She called out to no one. "You don't do this to someone you love!

Her body rolled over on its side and released its anguish. "I didn't know, God, I didn't know. What do I do now?" She dropped her head to her knees, "What do I do now?"

Dave Ripke had his one leg crossed over the other and his large video camera resting on his lap. He steadily worked, cleaning the lens with a soft cloth. "So marry her already. That's all she wants."

"Yeah, but, does she want to marry me or a TV personality?" Nick Penn sat in his director's chair that bore his name. His feet were kicked out in front of him and crossed at the ankles. His tell-tale ball cap slanted down to cover his eyes. His head rested on his hands, which were folded behind his neck.

"I know... I know... the burdens of showbiz."

"I don't love her, Rip. There's the problem." Nick stretched, lifting his hat from his head. He ran his fingers through his hair, once, then twice, then plopped the hat back down right where it was before. He resumed his former stretched out position. "I don't even know if I'd recognize love if it came right up to me. I've just... settled for so long, and now she throws this 'let's get married' thing at me. It's like a wake up call. What have I been doing for the past five years?"

"C'mon man, you've got a pretty good gig going. You have a major hit tv series, a hot girl on your arm... dude, you're writing your own future!"

Nick sat up and rested his elbows on his knees. He picked his hat up again... once... twice and plopped it back down. "You're not hearing me either. I feel like I'm speaking another language or something. Yeah, the money is great. I love doing the work and Christy is a great gal... and I know I sound selfish, but... there's something missing. I'm not... happy. There's just something missing. It feels like... like... I'm living someone else's life."

Ripke burst out laughing. "Living someone else's life!!" He laughed through his words. "Cause... cause that's kinda your job. What the whole tv series is about? Get it?"

Nick just looked over at his friend and rolled his eyes and wondered how their friendship had lasted so long. They were so different.

Nick sighed and leaned back in his chair assuming that the conversation had ended. He felt stupid for not being content with his dream life.

"Okay, okay, so seriously then, how do you find love?" Dave blew hot air onto his lens again.

Nick chuffed, "I dunno, but I know it's out there. Look at my parents."

"So why'd you stay with Christy so long if you didn't love her?"

Nick shrugged and peeked out from under his hat at his best friend and camera man, "Convenience, I guess. She just didn't leave..."

"Well, if you're looking to meet someone new, I know about these twins..."

Nick lifted his hat slightly just to make eye contact and mouth the word, "No," along with a slow shake of his head.

Chapter Two

Present Day

"God! How could you?" Guinevere whimpered as she sat alone on the stage painting a set. "I thought you wanted me to have children! How am I supposed to have a family now? I'm all alone! Why would you put such a need inside me and then leave me all alone?" She struggled to see the task before her as tears poured from her eyes.

Mark had tried to call several times, but she refused to answer. The entire divorce proceedings went surprisingly easy. Gwen barely had to participate at all. Just sign a few papers and it was done. Six years of marriage... over with a signature or two.

Evelynn St. Lawrence, the Executive Director of the Bakersfield Fine Arts Centre and Gwen's best friend, came into the theatre to bring Gwen some food and tissue. She

45

wore her ballet clothes but had a pair of sweat pants on over her tights. Her dark brown hair was swept up in a bun and she wore a pair of bedroom slippers since she was between classes. She opened the Styrofoam lid and unsheathed the plastic silverware from their wrapper. She sat down on the stage floor beside her friend. "I know you know this, but... God does have a plan for your life. It may not seem like it right at the moment but..."

"He doesn't! He took all my dreams away from me!"

Evelynn reached out her hand and placed it on Gwen's knee, "That means he must have something better planned for you."

"I know you're trying to help, believe me. I know all the things you're going to say to try and make me feel better, because I've said them to everyone else. I've been a Christian all my life..." her voice hitched as she tried to finish her thoughts, " but... but... I just don't believe God cares about me. I... I... I'm not important enough." Tears of self-pity poured down Gwen's cheeks. She avoided looking at Evelynn's face, knowing that pity was looking back at her. She raised her hand, "And... don't. I know He knows about the hairs on my head and sparrows that fall... I know all that... so please... just let it go..."

Evelynn let out a breath she didn't realize she was holding and straightened her posture. "Okay then," she began, "Let's look at this another way." Moving to the front of the brain was the business side of Evelynn. The side that makes her good at what she does.

"Mark has left you. It doesn't matter why. At this point he is gone and he is not coming back. It's been months now. You have two choices. You can throw your life away letting him control your emotions, or... you can step up and take control yourself. I propose the latter. You are far too valuable a person to allow someone else to make your decisions for you. Life isn't easy. Sometimes you really do have to roll with the punches."

"But you don't understand..."

"Gwen. You know that I love you more than any other human on this earth." She took in a deep breath and continued, "We have all had hard times. Yours are no more or less painful than others." She swallowed hard, but continued, "You have to choose if it's going to beat you, or you are going to beat it."

Gwen looked up at her best friend and saw that glimmer of pain cross over Evelynn's eyes that no one else would ever be able to perceive. Evelynn's husband left her only two years before. She was truly alone. No family, just the Centre.

"I'm sorry. You're right…"

Evelynn's voice and posture softened. "This is only a season. Things will get better."

"I am so lost…"

"I understand." Evelynn leaned in and wrapped her friend in an embrace. "But do you really think that the God that created the sunrise and sunset can't get you through this?" She pulled back to look at Gwen's face. She grabbed a tissue and wiped away Gwen's tears. "Your words and your prayers for me got me through my season. Your love and faith helped heal me. You. Gwen Collins, were my rock. Please, don't turn your back on it now."

Gwen nodded as another stream of tears slipped from her eyes. Evelynn sighed with a smile and just handed her the box of tissues.

Evelynn smiled lovingly then switched back to business and stood. "I have to go and you need to eat." Evelynn stood and brushed the dust from her sweats. "Oh, there's one more thing. Your student... Erin? Not only has she been absent from her classes here, but I was told she also hasn't been at school for two weeks. The mother paid until the end of the month here, but I thought it was strange that she wasn't at school, as well. It's like she just disappeared. I know how much she loved your classes."

"That is strange."

"Well, you think on it, and let me know if you want to pursue it."

A smile spread across Guinevere's face. "I know what you're doing..."

Evelynn smiled back but said nothing, only raising her eyebrows in question.

"Distraction?" Gwen leaned against her wrist holding a paint soaked brush, being careful not to get paint on her face.

Evelynn winked at her friend. "Call me later." She turned and walked down the front steps of the stage and off toward the lobby.

"I will." Gwen watched her walk down the center aisle, "Hey Evie..." Evelynn turned back to the voice. "Thanks."

Gwen sighed and replaced her paintbrush with a plastic fork. She heard Evelynn's words going through her head but couldn't stop the tears from returning. She's stronger than I am... she reasoned. I can't do the things she can... Even Gwen's mother, Judy, showed her God's provision time and time again throughout the Bible, but Gwen was angry... hurt... betrayed. It had nothing to do with God... except He allowed her entire world to be shattered and her dreams to be forsaken... Her muscles tightened and her lips pursed at the thought of His betrayal. "I haven't asked for much, God." Her brows drew together as the anger welled up inside her. "I have been a good person. Why would you make me want to have children if you had no intention of giving them to me? That's just mean!" She dropped her fork onto the portioned foam plate of food and laid back on the stage. She clenched her teeth and gave a deep guttural scream, feeling release when she heard it bounce off the walls of the theatre.

Breathless, she flung her arm over her face. She couldn't stop the tears. Evelynn's words came back to her... "Don't let him control your emotions..."

"Pfft... easier said than done. You have so much... too much control over your emotions..." she said out loud.

It was her mother's turn to remind her of all she should be grateful for. Her mother would not approve of her carrying on this way when there were other things to take precedence.

Her mother, Judy's voice was crystal clear in Gwen's mind, as she has reminded her on many occasions, "Reflect on the many ways you have been blessed..."

Gwen tried to block her thoughts but, perhaps, out of sheer obedience, she reflected...

I have the best job in the world, her mind told her. *I get to work with kids everyday and watch them grow and become more confident little human beings. I get to use every single part of the liberal arts degree that my father said would be a waste of time. I dance. I sing. I build sets.; I direct. I choreograph. I paint. I run an entire arts department... I get to work with my best friend... I love the kids and they love me...*

I wonder why Erin hasn't been in class?

I'm strong and healthy... She loves her classes...

I have a nice house- that I'm all alone in... I have nice neighbors- who are probably gossiping about me right now...

I hope she's not sick... She seemed fine the last time I saw her... oh! But her mother!

Did I put the costume order in?

Gwen sat straight up. "I know what you're doing, Lord," she said out loud. "This is the part where you're going to make me get up, get my big-girl panties on and get back to work, isn't it?" She sulked for a moment more. *Did she mention anything about being absent? Moving? Vacation?* Gwen looked around the room not really seeing, but searching her brain for clues of Erin's absence. "Fine... I'll call."

Gwen unglued her wet hair from across her face and took in a deep breath, knowing she must absolutely look a mess.

She reached for her phone, which has been on silent for days, and clicked it to life. "Hmm, four calls from Mark... don't care."

She tapped the screen making the missed calls disappear.

She tapped it again and pulled up the phone number for Mary Ann Cavenaugh. She tapped the number. It rang two times and went directly to voice mail. Gwen disconnected and frowned. "Something just isn't right."

She decided to stop painting for a moment, since she wasn't really getting anything done anyway, and concentrate on finding her missing student.

Gwen put away her paint and rinsed out her brush and made her way to the office where Miss Betty was pasting together the new programs for the next show.

"Hey, Betty." Gwen called out entering the office.

Betty looked up from her work and smiled, "Hello honey. It's nice to see you."

Gwen smiled, knowing her meaning, "I know, I've been a little absent lately." She could feel the tears trying to flow again, but she fought against it.

"It's alright, sweetie. I'm just happy to see you." Miss Betty. So much more than the office manager of the Bakersfield Fine Arts Centre, but also the resident grandmother to every soul in the building; always ready with a hug or a slice of wisdom to share with anyone who might be in need.

Gwen sighed, "Speaking of being absent, I was wondering about my student Erin. She's in my six o'clock Tuesday class. Evelynn said that she is basically missing from everywhere. Have you heard anything?"

"I haven't. Let me check her file." Betty went to her filing cabinet and in her own special system was able to pull out every shred of information the Center has on little Miss Erin. She tucked her pure white wavy hair behind her ear and licked her finger tips before she started riffling through papers. "It says that she has paid for the rest of the month but she hasn't been in attendance for your class or her drama class or ... Jeanne's art class." Betty bit her bottom lip and raised her eyebrows in concern.

"I guess it really is none of my business. I mean, kids come and go here all the time, but I just have this niggling feeling that something is just... off."

"Let me know how I can help," Betty called out as Gwen turned to exit the office.

The shower helped her to clear her head. Her eyes were still a little puffy, but the redness had faded to pink. She decided to regain her life in small steps. She'd conquer the world next week, but first she needed some food. Her stomach growled as she remembered the untouched food Evelynn brought her. She didn't want real food. She needed magic, healing food. Like, ice cream. Mint chocolate chip, to be precise.

She walked into Walmart keeping her head down, hoping no one would make eye contact.

This being the small town that it is, the people in her circle of life already knew the humiliating details behind her crying jags and pity-party, so either they will keep their distance or the busy bodies will swarm her looking for the dirty details and disguise it as sympathy.

She walked down the aisles trying to remember that she didn't need to shop for Mark... who would still not be at her home when she returned. When do those automatic thoughts and feelings stop coming?

Her eyes scanned the men's clothes remembering that Mark needed a shirt for... "He can get his own shirt," she growled under her breath and gripped the bar of the shopping cart a little tighter.

She turned left down a completely different aisle and perused the wall of sweets.

"That's what I need..." She dropped her gaze and shook her head. "I'll get the kids some treats to apologize for my moodiness. It's not about me at all, is it?" she laughed to herself finally "getting it."

Out of the corner of her eye, she saw someone enter the same aisle then quickly back out. Instinctively, Gwen looked up and saw Mary Ann Cavanaugh as she was trying to maneuver her cart around the cereal end-cap.

"Mary Ann?" Gwen called out. She didn't answer. Gwen pushed her cart to the side and went after her. "Mary Ann!" she called out again.

Mary Ann stopped, "Oh, Gwen, how are you? I didn't even see you there," she laughed nervously.

Gwen ignored the blatant lie and got straight to the point of her pursuit. "Mary Ann, I heard that Erin hasn't been in school or her classes for a while. Is she okay?"

"I'm sorry. I don't know who you mean."

Gwen furrowed her brow in confusion. "Erin... your daughter?"

"I don't have a daughter named Erin." Mary Ann straightened and looked... insulted?

"I... I'm sorry... your... foster daughter. Is she all right?"

"I don't know what you're..." Mary Ann sighed. She looked uncomfortably around the aisle at nothing and habitually adjusted her bun, "She's gone."

"Gone? What happened?"

"Gwen, she just wasn't bonding with the family."

"I don't understand," Gwen looked at her confused "that can't be right. She loved your family. She talked about you all the time!"

Mary Ann pulled her shoulders back ready to face off and cocked her eyebrow. "Well, she was quite the little actress then, wasn't she? She was an entirely different child at my home."

"Forgive me if I don't believe you. She called you mother!"

"Gwen," her accent was syrupy sweet, "I heard about what happened... you must be under a terrible amount of stress..."

"What happened to Erin?"

"We sent her back." Mary Ann shrugged as if the answer was obvious.

"What?" Gwen's jaw dropped, "This is a little girl, not a pair of jeans! You don't just 'return' them when it gets difficult!" Gwen could feel her body shaking and her voice rose in octave as well as in volume.

Mary Ann snapped back in loud staccato words, "You. Don't. Understand." Her lip curled in disgust as she spoke. "She's mentally handicapped. I was going to save her. Make her beautiful." Tears began to rim her black lined eyes, but Gwen knew the tears weren't for the child, but for herself. "My friend adopted a child and she's dainty and sweet... She's smart and wins pageants..."

58

a tear slipped over Mary Ann's cheek, her words painful ... broken.

"But Erin loved you."

"She was UGLY and STUPID!" Venom filled her voice now. "I put her in the prettiest dresses but she was clumsy and awkward. I bought her contacts, but she refused to wear them! Why do you think I put her in your stupid classes? She's obviously broken and retarded beyond repair. I would tell her somethin' and she would just stare at me. She refused to speak. Like she's some kind of animal."

Gwen looked around self-consciously positive that there must be a crowd gathering.

"She's not like other girls," Mary Ann sneered as she continued, "I am a professional and pillar of this community! I cannot have an ugly, retarded daughter!" Mary Ann spoke with conviction as if she had somehow been tricked into taking a poor little orphan-girl that was just... a girl and not the next cover of People magazine.

Local Pillar of the Community Turns Pauper Into Princess...

Gwen could physically feel her stomach turn over. She saw the woman before her in a new light. A selfish, arrogant being, feeling completely justified in the actions she'd taken to save herself and her family the humiliation of adopting a less than perfect child.

"What have you done?" Gwen breathed out and backed away.

Guinevere ran down the center aisle of Walmart completely forgetting about her own reasons for being there.

God! What are you doing up there? Gwen screamed in her head. *Isn't it enough that you've taken away my dreams? Why would you let that little girl be treated like that? It's bad enough that she'd been taken from her OWN HOME but now this? Why won't you DO something?*

Gwen slid into her car and slammed the door shut behind her. "Well if YOU won't do anything, I WILL!" she yelled out loud inside her car.

Gwen drove the few minutes from the Walmart to the parking lot of the Centre.

She burst through the office door and startled Betty. "Gwen! Are you all right? What is it?"

"Do you know what she did?"

Betty's eyebrows raised and she wondered if an answer was really required in this instance.

It was not.

"She sent her back!" Gwen shouted. She paced in circles around the office dodging the desks and copier. "Like a used pair of jeans!"

Betty, although confused, didn't interrupt, but was secretly thankful that there were no children or parents in the office.

"How could God let this happen?" Gwen continued.

"I'm not sure of all the details here, but if God allowed it to happen, I'm sure it fits into His grander plan," Betty offered.

Gwen snapped her head back to Betty in anger. "Whatever. I'm just not buying that anymore. Not any more."

"I'm sorry to hear that," Betty acknowledged. "But He does tell us that He will turn things around for good for..."

"Yeah, yeah... for those who believe in Him... Well, I believed. And look where it's gotten me?"

"Well, I have a few moments... let's look into that, shall we?" Betty calmly took out a blank sheet of paper fully intending to continue the exercise.

"Nothing! All I wanted was a family!" she paced.

"Families come in all shapes and si..."

"He can do whatever He wants to me. I don't even care anymore. But poor Erin..." the tears broke through the anger. Betty rose from behind her desk and wrapped her arms around Gwen halting her pacing.

"Why don't you sit down and tell me what's happened." Betty led her to the chair that set at the end of her desk. She took her usual place in her office chair and folded her hands to listen.

Gwen told her the whole story about meeting up with Mary Ann. Miraculously, the Centre's phones managed to stay quiet.

When she finished, Betty stayed silent for an extra moment sending up a prayer for all involved, then she quietly placed her hands over Gwen's.

"If I may..." Betty started cautiously, "I'd like to suggest we talk to my daughter, Gillian. As you know, she has a lot of experience with the foster care system and she may be able to shed some light on this situation." Betty looked over her shoulder at the clock on the wall and noticed that there was only six minutes left until the classes let out.

"Why don't you go to your office," Betty suggested, "and get freshened up and meet me back in here when all the parents and kids get moved about." Betty traced her finger down the day's schedule. "Gillian doesn't have a class next hour, so we can talk."

Gwen nodded, exhausted by the swarm of emotion. She disappeared out the back door and retreated to her office.

"That's terrible!" Gillian exclaimed after Gwen and Betty retold the Erin story. "That poor girl! I just can't believe it! ... of all the selfish, self-centered... pillar of the community... what a bunch of..."

63

"Yes, dear, we all feel the same way. But what can we do about it?" Betty tried to calm down the emotions in the room. She really was the "office Mom/ grandma"... all of it.

"Well," Gillian sighed, "my first thought is to call Susan Carter. She's the social worker for this area and a good friend." Gillian's mind was going a mile a minute. "Are you free tonight?" she directed the question toward Gwen.

"I... I guess so..."

"Let me give her a call and see if we can meet at my house around eight?" She was talking and looking through her cell phone for Susan's number. "Wait... all the kids will be home tonight and we will find no peace..." Gillian rolled her eyes. "Do you want to meet up here?"

"We can meet at my house," Gwen offered. "It's quiet and empty."

Gillian gently reached out and squeezed Gwen's arm. "Okay. Your house," she smiled. "I'll call you if anything changes." Gillian pushed the call button and stood to leave the room. "It's going to be all right," she whispered. "Hey Susan, it's Gillian...." ...and she was down the hall.

Betty beamed and chuckled to herself, "My girl gets stuff done." She smiled at Gwen who was feeling more than a little lost. "Do you mind if I tag along?"

"Of course not," Gwen blinked getting her bearings. "I guess I'll see you tonight, then."

Chapter Three

"Nick Penn leaves big time for small time living," Nick read aloud from the headline of the Entertainment section. His light brown hair was in need of a haircut, but he tucked the extra pieces around his ears under his ball cap.

"Is that really what you're going to do, Nick?" one of the sound girls asked him.

"Well Terenda, it says it right here," he held up the tabloid and pointed to the large black, block print. "It must be true," he smiled warmly at her.

"We sure are going to miss you 'round here."

"Well, I'm going to miss it too."

"Really?" she asked, surprised.

"No... probably not." He laughed and was joined by those around him.

"C'mon, Nick! Let's cut the cake!" Rip called out to him, drooling over the three-tiered decorated confection.

The cake was splashed with color and had the words *"Real People, Real Lives"* dominating the top two tiers and a big, red 500 on the bottom tier.

Nick made his way through the cast and crew shaking hands and being the congenial person who won a spot in the hearts and homes of those around him and fans across the globe.

Nick never took on the "star" attitude. He claimed that by being so close with his fans and co-stars, real people, it kept him humble. Real. It's that real-ness that has made Nick Penn a household name for the past eight seasons.

"Five hundred episodes..." he smiled. "It's a good number to ride off into the sunset."

Dave leaned over to Nick's ear, "Are we sure we want to do this?"

Nick grabbed the large cake knife and posed for the flashing lights of the cameras. "Yep."

When she filled a glass for each of her guests, Gwen put the bottle of wine back in the fridge. She grabbed the tray of assorted fruits and cheeses and set it in the center of the table.

"Oh, what a nice treat!" Gillian commented. "I never get to have a nice glass of wine!"

"The only time I get to have wine is on the sacrament," Betty laughed.

"And that's just grape juice!" Susan added.

Gwen sat down nervously at the table and took a sip of her wine.

"You have a lovely home," Susan said, looking around. "It's so nice to finally meet you."

Gwen smiled politely and furrowed her brow slightly.

"I've known Gillian and Betty for so long and they both talk constantly about their theatre family, and of course, I've been witness to some of your work at the productions and art shows. Your voice is amazing. You are very talented."

A little taken aback, Gwen was not expecting such a generous compliment. "Well, thank you. Thank you very much."

"And Gillian tells me that you are great with the kids."

Gwen nodded absently when a sudden flood of guilt rushed through her. "Yeah... I... really do love the kids. I usually can't wait to see them..." Gwen's smile all but disappeared as she realized she had practically abandoned them for her own pain. When she was present, she was like a zombie, just going through the motions. If she chose to look deep enough, she'd see that her "kids" noticed and her classes weren't nearly as lively. "I've recently... had a... set back." She struggled with the right words not wanting to get into a heavy discussion about divorces.

"Gillian told me. I'm sorry." Susan touched her hand.

"I hope you don't mind," Gillian added. "I thought you might not want to talk about it."

"You thought right. It's fine. And... and thank you all for coming tonight." Gwen put on her professional face. "Susan, can you tell us anything about Erin?"

Susan's face filled with concern. "I'm really not supposed to divulge any details about any of the children in the foster care program, but... this is turning into a unique case. But please, I was never here and what you hear tonight cannot leave this room.

All the women nodded.

Susan took a deep breath and leaned back in her chair. "Erin was brought to me." There. She said it. The room reacted exactly how she expected.

Gillian spoke first. "What? Why didn't you tell me?"

"Gill, now you know I wanted to tell you. You were the first person I thought of. I thought she would have fit perfectly in your little hen house." Gillian and Susan smiled at each other.

Susan continued, "Mary Ann dropped her off in the middle of the night and then she and her family went on vacation."

The shock in the room was audible. Betty teared up. "Oh, that poor child."

"It gets worse," Susan went on despite the raw emotion each woman was feeling. "I was going to keep Erin for a few days until I could place her locally so as not to disrupt her *entire* life... but came to find out that Mary Ann Cavanaugh had called my supervisor and told her that Erin was incapable of fitting in with a family situation. Her retardation..."

"She's not..." Gwen interrupted.

Susan held up her hand and continued, "...her retardation seems incurable and unmanageable. I was ordered to take her immediately to the institution." Susan breathed out as if she'd been holding her burden for months. Guilt wracked her body for not being able to fight harder.

"I don't understand," Gwen spoke, shaking with fury. "What does that mean?"

"What it means is, Mary Ann Cavanaugh sealed Erin's fate. Once a child reaches the institution, they are taken out of the foster care system," Gillian explained.

"Can she do that?" Betty asked, shocked.

"I'm afraid that if you're 'friends'," Gillian air-quoted the word, "with the higher-ups, then sometimes rules can be bent."

"But really, why would anyone believe her? If only they would talk to Erin..." Gwen pursued.

"Because," Susan sighed with disgust, "*she* is on the school board and she holds a hoity-toity degree."

"This is terrible!"

"Awful!"

"Now wait, ladies. God has given us provision. Provided a silver lining, if you will," Susan smiled.

Gwen tried not to roll her eyes at the mention of "God's provision". She was convinced that God got them all in this mess in the first place.

Nick drove his shiny black Ford F-150 down the long driveway. He turned off the air conditioning and rolled down his windows to breathe in the deep rich smell of pine.

His memories conjured up images of a crisp winter morning when his father and brothers would go out into the woods and choose the Christmas tree.

He smiled his Emmy-winning smile for no one but himself.

"If I really am missing something... if I am searching for something... here's where I'll find it."

Searching or hiding? his thoughts chided...

He turned up the stereo to drown out his thoughts and caught up with the thrilling crescendo of Pavarotti singing *Nessun Dorma*. Nick joined in with the emotional ballad with his pitch perfect, clear baritone voice.

He saw the two story Victorian home with wrap around porch come in to view as he sang louder to match his heart swelling in his chest. His home.

The faded blue paint, the porch swing, the garden. His old room, on the second floor, last window on the right. The one closest to the trellis, making evening escapes almost too easy.

The barn... It used to be the traditional red-painted wood, but has long since been replaced with the more modern galvanized metal and Nick knew that the very latest, newest, best-that-money-can-buy farming equipment was safely inside.

What's the point of having money if you can't help the ones you love, he thought.

His home. His family. Maybe the emptiness he was feeling was to be cured by coming home.

His highway life, traveling from city to city, hotel room to hotel room was satisfying and exciting for a while, but eventually, even though he was surrounded by hundreds of people at any given time, he felt lonely. Nothing felt permanent. Everything in his world was temporary. Maybe he needed to return to his roots.

He could see his front porch come in and out of view as he made his way down the long twisting road of the driveway. He could see his mother, Loraine, come out on the front porch and look in his direction. She was wearing faded jeans and a button down blouse with one of her husband's flannel shirts over it even though it was easily eighty degrees outside. She dried her hands off on a dish towel and saw the sun glint off her son's shiny black truck. He could see a smile cross her face and as if he wrote the script, her towel started flapping toward him.

That was a motion that was so familiar to him as he has seen it a million times before. Every time he came down that driveway, there she was. Even to call her boys home for dinner from the field or from their playing, she would wave that dishtowel. Nick swore he could even hear it flapping in the wind, so in tune to it he was.

He hung his arm out the window and waved while making that final curve. The towel flapped back in greeting.

Nick drove the truck up near the house and threw it in park while Loraine made her way to meet him.

Before Nick could turn off the vehicle, he had to finish the song. So he and Pavarotti sang on to the tearful crescendo. Nick, hitting every single note, spot on, holding out the final note until, it faded into the roar of pre-recorded applause.

"Oh Nicholas, you should have gone into the Opera," his mother cooed at his window. "How beautifully you sing."

She reached in and grabbed his face with her wrinkled hands and placed her forehead against his. Their tradition since the time he became "too old" for his mother to kiss him.

"You know I only sing for you," he flirted.

"Oh, you." She brushed away the fib with her towel. "Come inside. Dinner's almost ready."

"Just as I planned." Nick grabbed a couple bags from the back of the truck and followed her up the stairs and through the front door.

"Well, don't keep us in suspense! Tell us!" Betty blurted out.

Susan set her wine glass on the table with her neatly manicured, calm hand and a slow smile spread across her face. "There was no room at the inn."

The other women looked at each other blankly, wondering if she was the only one not getting the clue.

"What?" Gillian finally asked.

"There were no available beds at the institution," Susan explained.

"Oh!" Betty bonked her forehead with the palm of her hand. "No room at the inn... baby Jesus... yeah... I got it... I'm with you... carry on." Betty leaned over to Gwen and

77

whispered conspiratorially, "Might want to cut me off, dear. Wine goes straight to my head."

The two ladies giggled to themselves while Gillian asked the next question.

"So what does that mean for Erin? Where is she?"

"Right now, I'm sorry to say, she is in a Mediary Care Center just outside of Little Rock. While that sounds like a nice place, what it really boils down to is that she is in the basement of a church that has been turned into a homeless shelter. And, any orphans pending trial or the institute stay there until a bed opens up.

"She's there with homeless people?" Gillian stood up. "They don't know those people! That doesn't sound safe at all! We have to get her out of there!"

"Technically, the homeless stay on the upper floor. The children are downstairs."

Gillian paced the room, completely agitated by this turn of events.

"What's it like there?" Betty asked, hoping for a better answer than her imagination was pulling up.

Susan furrowed her brow looking for the right words. "It's a basement. It has two rows of beds. That's about it." She shrugged her shoulders, not sure what else to say at this moment. It was important not to sugarcoat the information so that the severity of the situation was not overlooked. "I do know," she added, "that at the present moment, Erin is the only child there."

Gwen felt sick to her stomach and so utterly helpless. She could not think of a way to help this poor child who was going to be locked away for the rest of her life because of one woman's selfishness and pride. Gwen could hardly bear to hear anymore. She was sorry she'd heard this much. Why would God allow this to happen to that poor innocent child?

Gillian walked back to the table after wearing a path on the living room floor. "Susan," she said sitting, "you said there was a silver lining. What can we do to help Erin?"

"She can be adopted."

"Adopted?" Gillian took Susan's hand in hers and squeezed it. "That's wonderful! Let's get the paperwork started right away!"

Gwen looked at her confused. "You... would... adopt her? Just like that?"

Gillian didn't hesitate, "Of course I would."

"But... " Gwen looked at all the faces around her table and didn't want to sound cruel, or insensitive... "But... you barely know her. Adoption is... a lifelong commitment."

Gillian looked at her like she didn't speak English. "Gwen," Gillian took in a deep breath for calm, "Erin is headed for an institution. She is an eight year old girl whose only sin was not being pretty enough for a *pillar of the community*!" Gillian tried to make her voice gentle, but there was passion woven in her words. There was a look of desperation in her eyes as if she were imploring Gwen to understand.

"Yes," Susan interrupted, "It is a very important decision to adopt and shouldn't be taken lightly, but you have to understand also, that foster care is no longer an option for this child. Either Erin is adopted or institutionalized. She has no third option."

Erin sat on the edge of the thin mattress and stared down the empty room of beds before her. The trash bags filled with her entire life sat beside her on the floor. She could hear the bustle of life continuing without her on the floors above, but this room was still. Quiet. Alone.

The woman who brought her down to this room put her things beside her and told her to wait.

She rested her hands, folded neatly, on her lap. Her face was expressionless. Her eyes scanned her surroundings and she numbly counted the cracks on the walls and the tiles on the ceiling... but her thoughts kept going back to the same thing playing in a loop over and over again, *What did I do wrong?*

Chapter Four

Gwen lay in her bed drifting in and out of sleep, so many thoughts keeping her from falling into deep slumber. She rolled over to wrap her arms around her husband only to find the other side of the bed empty and cold.

She opened her eyes remembering instantly why she was alone.

She shook off the painful thoughts and tried to go back to sleep. Knowing that sleep wouldn't come, Gwen sighed and rolled onto her back to try and work through the thoughts that were plaguing her tonight.

She used to try and fight it, forcing herself to try and sleep, but soon figured out that some of her best ideas and plans came through these restless nights. Her deepest inner workings were trying to speak to her.

There was always a notebook at her bedside so she could jot down new production ideas, choreography steps, new music class plans...

"Okay, brain, what is it you're trying to tell me?" Gwen spoke out into the darkness.

While she waited for her inner-self to give her brilliance, her eyes looked around her bedroom. The light from the window cast just enough of a glow to illuminate her small bedroom.

The walls... they were empty. She had taken down all the pictures of her and Mark as it pained her every time she looked at them. She missed him. She missed the idea of holding a baby. Their baby...

Her memories filled in the blank spaces of the wall, so it was as if she'd never removed the photos at all. She closed her eyes and rolled to her side to look out the window.

The tree limbs reached over the window only allowing her to see a small portion of the giant oak. She stared mindlessly at its shape and shadows, seeing beauty in its structure and sturdiness. The leaves fluttered at the hint of a breeze.

Gwen sighed deeply giving in to the notion that there was no brilliant idea coming... that she was just... awake. She felt... empty. Her thoughts were blank. She felt completely alone.

A flutter of pain pricked her heart and Erin's face passed in Gwen's mind. *Oh, Erin. I have no reason to feel sorry for myself,* Gwen thought. *Erin is there in that old church, all alone. I wish there was something I could do.*

She rolled onto her back to justify to herself why there was nothing for her to do. *Gillian is taking care of it,* she reminded herself. *Gillian will adopt Erin and all will be fine. Erin will have a...* Gwen's throat caught.

She lifted her arms off the sheets and let them flop back down. "Even Erin gets a family before me!" Gwen said out loud and instantly regretted her line of thinking.

She furrowed her brow as God opened the door to her heart. "No wonder I haven't got a family... I... I... I have been so selfish." The realization came crashing down on her and almost knocked the breath from her. "Is it true? Is that what you've been trying to tell me?" she asked out into the darkness. "I am so..." Gwen shook her thoughts off, *ashamed.* "You're right," she spoke directly to God. "I have been selfish. I was only thinking of myself and what I wanted. Is that wrong? Is it wrong to want a family? Do you not tell us to ask for our heart's desires?"

I wasn't thinking about anyone else BUT me. I was so focused on wanting a baby that I couldn't see I was pushing Mark away... A tear slipped from the corner of Gwen's eye as God gently spoke to her heart. "What do I do? Should I try to get him back? We can still get pregnant..." Gwen caught herself. *I see. I see it. I am not thinking of others... Tell me, Lord. What should I do? I promise, I'm listening.*

Erin.

Gwen furrowed her brow as the little girl kept appearing in her mind's eye. "I don't understand."

Erin.

Gwen saw an image of the sweet girl sitting in a giant hall of a room all alone.

"But what am I supposed to do? It's being taken care of. Gillian knows what she's doing. It's all being handled... She doesn't need me."

Again, the same vision of a confused, but still Erin flashed in her mind. Dry-eyed, Erin sat at the edge of her bed in the darkness staring blankly at the row of empty beds.

Gwen's heart lurched. "Okay. I'll call Gillian in the morning."

Gwen blinked heavily and allowed the tears to spill, *how could I have been so selfish...* she repeated in her mind.

Forgive yourself... I have a plan for you...

Shalisa, a volunteer for the Good Faith Church of Little Rock came down the stairs to the basement with her arms full of neatly folded sheets. She wore a denim dress with white sandals and had long rows of braids tied back into a ponytail decorated with flowers. She flipped the switch that brought the two rows of florescent lights to life.

The lights startled Erin who had fallen asleep on top of her blankets, feet still dangling off the edge.

Shalisa gasped and ran to the bedside of the child. "Oh, girl! What're you doin' down here? I'm so sorry. I didn't mean to startle you. I didn't even know there was anyone here."

87

Erin rubbed her eyes, but said nothing.

Shalisa set the sheets down and sat on the edge of the bed across from Erin. "My name is Shalisa. But everybody calls me Lisa. Don't ask me why, I guess the Sha is just too hard to say when you add it to a Lisa!" she laughed at her own story. "You can call me Miss Lisa if you want to." Her eyes scrunched at the corners as she leaned in, "Tell me lil girl, what's yours?"

"Erin."

"Erin. That's a pretty name. I like it. When did you get here?" Miss Lisa asked, looking at the trash bags under her bed.

"My friend, Miss Carter, brought me here yesterday." Erin's voice was thick with sleep but her deep Southern drawl was crystal clear.

"Susan Carter?"

Erin nodded, rubbing her eyes again.

Lisa searched her memory for any paperwork for this little girl.

"My mother should be here to pick me up soon," Erin offered. "She and my brother and sister went on vacation but they'll be back."

88

Confused, Lisa asked, "Is that what Miss Carter told you?"

"No... but..." Erin stopped short, thinking. "Am I in trouble? Did I do something wrong? Is that why I don't get to go on vacation?"

"Oh, honey, I'm sure that's not the case..."

Erin said nothing, just looked down at her hands in her lap.

"Have... have you eaten?"

"No ma'am. The lady told me to wait here."

"Since yesterday? What? Who told you to wait here? And they jus forgot about you? Oh, no. No, no, no, that's not gonna work. You ain't et since yesterday?" Lisa asked alarmed. Her long nails clicked as they touched each other. She stood and flailed her arms as she walked in a small circle.

"No, ma'am."

Lisa rolled her eyes and breathed in deeply praying silently to calm her emotions. She flipped her wrist to see the face of her watch. Eleven. Eleven o'clock in the morning. She breathed in deeply again. "So, I

89

guess you hungry, then, huh? You wanna get something to eat?"

Erin looked at the face of the young woman and nodded.

"Okay then..."Miss Lisa smiled. "Let me put these sheets away, and you and I will go scavenge the kitchen. Sound good?"

Erin smiled at the invitation and accepted.

"You can't find her paperwork? Are you kidding me?" Gillian was trying her best to stay calm as she listened. "Carter. Susan Carter took her to the church two days ago." She spoke sternly into the cell phone. "I'm the one who wants to adopt her, that's who and you've lost her!" Gillian paused letting the other person speak. "That's impossible. I have worked with Susan Carter for years. The paperwork, and more importantly, the CHILD is there." Gillian paced the floor of the office while Betty watched, helpless to do anything. "I don't care where the office is! She is at the church!" She wrote down a number that came across the line. "I will do just that," Gillian spoke sharply and hung up the phone.

"Dare I ask?" Betty spoke up.

"They have no record of Erin being dropped off OR any record of Erin anywhere!" Gillian paced again. "Oh! I am SO mad!"

"Can we call Susan?"

"Oh heck yeah, that's my next call. She'll be furious!" Gillian frowned and stood perfectly still for all of forty-five seconds. "I've gotta go. I'll stop in later, okay, Mom?"

"Go do your thing, honey. I'll be here," Betty smiled proudly at her daughter.

Gillian walked over and kissed her mother on the head and stormed from the room.

"That's my girl," Betty beamed.

Just then, Gwen came into the office. "Hey Betty."

"Hello, sweetie. You're here early."

"I know," Gwen came in and sat in the chair at the edge of Betty's desk. "I was just wondering if there was something I could do to help with the whole Erin ordeal. I feel like I should be doing something. I mean, I got everyone all fired up and then kinda dropped the ball..."

"You aren't the only one," Betty scoffed.

Gwen looked at her questioningly and Betty caught her up on the details.

"Lost her? How does that happen?"

Betty shrugged her shoulders, just as helpless as before.

Gwen's face shrouded in anger. "What have I done?" And in a moment, when Gwen rushed back out the office door, Betty was alone again.

Susan walked down the aisle to the booth where Gillian was waiting. She threw her cavernous leather bag, doubling as a purse, on the bench before she slipped in. "You know, I admire your enthusiasm," Susan grinned slyly, "but you're going to blow my cover."

Gillian blew air across the top of her Styrofoam cup, trying to cool down the steaming contents. "What are you talking about?"

"Erin."

Gillian couldn't help but laugh, "What are you up to?"

"Well, while you were berating those poor workers at the offices of the church, you should know that it was *me* that 'misplaced' Erin's paperwork," Susan used air quotes to emphasize her words.

Susan was put together, as always. It must be court day, because she was dressed in a suit and was wearing make-up. Gillian knew from working with her for many years that that was the only time the mascara came out. Susan's nails were painted in a shiny royal blue color and Gillian would bet money that her toes matched. Susan was one of the hardest working-women that she had ever known and her mani/pedi was her only treat for herself. It didn't hurt that her "put-together" appearance made her a formidable-looking opponent.

Gillian smiled at her friend and tucked a strand of hair behind her ear waiting for the social worker to continue.

"When Erin and I got there, it was late in the evening." When Gillian looked at her questioningly, Susan added, "We stopped for a burger. I just feel so bad for that girl."

Gillian nodded, agreeing.

"Anyway, I put the paperwork on the stack on the main desk, but it might have accidently slipped to the bottom of the pile. I knew that the workers would find her, but the office people and the worker people don't usually communicate, so... " Susan hung her head in shame but felt a little easier when she heard Gillian giggle.

"Oh, Miss Carter," Gillian teased. "I think you've been hanging around me a little too much." Gillian covered her face with her hand and giggled again like a school girl who just passed a note in class and got away with it. She leaned in across the table conspiratorially, "So, what's your plan?"

Susan scolded her friend with her eyes, "Well, if a certain someone hadn't called and set a fire under their feet, our Erin would have stayed 'hidden' until you could get your end of things in order."

Gillian nodded, feeling the scolding. "So now I have to work a little faster getting my stuff together."

"It shouldn't be a big deal, the courts know you..."

"On a first name basis..." Gillian added. Being a foster parent sometimes brings you in front of the court system on a fairly regular schedule. It does or does not help that Gillian is very vocal in the care of "her" kids.

"Right," Susan chuckled. "But as always, there is protocol."

Gillian rolled her eyes. "That poor little girl is in that place all alone, not knowing what her evil foster-mother is up to."

"I'm working on it." Susan pointed to the second steaming cup on the table. "This for me? she asked. Gillian nodded and Susan continued her train of thought, "In the mean time, you can go and visit her. She's allowed to have visitation and..."

"Can we..." Gillian interrupted.

Susan held up her hand, "... you are allowed to bring gifts."

Gillian laughed, "You know me so well, Susan."

Susan smiled back, "That, I do. But now I've got to go."

"But you didn't get to..."

95

"Kids need me. I gotta go."
"You go get 'em, Super Woman."

Chapter Five

Nick Penn was built broad and strong, like his father. He was one of five brothers. Right in the middle, so he had the reputation for causing trouble in typical Penn Family tradition. But he was also the one who was the closest with the parents.

As Loraine sat back and watched father and son conversing, she noticed how much they resembled each other. Nick looked almost exactly like Curt when he was the same age; sandy brown hair just slightly beginning to thin, blue eyes that could melt any woman's heart and that beautiful smile that had first attracted her to Curt all those years ago.

The talent and good manners he gets from his mother, she smiled to herself.

"So what do you plan to do with yourself?" Curt was asking him.

Nick scraped his plate with his fork and mashed the last of the pie crust between the fork tines. "Nothin'."

"Nothing?" Loraine giggled, coming out of her reverie. "You've never done nothing in your life."

Nick stopped and gave her comment a thought before he answered. "I know," he finally said matter-of-factly, "I wanna give it a try."

Curt chuckled to himself, "That's not going to last long."

"Now you know, whatever I put my mind to..."

Curt nodded then stood up from the table. "Good supper, Mother, thank you. So..." he looked over at his son, "What time you want to tackle that back field tomorrow?"

Nick set his empty dessert plate and silverware on his dinner plate. "I guess around seven, if that suits you."

"Ha!" Curt laughed out loud and slapped his son on the shoulder. "You can't even do nothin' for one day!"

Nick laughed and leaned back in his chair. "This might be tougher than I thought."

Erin followed Shalisa around the kitchen prepping for the afternoon meal. She chatted as she worked, barely taking a breath before changing the subject. "And my brother, he plays basketball. His name is Evan. He doesn't like ballet. He doesn't like coming to my dance shows. But sometimes Mother makes him. My Mother always does my make-up for the shows. She says I need to look the most beautiful so she can see me from the audience. I guess they are having fun on the vacation, huh?"

Erin paused only for a moment, a flash of pain crossed her deep brown eyes but then it flickered away... "Can I have the scraps from the turkey slices?"

Now that Erin has warmed up to Shalisa, she was a bundle of conversation. Most of the time she wasn't looking for a response, but was merely filling up the silence.

"Why would you want the scraps?" Miss Lisa asked.

"Yesterday when I took the trash out, there was this poor little dog. He looked hungry so I was thinkin' that maybe if he was out there again today, I could give him some scraps or something."

Shalisa smiled, "I sure don't want no scrappy dog hangin' around here. Girl, what were you thinkin'?"

Erin looked up at her new friend and sadness crossed her face, "I was just... he looked lonely... and maybe he was missing his family or something..."

Shalisa raised her right hand up to the heavens and waved her long hot pink nails around, making them clickity-click, "Lord Jesus, you sent me this lil girl who is tryin to save the world, an I'm just gettin' in her way!" She closed her eyes and raised her eyebrows and shook her head, just whispering, "Lord, Lord, Lord..." When she reopened her eyes, she looked down at Erin with the most love and compassion, "I'm sure we can find him something. After all, we here to feed the homeless."

A smile spread across Erin's face, "Hey! That's right! I didn't think about that!" She went back to her kitchen duties and continued randomly chatting, "Although, I'm not homeless. I'm not sure why I was brought here, cause I have a home. And a mom and a dad and a brother and a sister, but I don't have a dog. Do you think I could pretend that the dog is mine for just while I'm here?"

Shalisa hurt for her, but allowed her to continue to reminisce because the truth would come to the surface all too soon. "Well, I guess you should, you feedin him, ain't you? I guess you should call him somethin' too, while you're at it. What should we name him?"

Erin's face lit up. "I've never named a dog before!"

Shalisa smiled at her. "Oooo, girl, then today is a good day. Or maybe we should wait? He might have found his way back home.

"Yeah, that's probably a good idea. His family might have come and picked him up. Like my family. When they get done with vacation, they will be back to pick me up. So... I guess we can see if he is here after lunch, right?"

"Right. That sounds like a great plan. But in the mean time, we have to get ready to feed these humans!"

Erin laughed, "Okay. I'm going."

Shalisa could not understand why she was being pulled from the foster system. She wasn't able to read her file, but she seemed like a perfectly normal eight year old. Sweet, loving, very helpful. Sadly, if she *was* here, her "family" would not be returning for her. Shalisa knew that all too well. Usually, the small church hosted kids who were getting ready to age out of the system and needed some help with placement, or the kids were mentally challenged and were on their way to the institution for life care. Some are able to be habilitated to live in a group home when they are older, but the majority of their family would be the other kids and staff of the Behavioral Services.

Erin was getting quite comfortable in her new surroundings and enjoyed plating the food for the homeless people that stayed in the shelter. She was never far from Shalisa's side, and that was fine with her. The other workers were kind to her, but were happier when she would spend the day outside. But her new friend, Shalisa, would let her help.

She has been waiting for a whole week for her foster family to return for her, but while she waited, she enjoyed being needed. When the indigents would come through the mess hall, Erin would happily scoop their choice of food on a plate for them as they walked through the line. Today she was in charge of green beans and macaroni and cheese. She would beam with delight when they would comment on how good the food looked. "I helped make it for you!" she would tell them. She blossomed under their praise and was always available if they needed a hug. She was a blessing with a heart to serve.

Shalisa watched her and was so happy that if she had to go somewhere that it was here. *Surely God has bigger plans for this angel than the institution*, Shalisa thought to herself.

"What? Oh, Come on!!" Gillian dropped her sandwich bread on the counter and flopped her arms to her sides.

Susan sat at the table with her files spread out in front of her. She scanned her notes for more details. As Gillian ranted, she stopped her scanning and took in a deep, eyes closed breath knowing that this was only the tip of the iceberg.

The two women were in Gillian's farmhouse kitchen. The large table filled the center of the room and a long counter took up the left wall where Gillian was attempting to make sandwiches.

Gillian stormed over to the refrigerator and grabbed the deli meat, cheese slices, mayo and pickles. "They know me!" She squawked. Back over to the counter where she roughly tossed her items down beside the bread. "This is the stupidest... dumbest... what are they thinking...." Gillian had her back to Susan while she flung items in various directions. "Behavioral health needs? Seriously?"

She wasn't expecting answers, but merely working through the disappointment in her own way. "She's just a little girl! She doesn't take up much space! Look at this table! It's built for a dozen!"

Susan opened one eye and saw Gillian staring at her expectantly. "Oh. Are you ready for me now?" Gillian exhaled with a slight smile, realizing that she might be slightly over re-acting. "Cause I can wait..." Susan was teasing her now, "I was gettin' my meditation on..."

Gillian laughed at herself and loved how well she and Susan got along. "No... I'm done... I think."

"Okay... then go back to your sandwich makin' cause you're about to starve me to death."

Gillian laughed again, "Sandwiches. Right. Continue."

"Yes, the court knows you, and therefore knows exactly how many beds you have and how many kids you were permitted to have at one time."

"Yeah, but I could always..."

"You said you were done..."

Gillian dropped her defeated shoulders and went back to her sandwich artistry of creating calm out of her sandwich ingredient chaos.

"I'm sorry, honey. They said no. They are maintaining that she needs the extra care that the Behavioral Services can give her in Virginia."

"Virginia?"

"The courts maintain that it is the best option for Erin, they believe that..."

"But they're wrong! She is not mentally challenged!"

Gillian's back was to Susan, but she knew that her very dear friend was crying. Susan didn't move to console her and was really at a loss for words, so she just continued with her findings, "Erin's file has been examined and they have decided to allow that first test to stand as reason enough for her to be removed from the foster care system."

Gillian turned around to face Susan, waving her butter knife, tears pouring down her cheeks, "But that's not fair! That test was done a day after they pulled her from her abusive home! She had barely been to school. She'd been sexually and mentally abused... by her own family! I don't think anyone could pass that evaluation test with flying colors under those circumstances!"

This brought Susan to her feet and over to Gillian's side. "While that's true, and under normal circumstances, the court would take that under consideration, but Mary Ann Cavenaugh has pull... and an agenda. For whatever reason, she wants Erin out of the system. Erin has two weeks before she is moved." Susan linked her arm and fingers with Gillian's, the most she could offer. Gillian accepted it and dropped her head on Susan's shoulder.

"So that's it?"

"She can still be adopted, just not by you."

"That poor, poor girl... I feel like I have failed."

"Girl, you know you can't save them all."

"I know but..."

"Then let the Man do His work. If she is meant to be with you, she will be. Don't forget that He always has a plan."

Chapter Six

The theatre was dark as Guinevere made her way out on to the stage from the back curtains. Even though her steps were light, her heels still echoed off the wood floor filling the auditorium with staccato moments of sound.

The only lights to be seen were the thin strips of rope lighting that illuminated the edge of each platform of seating in the audience.

This... was her cathedral. This was where she came to commune with God and search her soul. And her soul was hurting...

She had now been officially divorced for a little less than a year, but it still felt like yesterday on some days and then the news that Gillian could not adopt Erin had disrupted the entire Centre. The only option that Gwen could see was that she could visit Erin one last time at the church-turned-shelter. Gillian said she had two weeks before they were moving Erin to her new, permanent home.

Her heart was heavy as she walked to center stage and breathed in the mixture of smells that made up her familiar world. Fresh paint... turpentine... fresh cut wood, grease and a lingering smell of canvas...

She let her eyes adjust to the darkness and let the spirit move her.

Her voice started off low, barely audible. *"I sing...because... I'm happy..."* A little louder, *"I sing... because... I'm free..."* she sighed and dropped her shoulders.

"I can't!" she called out to the empty auditorium. Her crisp, clear voice bounced off the empty walls.

As hard as she tried to get the lyrics from her mind, *The Eye Is On The Sparrow* kept running through her thoughts.

Gwen crumbled to the floor and sobbed. Her lungs filled with air and expelled again with the pain stored in her heart.

"Oh, honey... Oh, honey..." Betty shuffled up the stairs from the auditorium to the stage. She dropped to her knees and put her arms around Gwen's shoulders.

"He's not listening," she cried into Betty's embrace, "He's not listening."

"Oh honey, He is. I promise you, He is."

"He took away my one chance... for... for... a baby..." Another wave of sobs...

"Gwen, honey... now... uh..." Betty shifted their bodies so that she could see Gwen's face. "You may not like what I'm going to tell you..." Betty pulled her sleeve down to cover her palm so as to wipe the tears from Gwen's face. "There is no such thing as only one chance. If God meant for you to have a child, then you will have a child."

"But..."

Betty held up her finger causing Gwen to pause, "He gave us this little thing called 'free will'. It is not God's fault that your husband decided to leave you. He does not like to see marriages dissolved. So, I need you to stop blaming God for that."

Guinevere blinked at her sternness, which caused more tears to slip from her eyes. Betty wiped them away without missing a beat and continued, "What you need to understand is that God fulfills His

111

promises. It may not be *how* you had things planned, but it is what is best for you. He always wants what is best for His children. You think a little human interference is going to thwart His plan? No ma'am. My God is bigger than that."

"How am I supposed to have a family now?"

"There is more than one definition of family."

"I know that, but..."

"I know," Betty nodded. "He knows your heart. He knows what you need. And soon, you'll look back on this time in your life and realize that you had to go through this very struggle before He could get you where you need to be. He's watching over you, I promise."

Gwen met Betty's eyes, recognizing the lyrics she so recently tried to sputter out and saw the sheen in Betty's eyes.

She has a family. This woman in front of her, feeling her pain with her was the Mom/Grandmother to this entire theatre family.

Gwen had sisters a-plenty. And children... she had dozens of children to love on and watch grow. Gwen wasn't as alone as she originally thought.

But it's not what I... she pushed the negative thought from her mind and decided instead to embrace this dear woman instead. "Thank you."

"Of course," Betty smiled, "It's what family does." A tear slipped from the older woman's eye and Gwen returned the favor by removing the lone tear from her cheek with a gentle swipe of her thumb.

"Now," Betty put her emotions in check, "help an old lady up. I'm supposed to be meeting Loraine in the kitchen any minute now. She's bringing pies for this weekend's Coffee and Dessert Night."

Gwen stood and helped Betty to her feet. "And you... try the song again. You know how I love to hear you sing."

Gwen hugged the matriarch of the theatre family again.

"Okay, alright..." Betty patted her back and quickly pulled away, "We've got things to do." Betty tried so hard to be gruff, but was completely transparent.

Gwen watched her walk back down the stairs and disappear into the darkness of the back rows of the theatre. "Sing!" she called out from the darkness. "And I want to be able to hear it from the kitchen!"

Guinevere giggled to herself and walked softly in small circles, humming, trying to find the right note.

She started again, meekly, "*I sing... because... I'm happy...*" she giggled again, embarrassed and suddenly filled with... joy? Contentment? She shook it off, ready to concentrate.

She circled around one more time and stepped into center stage. She shook the stress from her hands and drew in a deep breath. She closed her eyes and let the air and anguish release from her lungs slowly. With her eyes still closed she began again: "*Why should I feel discouraged, why should the shadows come...*" her voice broke, and she swallowed, pushing on...

"*Why should my heart feel lonely, and long for heaven and home...*"

She walked around in small circles, clearing her throat.

"*I sing... because... I'm happy...*"

The notes were rich and pure shaking with emotion.

114

"I sing... because... I'm free..." A little more confidence.

"His eye is on the sparrow, and I know... he watches me." Her heart swelled with warmth and her voice matched her gratitude. Again, she sang. *"His eye is on the sparrow and I know he watches me... I know he watches me..."*

She took in a deep breath and sang out filling the auditorium *"I sing..."*

"I sing..." a deep baritone voice joined her own from somewhere in the darkness.

She continued, a little confused, she pulled back a notch listening and trying to see into the shadows...

"...because I'm happy..." The deep voice grew stronger filling in the gaps.

"I sing..."

"...because I'm free..." The two voices split into harmony and Gwen's skin had goose bumps. As the two voices continued from opposite ends of the theatre, Gwen's mezzo-soprano blended perfectly with the never over-powering invisible baritone.

"His eye is on the sparrow..."

"...and I know..." he sang.

"...aaand I know..." she sang.

115

"*He watches....*" He sang.

"*...me....*" They sang. And a figure emerged down the center aisle.

He stepped into the dim light from the stage and they just silently stared at each other for a moment.

Gwen could barely see his features but could make out a broad shouldered man wearing a ball cap backwards holding a large flat box.

"Can you tell me the where to find the kitchen?" he spoke.

Gwen laughed nervously, "I'm sorry, what?"

"I brought pies for something. I'm Nick Penn."

She obviously didn't recognize his famous name and he wasn't sure if he was insulted or pleased.

"I'm Loraine's son," he offered more clarification. "She asked me to drop off these pies for her?"

"Oh! Oh yes! Yes, of course, I'm so sorry. I can show you."

"That's okay, I didn't mean to interrupt, if you could just point me..."

"Oh no, you're fine... I was just..."

"You have a beautiful voice," he offered sincerely.

Gwen laughed and signaled him to follow her back up the center aisle, "I was thinking the same thing about you."

"I hope I didn't..."

"No... no, not at all. It was... nice." She brought him back into the lobby where she saw his face for the first time. There was a moment of recognition, but the kind that you know you've seen someone but can't remember where. His eyes were the deepest blue and his smile was brilliant. "In fact," Gwen teased, "how have we not snagged you for any of our shows here?"

Nick shrugged. "I've been busy. Working... out... West mostly."

Gwen nodded, understanding. "So you're just visiting then? That must make your mom so happy." She smiled, making casual conversation.

"Uh, not sure yet, on the visiting part," Nick answered, honestly. "Whenever I get stuck, I always come back home to clear my head."

"Sounds like good advice." She took a few more steps toward the edge of the lobby.

117

"Just down this hallway and the last door on the left."

"Thanks." He balanced the box on his forearm and reached his right hand out, "It was nice to meet you..."

"Oh gosh, I'm sorry. Guinevere... uh, Gwen."

He raised his eyebrows, "Guinevere," he repeated. "Beautiful name."

She laughed. "Yeah, my mom was kind of a romantic. Completely in love with the whole *Camelot* thing."

He caught her glance and gave his million-dollar smile, "It suits you."

After an awkward pause, Gwen broke the silence. "Well, I have to get ready for my next class."

"Right." He turned. "Down the hallway to the right."

"Left."

"Right. I meant left."

Gwen laughed, "And thanks for the duet."

"Hey, anytime."

And down the hall he went.

"Come here... come on... you can do it. Don't be scared." Erin was hunched over with her arm extended reaching out toward the huge, furry stray dog that looked like it could completely take her arm off if it chose to. His ears twitched at every little sound and his eyes were cautious.

Erin scooted a couple steps closer to the wolf-looking dog, completely unafraid. The dog allowed her to close the gap without retreating but only stretched forward slightly with his muzzle trying to get a better whiff of the treat the child was offering.

The dog crouched down and could choose to either pounce or lay down. He chose to crawl closer to the lunch leftovers.

"That's it. Come on lil guy. I got a treat for ya."

The pair inched their way together and with the gentlest touch, the stray removed the leftovers from the child's fingertips.

Erin was so excited that she jumped up and squealed, spooking the big dog. "Oh, sorry!" she giggled. "Please come back. I've got some more treats for you." Erin went

back to the bowl setting by the back door of
the church and chose another piece of meat.
They went through their dance once again,
and this time Erin didn't jump.

By the time they reached the bottom
of the bowl, the two were fast friends. Erin
sat on the stoop of the door to the church and
the wolf-dog towered over her. He sniffed her
hair and her face and she giggled and petted
his fluffy, thick fur. It's official, they are
friends.

Erin led him into the fenced-in
playground and he followed her willingly.
She talked to him and played around him and
he was happy with any and all of the
attention directed at him. They made a good
match.

Just as the sun was beginning to set
and dinner needed to be served, Shalisa came
outside to look for her wayward eight year
old.

Shalisa gasped when she saw the giant
husky mix towering over the child. "Oh, Lord
Jesus, Jesus, Lord, that dog is gonna eat that
child." She tried not to cry out so as not to
alarm either the child or the dog. But, Erin
saw her and climbed out from underneath

the fur and girth. "Hi, Miss Lisa!" Erin squealed. "This is my new friend!"

"This your little stray?"

"Yeah! Isn't he cute?"

Shalisa was nervous and spoke under her breath, "Please Jesus, don't let that dog eat her."

"C'mere! I want you to meet him! We can all play!"

"Honey, I can't right now, and actually, I need you to come inside. It's time to help with dinner."

"Oh! Okay!" She turned to her new furry friend, "I have to go for now, but you can wait here and I'll bring you some more left overs, 'kay?"

"Erin, I think you should let the dog out. What if he has a home he needs to go to?"

"He doesn't. That's why he's here."

"Just in case, sweetie. We don't want to keep him away from his family."

Erin sulked and went back to open the gate. The big dog trotted right along beside her. She had to raise her arm above her head to rest it on his back. "You have to stay here... or, go back to your home if you have one." She cupped her hand around her mouth and whispered to her new friend, "But if you don't, you can stay here with me. I can bring you some food later. Okay? Okay puppy?"

Shalisa tried to smile as the dog seemed to understand and chose a spot near the door to lay down and wait. She shook her head again and her hand went up, "You know, Lord... you know... Imma let this go."

Erin twisted a piece of grass around her finger as she walked toward Shalisa. And the dog followed her movements with his eyes. "He pretty, I give 'im that," she offered.

"Yeah, he is." Erin beamed. "I can still pretend that he's mine, right? Until my family comes for me, right?"

Shalisa wanted to pull her close and just hug her so tight so that she might stay happy and oblivious forever, but she knew that it was only a matter of time. "Sure you can. He can stay here for as long as you do. Deal?"

Erin ran back over to the sleeping dog and threw her arms around his furry neck. She easily knocked the wind from the gentle giant but you wouldn't know it. He laid still and let her squeeze his neck with her tiny arms.

"But then what?" Erin still had her arms wrapped around the dog as she looked up at Shalisa.

"Well, if he doesn't have a family, we'll have to find him a puppy homeless shelter so that he can be taken care of, too. C'mon, now, we gotta get inside." Shalisa waved at her to come back.

Erin's demeanor changed. She petted the dog's fur in long strokes and she looked like she was near tears.

"What's wrong, baby? Don't you want your friend to have a nice home and a safe place to sleep?"

She looked up at Shalisa and Shalisa's heart almost broke in two. "But what if he is afraid? What if he is sad and he misses me?"

"Come on now, let's worry about that when we have to. Right now, you have hungry friends inside that're missing you." Shalisa gave her best convincing smile.

"Oh! That's right! I'm not doing my job!" She turned back to the dog and grabbed both sides of his face and kissed him on the nose. "I'm sorry puppy, I have to go inside

and feed the homeless people. They are
waiting for me." She kissed him again,
hopped up and took Miss Lisa's hand. They
went inside and the door closed behind them.
The dog stood up, sniffed at the base of the
door then stepped back off the stoop. He
circled around... circled around... circled
around again.., and lay back down in the
same spot.

Gwen looked up from her work when
she heard the tapping at the window of her
office.

Nick nodded and held up two
Styrofoam containers as a bribe for entrance.

Gwen smiled and nodded for him to
meet her at the Centre's door.

"Hey you," Gwen smiled in greeting.
"Twice in one week, I am honored."

"Two things," Nick passed her in the
doorway and made his way toward her office
as she followed. "One, I recognize a fellow
work-aholic when I see one, and two, Sonic
had ice-cream slushies on sale for seventy-
nine cents... how could I pass that up?"

124

He followed her into her office. "You haven't eaten today, have you?"

Gwen darted her eyes away, "I've been busy."

"Ah yes... I recognize the symptoms..."

Gwen looked at him skeptically, "You're a work-aholic? You seem to spend a lot of time not doing work and then taking me down with you."

Nick laughed. "What can I say, I had a nice time when we accidently bumped into each other in the theatre lobby when I was looking for excuses to come and see you again."

Gwen couldn't help but blush. "I did enjoy our visit. You are well versed in your Broadway..."

"I was raised well..."

"I can tell. Your parents have been big supporters since we opened the Fine Arts Centre."

"They are good people."

Nick looked down the hallway and everything was pitch black. "Kinda creepy here at night. Do you ever get scared here by yourself?"

She shrugged. "No, not really. The auditorium does make some pretty unsettling noises though. I usually stay over in the office side if I'm here by myself. Besides, I know every inch of this place. If anyone tried to get me, I could just turn out all the lights and get away."

"That reminds me of that one play, where they were after this doll and a blind woman had it... oh man, what was the name of that?" Nick frowned forcing his brain to remember.

"*Wait Until Dark?*" Gwen offered.

"Yeah! Yeah! I love that one. I saw it once with Stacy Keetch... man, he was a good bad guy!"

Gwen smiled, and flopped back down in her office chair, and extended her hand, gesturing that Nick sit in the chair on the other side of her desk.

"That's one of my favorites too," Gwen nodded. "A great suspense!"

He set the cups on the desk between them.

"Oooo! Which one is mine?" Gwen fluttered her fingers like a little girl excited to get her hands on her dessert/dinner.

126

"I got a cherry limeade for you." He pulled a straw and spoon from his back pocket.

"Oh, I love the cherry limeade! Thank you!"

He grabbed his cup and took the lid off and sat back down in his chair.

"What kind did you get?" Gwen asked.

"Watermelon."

Gwen stopped short and gasped at him. "Watermelon? They have that kind?"

"Um, yes? Did you want to switch?" Nick laughed.

"No, uh... no... but could I taste yours? Watermelon is my favorite!"

Nick laughed, "Of course you can."

Gwen hopped out of her office chair and scooted to the other side in front of Nick and slid back onto the desk. She swung her legs waiting anxiously for him to take the lid off.

He stirred the contents, exaggerating his movement. "Mmmm, this sure does look good." He lifted the cup to his nose, "Oh, and it smells... heavenly".

Gwen giggled, "I know what you're doing..."

127

Nick looked at her innocently.

"And it's totally working!" she laughed.

Nick dipped his spoon in and lifted it toward Gwen before circling it back around and eating it himself.

She squealed and playfully smacked his arm.

He laughed, "Oh, now this... this is good."

Gwen laughed and tried to reach out for the cup, "I can only imagine."

"Oh, that's right. You wanted to taste this heavenly treat, didn't you?"

She reached for it again and he tugged it away just seconds before she could get her hands around it.

"Hey!" She complained.

"Okay, okay, don't bite my arm off... that's not very ladylike."

"In my defense," Gwen laughed, "You are teasing me with watermelon."

"So, I've discovered the way to your heart." He scooped up a spoonful and lifted it up for her to taste."

"Ooo... cold... cold... cold... but so good!" she fluttered her hands and scrunched her face fighting off the cold rush. "Mmm, that IS good. I'll have to remember that for next time."

Nick sat back and smiled at her.

"Well, I can see that you really are busy. Why else would you be here at 10:30 at night? I can go, if you'd like."

"Well, I *am* very busy... there is always work to do around here," Gwen looked behind her and under her at the papers spread out on her desk "but how rude would I be to pass up a seventy-nine cent slushie?"

"Ice-cream slushie."

Gwen snickered, "*Ice-cream* slushie. I stand corrected."

"You just love me for my watermelon flavor..."Nick teased.

"Yep. That's it... you caught me." Gwen rolled her eyes.

"Did you want another bite?"

Gwen chuffed, "Uh... yeah!!"

Gwen pulled into the small church lot and found a place to park. She slid her sunglasses on top of her head and gave herself a quick check in the rearview mirror. She tried to smooth away the sunglasses marks on her nose but gave up after a few swipes. She freshened up the lipstick and ran her hands along her ponytail smoothing it.

Gwen reached into the back seat for the pretty little package tied with a big purple bow and smiled. She was actually excited to visit with Erin.

She didn't have long to wait because Erin was at the front door waiting for her ballet mistress to arrive.

Gwen was greeted with a huge hug and words of love.

"Oh! Miss Gwen! I've missed you so much! I can't believe you're here! You came to visit me! I love you so much, Miss Gwen!"

Tears formed in Gwen's eyes. She wasn't expecting to be so overwhelmed with emotion.

"Erin, I'm so happy to see you too! You look so pretty in your beautiful yellow dress."

"My friend Miss Lisa ironed it for me since it got smushed in my bag, but she made it all pretty for me. And I brushed my hair and I even took a bath last night."

"Good, good. Well, Miss Lisa did a fine job. You look like sunshine."

Erin beamed. "And look! I made you a plate for lunch! We feed the homeless people, but I saved some so I could eat lunch with you. I helped cook it and I put it on the plate. Do you want to eat?"

Gwen followed Erin to the kitchen where a table for two was set up just for them. They sat together and talked mostly about ballet and her friends that missed her. Gwen gave her the gift filled with goodies and some necessities that she might not have access to while she's here or at the ... Gwen couldn't imagine this lively little girl having her life completely altered because one woman decided she didn't want her and didn't want to be reminded of her mistake. How does someone get that much power? And this sweet child doesn't even know what's coming.

They spent the rest of the afternoon playing cards and dominos, both from the gift bag, and coloring in a My Little Pony coloring book with brand new crayons. "Even though

My Little Pony is for babies, I don't mind coloring in it with you."

When the time came for Gwen to leave, Erin was beside herself. She cried and didn't want to let go of Gwen's hand.

Gwen cried right along with her and had to pull her tiny little arms from around her neck to break the embrace.

"I'll come back to see you, I promise," Gwen said, as she was still eye level. "You keep being your sweet self and help Miss Lisa as much as you can, okay?"

Erin nodded, tears rolling down her cheeks.

"You are such a good girl. So smart and so kind. I am so proud of you. You'll always remember that, won't you?"

Erin nodded.

"Okay... I have to go."

"I love you Miss Gwen."

Gwen's heart was in her throat. Her voice cracked as she answered, "I love you too, sweetie."

Erin threw her arms around her teacher's waist not wanting the visit to end. Gwen leaned over and kissed the top of her head.

"Is there anything special you'd like me to bring you next time? A different coloring book?"

Erin shrugged as she backed up and leaned on Shalisa.

"Maybe butterflies?"

"I like butterflies."

"Okay. Butterflies it is. I'll see you soon, okay? Can you smile for me before I go?"

Erin gave her teacher the best tearful smile she could muster and Gwen blew her a kiss and walked out the door.

Erin turned into Shalisa's stomach and cried.

Gwen got behind the wheel and cried.

Chapter Seven

"I want to adopt Erin."

Susan looked up from her paperwork to see Gwen standing over her desk. She set her pen down and a half smile crept across Susan's face. That's the determination she loved to hear in parent-hopeful's voices.

"Well, hello Ms. Collins."

"Can you help me?"

Susan indicated a chair in front of her desk and Gwen sat down. "I am honestly unsure if I can."

"Oh please don't say that. I know I took a long time to decide, but now I'm sure. I can't let her go to that awful place. She is not mentally challenged. She is bright and funny and sweet and so, so loving. Please say there is still time for me to adopt Erin."

"That's just it, Gwen. Time is the issue. You are not currently in the foster care system and it takes weeks just to get that to happen, not to mention the adoption proceedings."

"Isn't there something we can do? Can't we point out that this is a unique case?"

Susan laughed and shook her head. "You've been talking to Gillian, haven't you?"

Gwen looked sheepish and shrugged her shoulders, "Maybe? A little?"

"That girl," Susan sighed. "Let me see what I can find out. If we fail, it will be because time was just not on our side. But I will try everything in my power to get that sweet child out of her current life sentence."

"Thank you. Is there anything I should be doing?"

"Yes," Susan said matter-of-factly. She pulled out a booklet from her desk drawer and handed it to Gwen. Start reading this and memorize as much as you can."

Gwen nodded, not even the least bit intimidated. She now knew that she could have the family that she wanted even if it wasn't the traditional version. She would be a single parent. She would adopt an eight-year old girl and they would be a family. And she will have an entire theatre full of aunts, uncles and cousins.

"Thank you. Thank you so much."

"I'm not making you any promises," Susan warned.

"I understand. I appreciate your efforts."

"But your Honor," Susan pleaded in front of Judge Middleton as she only cocked her perfectly shaped eyebrow. "This is an opportunity for her to have a home."

"Didn't we put this case to rest last week?" Judge Middleton was not amused.

"But I am not putting the question of her sanity to the courts. This woman, an honorable member of the community, a perfect record, not even a traffic violation wants to adopt this child just the way she is." The judge looked down at her file. "Please, your Honor, don't let this child be punished just because..."

Judge Middleton held up her hand to silence Ms. Carter, "Don't... even go there," she warned.

Susan nodded and backtracked. "Your Honor," she began, "this is a child. An innocent child. This is her very last chance to have a real home."

The judge took in a deep breath and tapped her finger while her mind raced.

Susan stood quietly and let her ponder.

"This woman, this... Guinevere Collins would have to go through the Parent Courses and the home inspection. I won't budge on those."

Susan fought the urge to run up and hug the judge, but couldn't stop smiling, "Yes. Yes, of course, your Honor. Thank you."

Susan breathed a sigh of relief and added, "The child only has a week left before she is sent away, is there..."

"Then Ms. Collins had better get busy."

"So, she is allowed to expedite the classes?"

"She is." Judge Middleton clacked her gavel and the matter was closed.

Susan sent up silent prayer as she gathered up her files to get the news to Gwen.

Nick Penn walked in the office door of the Fine Arts Centre with a large flat box. Evelynn, the Executive Director greeted him. "Hi. Welcome, what can I do for you?"

"Hey, how are ya? I'm…"

"Oh, you must be…"

Nick smiled and shrugged, "Did you want an autograph?"

Evelynn stopped a moment mulling over his question. "For delivering desserts?"

Nick snapped back to reality, humbled once again, wondering if anyone owns a television in this town.

Evelynn tried again, "I'm sorry, are you Loraine's son?"

"I am. And yes, I have desserts. I was… just.. "

Evelynn reached out her hand. "I'm so glad to finally meet you. "

Nick graciously returned the handshake, "I tried the lobby door, but it was locked."

Evelynn laughed. "That's funny, because Betty is probably over there wondering where you are. I can show you the way through the theatre."

Evelynn began walking and Nick followed. "I'm glad you're here, actually. Gwen wanted to talk to you about something. She said she wasn't sure if you were staying long..."

Nick shrugged, "Things are kind of up in the air right now. I'm helping my dad out on the property. It's good work for... thinking."

"Apparently, theatre time is therapeutic for you as well?"

Nick smiled, "It is. Gwen is good company."

"She is," Evelynn measured out her next words, "She's had a tough year. She could use the distraction herself, but..."

"I understand." Nick saved her the trouble speaking the subtle, friendship threat that lurked just below the surface.

"Well, hopefully you'll stay in the area for a while. Gwen has big plans for you," Evelynn laughed.

"I'm sorry?"

"She said you have an amazing voice. She'll find some place in this theatre for you to be, I promise. She doesn't like to see talent go to waste."

"I'm beginning to wonder if I ever had any," he laughed to himself.

"Don't give up. But, if you do have any time, Gwen would love it if you stop by her office. She could use a break."

"Now I'm curious. I'll stop back by on my way out."

"Does anyone here own a TV?" Nick asked as he poked his head into Gwen's office. He found her sitting sideways in her office chair, ankles crossed in the air, making her body the perfect "V" shape. Her hair was up in a high ponytail on her head and she wore glasses that surely dated back to the nineties. She wore a men's white button down shirt over her ballet leotard and had her nose deeply imbedded in a book.

Startled by his entrance, in true ballet perfection, she pointed her toes, flipped around to a seated position and acted like she's been that way all day.

"Umm, we have televisions... as in that big box that shiny things come out of? But no one here really has time to sit and wonder at it's magical time-sucking ways," she laughed, "Why?"

"Oh, I was just... I ... there was this show, I was going to watch... no big deal..."

"I think there was a television here... somewhere... I can try and find it for you."

"No... it's...no, but thanks." Nick couldn't help but laugh. "Be careful what you wish for..."

"What?"

"Do you ever get out of here?"

Gwen took inventory of her disheveled office and her appearance. "Uh, no. Not really. I go home to sleep, sometimes, does that count?"

Nick shook his head. "No," he laughed. "Not at all."

"So what do I owe the pleasure?" Gwen smiled at him.

"Oh, I was delivering baked goods for the weekend."

"Nice! Did you want me to walk you over to the kitchen?"

"No, I was just there, actually. I'm on my way out."

A look of disappointment fluttered across Gwen's face and she started adjusting things on her desk so she hoped it looked like she was so busy that he wouldn't notice.

The awkward silence only lasted for a couple really long seconds before Nick absent mindedly massaged the back of his neck and said, "...Uh... your... uh... Evelynn said you wanted to see me?"

"Oh! Yes! Oh my gosh, I almost forgot!" She jumped out of her seat excitedly and came to stand in front of him. She placed her hands on his arms that were folded across his chest. "Okay, I know it's not much, but the owner of Hooper's Hardware came and asked if we had anyone in mind that could do the voice-over for a radio spot. And I thought of you!" She stretched up on her toes and smiled at him expectantly.

Nick smiled completely enamored at her enthusiasm.

Not getting the response she had hoped for, she decided she might need to sell it bit better. "It's not hard. Nothing too scary, you just go down to the local radio station and they will give you a script and everything. I don't know how much it pays, but it would look great on a resume and who knows, it may lead to something else!"

143

She was so excited and sincere about this offer, that he couldn't help but go along. He was sure she would be so disappointed if she didn't feel she was "helping".

"Well, if you think it would be a good opportunity for me, I'll give it a chance."

His smile made her stomach jump and she was instantly aware of how close she was to him. "Oh, it's uh... not for me... it'd be a great way to get your feet wet in the business... if you wanted..."

"I'm not sure that's the route I want to go, but I'd be happy to help out your friend."

"Oh, but your voice! And your personality, I'm just sure you're meant for bigger things other than tiny little Bakersfield."

"I happen to like it here."

"Oh, I do too. I love it here, but I'd hate to see talent wasted."

He just smiled at her. She had no idea that his talent had reached every goal she probably had in mind for him but he wasn't about to burst her hopeful bubble... just yet.

Their eyes lingered and she was momentarily lost in his gaze. Remembering the sting of lost love and the busy lifestyle she leads, she turned back to her desk. "I can get his number for you... or I can set it up, if you'd rather." She tucked her long leg underneath her as she sat at her desk looking for Mr. Hooper's contact information.

"Will you be there?"

She looked up at him from her paper, knowing that she has a full schedule in front of her and absolutely no spare time, "I can if you want me to be."

"Okay then. Set it up. Tell me when I should pick you up."

"Pick me up? I could just..."

"Don't be ridiculous! We're both going to the same place. And since you brought me this great chance, I'd be happy to buy you lunch."

Gwen knew that he was staying with his parents and didn't have a job... It just wouldn't be right. "You don't need to do that."

"I want to."

"I don't want you to waste your hard earned money on me."

"I have lots of money."

"Oh really?" she said skeptically.

He laughed, "Yes, millions."

"Oh, I'm not interested until you get to the billions."

"Okay, you caught me. I have billions."

"Oh... ok." She giggled sarcastically.

"Billions and billions."

"So, a fancy burger joint, then?"

"Only the best for my voice-over manager." He came and leaned his hands on her desk. "Say yes. Let's get you out of here for one day. Say yes."

She swallowed hard at his sudden intensity. "Yes?"

"Are *you* asking *me*?"

She blushed, and giggled. "No... I mean, yes... yes, I'll go to lunch with you."

"Great!" He knocked his knuckles on the desktop. "I'll look forward to hearing from you!"

"But I...."

"Here," Nick held out his hand, "Give me your phone."

Gwen looked confused, "My phone?"

"Yeah, " he looked at her like it was a perfectly normal question, "Unlock the screen and hand it over."

She tapped in her code and handed him her phone.

146

He took it and tapped away at the buttons before handing it back, "Here, now, you can text me the details instead of waiting for the next delivery."

She looked down at her phone and laughed. "The Incredibly Amazing Nick Penn?"

He shrugged. "It sounded better than, Deliverer of Mom's Pies."

She laughed again. "Okay, I'll give you that." She leaned back in her office chair and tapped away at her phone."

Nick's phone beeped and lit up. "I got a text message!" He feigned surprise.

"Hey, this is me... I'll text you the details."

He read it and looked up and smiled at her then typed back.

He smirked and winked and was out the door.

Her phone lit up and signaled her new text : "And don't forget about lunch."

Gwen giggled and was left speechless at her desk, not exactly sure what had happened, but was pretty sure she didn't object.

Chapter Eight

"But I don't have time for this! I can't believe I said yes!"

"Honey. It's not even anything to worry about." Evelynn sat calmly in her chair while Gwen paced in front of her.

"It's a date, isn't it?"

"Is it?"

Gwen stopped, "Isn't it?" She tugged on the sleeves of her shirt. "I don't know! Do you know how long it's been since I've dated?"

"Gwen, you're still not dating. You're over-reacting, that's what this is."

"But he was so charming and cute and he flirted with me!" Gwen paced back and forth in Evelynn's office. "He gave me his number!"

Evelynn stood and walked over to her best friend and grabbed both her arms. "You enjoy each other's company. He hangs out in your office for hours. You are singing again.

What is so different? Now you're just hanging out somewhere else, outside of your safety cave." Evelynn paused. You want to know what I think?"

Gwen nodded with her best pouty face.

"I think this is good. You need this. You need to be loved, you need to be flirted with, and you *do* need time away from the theatre."

"But I'm trying to adopt a child. I have classes to teach. I have programs to create... I don't have time for a..."

"A what? Has he asked to marry you yet?" She didn't wait for an answer, "No. He hasn't. We can handle it. Maybe it's time you take some time for you."

"Look who's talking!" Gwen teased, knowing full well that Evelynn puts in just as many hours as she does.

"I don't have a family. You are about to be the full time parent of an eight-year-old girl. You are going to have to make some adjustments. You are going to have to learn how to fit other people into your schedule. You are not going to be allowed to "live" here any more."

Gwen whined, "You're kicking me out?"

Evelynn laughed. "Yes. You're banned from your home away from home to raise the family you've always wanted. I know. I'm a terrible human being."

Gwen paused, "Overreacting?"

"Yes... maybe just a little..."

Erin sang as she concentrated on the work before her. Vibrant color filled in any trace of white background. "And I... will goooo to the Disney caaaastle... and then... I caaaan beeee a princess... cause my moooom will buy me a pretty dreeeesss and I... will be soooo happy...."

She slowed down as she came to the edges so as not to go out of the lines. "You know," she spoke matter-of-factly to her wolf-like companion, "I bet they will have missed me so much while they were on vacation, that they can't wait to come and pick me up." Her tongue slipped out of the edges of her lips to help her concentrate on

151

the tricky spots. "Miss Lisa said that I get to go and stay with my ballet teacher, Miss Gwen. You haven't met her, but she is really nice. I always think to remind myself to tell her about you, but I sometimes forget. She is so nice. She brought me a candy bar last time and this time, she says she will bring gum. I like gum. My mother says I shouldn't eat gum cause it makes me look like a cow. 'Cause cows do this," she stopped her coloring to face the dog and move her jaw in slow circular motions letting her jaw hang wide open. "Like that. She really, really hates that. But I won't do that around Miss Gwen. I don't want her to think I'm a cow... 'cause I'm not."

The big, beautiful dog kept his eyes on her, waiting to be called upon for some task, but was perfectly content listening; not having to be an active part of the conversation.

Erin held up her masterpiece and scrutinized her work. An oddly shaped, rough edged oval was brightly colored with the word MAX mostly in the middle. The brand new name tag was cut from a milk carton and Miss Lisa poked a hole in the top to put the yarn through.

152

She smiled at the finished product. "Well? What do you think?" Max thump-thumped his tail in response. Erin squealed with delight, "I just knew your name was Max!" She wrapped her tiny arms around his neck and they practically disappeared in the thick fur. "I love you, Max. You're the best friend I ever had." She nuzzled into his face and showered him with kisses. "You wanna wear your new collar? Do ya?"

She pulled away and picked up the flimsy yarn collar and slipped it over Max's head. "There you go! Look at that! You have a collar! And see? It has your name right here, so everyone will know it's you! Such a good boy." She stroked his head and Max didn't mind a bit.

"Oh, I love this place!" Gwen smiled and then just as quickly frowned when she lit up the screen of her phone revealing the time. "Rats, they don't open for another hour."

"It's okay, my mom knows the owner. He's going to open a little earlier for us."

"Man, your mom knows everybody!" she laughed.

Nick shrugged innocently and climbed out of the truck. He went around to attempt to open her door, but she was already sliding out. So, instead he held a hand out to brace her exit.

"Your mom got you a good deal on this truck, we get to eat at places before they open... there's a whole other side to Loraine I didn't even know about!"

"She's pretty amazing," Nick said.

Gwen noticed the love for his mom on his face as he spoke of her and it warmed her heart. *He seems so genuine*, she thought.

He lead the way to the door and opened it, "Shall we?"

She smiled, "We shall."

"Hey, Nicky, so good to see you!"

Nick stuck out his hand and grasped the owner's in a solid handshake. "You as well, my friend. And thank you, for uh... opening a little early."

"Anything for you, Nicky," he winked. "I've known this boy since he was knee-high to a grasshopper," he addressed Gwen. "Sit anywhere you want. I'll send my boy out to get your order."

"Thank you."

"Best chicken in town," he promised.

Nick nodded to a booth along the back wall and Gwen started in that direction. He sat with his back to the storefront window and she sat across from him. He leaned into the table and crossed his arms across it.

She smiled at him, "Are you nervous?"

"Me? Not even a little bit."

"Really?"

He shook his head, "I like challenges."

She laughed, "I'll keep that in mind." She dropped her gaze when she realized he was looking directly at her. Luckily, that's when Caleb brought their water to them. He had his tongue out in concentration and his almond shaped eyes never left the glass.

"Here's your water," Caleb said with a slight speech impediment. "I'll be right back with some silverware." He smiled at Nick and winked at Gwen and then sauntered off toward the kitchen.

Nick leaned in closer and spoke low to Gwen. "Caleb has down-syndrome, but you wouldn't know it from his parents. He's the last of eleven kids, and they don't let him off easy," Nick laughed. "He's a good kid." Nick searched his brain for a memory, "I think he's about twenty-four now?"

Gwen smiled, "I see him in here every time we come. And you're right, he works just as hard as everyone else." Gwen busied her hands by stirring the ice in her water with the straw. "Have you lived here your whole life?"

"Pretty much of it. Went off to college and stuff, but this will always be home. You?"

"No, oh no. I've only been here about six years. My... ex... husband," the words felt uncomfortable speaking, "and I moved here for his job and so I could open the Fine Arts Centre with Evelynn."

They ordered their food and shared in small talk while they enjoyed the 'best chicken in town'. Nick was intrigued. She wasn't like most of the women he's been around recently, but maybe he was looking too hard and tipping the scales in his favor.

"Rip and I met at a summer camp when we were like in sixth grade or something. We just, I dunno, hit it off. He

156

was the little fat kid. He wore striped shirts and khaki pants, like... every day. He had this," Nick paused laughing at his childhood memories, "...long, black hair and he would tuck it behind his ears every time he wanted to be 'cool'. He was the first one to tell me to blow into my drink box," He rubbed his eyes remembering the fountain of juice that spewed from his drink after he took Rip's suggestion. "You remember those?"

Nick was practically crying and Gwen couldn't help get caught up in his laughter as he explained the aftermath of the fountain of orange drink. He has such a great laugh, Gwen thought to herself. "...and after camp was over, like two weeks later, I got a letter from him. We stayed pen-pals for years and only got to 'hang out' at this summer camp every year." He laughed recalling their years of friendship. And Gwen smiled, happy to listen to his memories.

"So, when we graduated, he said that he had no plans to go to college, at all. That was unheard of in my household. Said he was finished with school. I told him that we should go to the same college, and we did. I helped him with his paperwork and when times got tough, we were really there for each other." Nick nodded reminiscing. "Of course, he's a pain in my ass most of the time... but that 3%, he's a hoot."

Gwen laughed. "A hoot? Don't think I've heard that word in a while."

Nick joined in her laughter, "Just wait till you meet him..."

"Well, if he's anything like you, then I'm sure I'll like him."

"He's not!" Nick leaned back and laughed. "He is nothing like me. But I love him to death." Nick shook his head with a smile on his face.

They were quiet for a moment trying to decide if they were full or not.

"So," Nick began while wiping his fingers with the moist towelette, "what would you do if you had a million dollars?"

"What? Where did that come from?"

"I feel like I've been doing all the talking. So now it's your turn... A million dollars... aaaand go."

"Oh, that's easy," she smiled. "I'd pay off my mom's house and definitely get her a new car and pay off her credit card bills. I'm pretty sure she spent them on me in the first

158

place, " she giggled. "Then, I'd pay off Evelynn's car. Build on to Gillian's house, she has a lot of kids, and I'd get a new roof for the theatre, new carpet for the lobby, Studio A needs new flooring... Oh, build a room just for the costumes..."

Nick laughed as she was lost in her million dollar spending spree. "Whoa, whoa, whoa," he pushed his plate away and held up his hands. "First of all, I said ONLY a million dollars. But, I'm noticing, there's nothing in there for you?"

Gwen furrowed her brows thinking, "No, not really. What's the point of having all that money if I can't do something nice for the people I love."

Nick couldn't help but smile. "My sentiments exactly..." He wanted to reach across the table and hold her hand so badly. "Okay, okay, so what happens if we take care of everybody else and you still have a million dollars that you *have* to spend on yourself. What would we spend it on?"

"Hmmm..." Gwen furrowed her brow again deep in thought. "I... I don't know." She shrugged her shoulders. "I don't really need anything..."

"Who said anything about needing? Think selfishly. It's all about you. What do you want?"

A timid smile brushed across her face with just a hint of blush on her cheeks. "Well, I've always wanted to live in the country." She snickered, embarrassed. "I... I don't know, maybe a nice little farm house with... the perfect view of the woods. I love trees."

"Maybe with a field on the other side?" he asked stirring her imagination.

"Of course," she giggled. "And some wild flowers," she added.

"So I can pick some for you on my way home for dinner.

"From working in the field."

Nick looked deeply into her blue eyes as they put each other into the same future, "We could have a bonfire on the weekends."

Gwen lit up, "Yes! And have popcorn and S'mores"

"The kids could roast their own marshmallows. There'll be quite a few. Can't let Gillian have all the fun."

"Oh yes," Gwen followed him into the future, "a house full of children... We could..." Gwen blinked back to reality. Nick saw sadness flicker in her eyes, even if it was just for a moment. Her hand went to cool her cheek as she could feel the heat from blushing. Embarrassed, and yet almost sad realizing that she was dreaming out loud. She really liked the way it sounded... and didn't mind a bit sharing it with Nick. There was silence as Gwen looked away. When she looked back up, avoiding his eyes, Nick could see that the moment was gone.

"It's uh... getting late." She pushed the home button on her phone bringing the screen to life, checking the time. "We don't want to be late for your first big radio break."

"I don't mind, I'd rather stay here and..."

"Oh, don't be like that... so many people are taking a chance on you, and trusting me, and... and the restaurant has to open for other customers..."

Nick put his hands out in front of him to brace against the scolding, "Okay, okay, you're right. I would never want to do anything that might tarnish your reputation." He slid out of the booth and held his hand out to steady her, "You don't get to dream much, do you?" he asked.

"I dream," she shrugged. "I just know dreams require hard work. I don't take things for granted and expect someone to just hand me a million dollars." The slight edge in her voice stung and he knew he was going to have to own up to his identity soon, because right now, at this moment, he realized, she thinks he is just a worthless sponge that still lives with his parents.

Nick pulled his truck up and parked in front of the radio station. He turned off the engine and touched Gwen on her shoulder, pausing her exit. She looked back around at him expectantly.

"Uh... um... before we go in..." Nick stumbled over his thoughts.

Gwen couldn't help but smile at his sheepishness, assuming that he was nervous.

"I... just wanted to say that no matter what happens in there, I had a really great time with you this afternoon."

Gwen smiled sincerely and responded, "I did too. I have to admit, it is nice getting away from the theatre."

"So, maybe we could do it again?"

Gwen shrugged, "We'll see... maybe?" Gwen could practically see the thoughts racing around in his head. He wanted to tell her something, but couldn't seem to find the words.

"How about this," Gwen offered. "No matter how it goes in there, we'll find you some work at the theatre. I may be speaking selfishly, but I kinda hope you bomb in there so I can keep you all to myself," she giggled. But when she raised her eyes to his and saw that he was smiling at her, she gulped, and added, "The theatre... I ... I mean the theatre has... roles... uh, lots of roles, uh parts for you to play...." She slapped her hand on her forehead and looked down to her lap wishing to be anywhere but in such close proximity to Nick Penn.

"So, did you just offer me a job?"

"I... would... uh have to run it by Evelynn, of course, and it may not be much... but... yeah, we could probably find you something."

He smiled at her but said nothing.

Gwen looked at him gently. "You'll do great. They will love you."

"I just don't want your opinion of me to change once we go in there..." Nick laughed nervously, "I like spending time with you, and I don't want..."

Guinevere dipped her eyes down and reluctantly admitted, "I enjoy my time with you as well. I have to admit that I like the excuses you find to "accidently" end up at the theatre," she laughed and blushed slightly at her admission. "I think I'd enjoy your company even if you weren't amazingly talented. It's just one little radio voice-over... it will be fine."

"You're right." Nick breathed in deeply. "Whatever happens, is gonna happen."

Gwen smiled, happy to see his confidence return. "Right. You ready?"

"I'm ready if you are"

"Then let's do this!"

Nick slid out of the truck but was too slow to help Gwen from her side so he opened the main door to the radio station. Gwen took the lead and walked up to the reception desk.

"Hi," she said, "Nick Penn is here for Hooper's Hardware... I think they said Studio 7?"

The receptionist stared at Nick and was brought back from her reverie when she realized Gwen had stopped talking.

"Oh, yes, of course... Mr. Penn, we've been expecting you." She pointed to the leather couch, "if you'd like to have a seat..."

"Nick! Nick Penn... Well if I ain't dancin' in high cotton..." A short, heavy-set man came walking down the wood paneled hallway. He was the only person in the building wearing a three-piece suit and his shoes had a high shine to them.

Gwen smiled and shook his outstretched hand. "Nick, I'd like you to meet Colby Thornton, owner of K-WIN and FLPN Country."

Nick nodded and shook his hand.

"Ms. Collins, when they told me that you were sending us Nick Penn, I didn't think you meant THE Nick Penn... Sir, it's an honah" His Southern accent was thick and his voice raised up several octaves when he spoke.

"Happy to help." Nick smiled, acknowledging the gathering crowd and hoped this was not about to take a very bad turn.

165

"Could I get your autograph, Mr. Penn?" The receptionist could hold it in no longer."

Gwen furrowed her brow at the sudden hustle and bustle in the lobby of the radio station. Autographs?

She caught Nick's glance and questioned him with her eyes and he just smiled, raised his eyebrows and shrugged.

"Mr. Penn, it is an honor to meet you."

"Mr. Penn, this is Mistah Hoopah, the man you gonna be puttin' on the map today."

Nick shrugged again, "I don't know about all that. Nice to meet you, should we get started?"

"Of course, of course! You're a busy man! We sure do thank ya for takin' time out of yo busy schedule to come on down here."

"It's actually all Gwen's doing, uh... Ms. Collins, she set everything up."

"Ms. Collins, shame on you. Keepin' Mr. Penn all to yo-self," Colby Thornton teased.

"What can I say," Gwen crossed her arms and leaned against the large front desk, "Mr. Penn is a well-kept secret." She cut her eyes to Nick as she begrudgingly played along, but it was just enough to let him know that he had some explaining to do.

He winked at her and followed the tubby man down the hall to Studio Seven.

In the mean time, Gwen pulled out her cell phone and did a quick search for Nick Penn...

Gwen waited for Nick in his truck outside the radio station. He was all smiles and waves and camera flashes as he left the building but when he turned to face Gwen, watching him from the front seat, his expression looked like that of a little boy who got caught with his hand in the cookie jar. He couldn't wipe the smile from his face, but there was the tiniest bit of guilt added in.

He shoved his hands in his front pockets and cautiously approached the driver's seat trying to read Gwen's expression. She just stared straight ahead... waiting.

Feeling that any second, he was about to get scolded, he tried to offer up his best smile. She turned to accept it, but gave a blank look in return.

"So..." Nick attempted, "I think it went well..." He settled into the drivers seat and flipped the sun visor so the keys dropped into his hands.

Gwen cocked her eyebrow at him and then turned back to the front.

"I really appreciate you getting this gig for me..." he tried again.

Gwen squinted her eyes as if he were speaking another language. She took in a deep breath and pulled up her phone... "Nick Penn retires after 500 episodes of *Real People, Real Lives*... Nick Penn stars in *Les Miserable* on Broadway... Nick Penn hosts an Evening of Opera... Nick Penn chosen as Ford's spokesman..."

"I'm pretty sure we can add Hooper's Hardware to that list... I think I really sold some power mowers today..."

Gwen turned to face him and he was pleased that the corners of her mouth lifted ever so slightly. She shook her head and grinned.

"You could have just told me." She peeked at him from the corner of her eye.

"What, and ruin the surprise?"

"Surprise for who? I was a little humiliated in there."

"No one noticed. They think you're the bomb!"

"The bomb? Do people even say that anymore?" She took in a deep breath, "Again, you could have told me."

"Well, speaking of humiliated, I don't usually *have* to tell anyone... and second, is it so wrong to meet and get to know someone for just who I am and not who they *think* I am, or what they can get from me?"

Gwen furrowed her brow for a brief second not thinking about it from that angle. "It *was* nice to know you before you became a super star..."she said smiling.

"I think so too. But maybe, could I go back to being an unknown who is sponging off his parents?"

Gwen feigned shock, "I never thought that!"

"Oh yes you did, admit it!" Nick teased.

Gwen smirked and looked out the window.

"That's why you wanted me to get this job so bad... I'm guessing you always find the good in people, don't you?"

"I just wanted to help. You are so talented and I was worried it wasn't going to be shared. Obviously, my concern was unfounded. And yes, I like to help people. I thought you were in need of... " she giggled thinking that Nick Penn needed help.

"It's only a season. I'll be forgotten in no time. Fame is fleeting. Real friendships, those are worth saving. And I do need help..."

Gwen turned back to look at him and he reached out and covered her hand with his own. "Say you'll be my friend for a long, long time."

She smiled, "I'd like that." He held her gaze until she averted her eyes to her lap.

"Good. Then we'd better get out of here before we both hit the tabloids!"

Gwen couldn't help but roll her eyes as he backed out of the parking lot.

"So about my job at the theatre..." Nick asked.

"I don't know, Mr. Penn. We are a non-profit... tight budget and all...

Chapter Nine

"What are you grinning at?" Evelynn smiled as she walked into Gwen's office.

"Was I?" Gwen looked up from her phone sheepishly.

"Oh, you were... and are!"

"Tomorrow is my home inspection."

Evelynn raised her eyebrows, allowing for a pause. "And...?" she finally asked.

Gwen couldn't hold back her grin even if she wanted to. "And... that was just Nick on the phone encouraging me and telling me that everything would be great."

"Ah... I *thought* that was the 'Nick' smile."

Gwen laughed, "There's no Nick smile."

"Of course not."

"And you were right, I just didn't get the chance to tell you, but I'm glad that I told him about Erin. It was silly to keep it to myself, like it was something bad... or something."

"...and?" Evelynn nudged.

"And... he was really happy for me. Didn't even flinch! I mean... if there was ever... I mean... if we were to...." Gwen could feel her face beaming a bright shade of red. "Nevermind, I'm just glad I told him. He's been a great help."

"And there's no 'Nick' smile... and you're not singing Disney song's in your head right now..."

Gwen was about to protest but Evelynn continued, "Don't deny it. I could hardly pry you away from your phone for the better part of last week."

"What?" Gwen asked trying her best at innocence. "He was helping me study for my foster parent's application."

Evelynn just smiled, saying nothing.

Gwen shrugged, "He's bored."

"Well, if I can steal you away for just a moment, I would like to talk about next year's calendar. There's a lot of stuff in the air."

"Oh sure, of course." Gwen un-tucked her legs from underneath her and sat upright at her desk. She pulled out her folder that she jots notes in for the next season's performance suggestions, class ideas, and thoughts for different summer camps.

Evelynn pulled the chair across from her and rolled out her "mock-up" calendar for the following year.

Gwen pushed the home button on her phone to light up the screen, mindlessly checking for... anything. She clicked it off again, flipped it over and moved it to the edge of the desk.

"Okay, so what's up first?" Gwen started their meeting.

"Well, Danni graduates high school this year. She's been teaching the little bitties."

"Yes, yes... she's been working so hard on her audition piece. It's going to be beautiful."

"I agree. And if she gets accepted to Rouchard, we will be short one amazing teacher."

Gwen sighed, "Well, I can take her Tuesday and Thursday classes... maybe even..."

Evelynn smiled. *Always the fixer... always stepping up to help even if there were*

173

no available hours left in her day, she thought. "No... you can't, you are going to be a Mom. And you can't be here all the time anymore."

"It's just... what... three classes? Maybe four? Oh, look, we could combine these two and then..."

"Gwen," Evelynn placed her hand over Gwen's. "You have wanted this for so long. Erin has got to be your priority. And..."

"She is... I mean... she will be, but..."

"I'm not asking you to give up the theatre, or your classes, but..."

"Good, cause I'm not." And as if right on cue, Gwen's phone sounded the double clang of a ship's bell, which accompanied a new smile on Gwen's face.

Evelynn leaned back in her chair and smirked at her best friend. "This is me not saying anything about your priorities changing."

Gwen stared back blankly trying desperately to pretend that the alert on her phone didn't make her heart skip a beat. "It's not that big of a deal. We're just friends."

"Right. Right. But hey, while we're on the subject of your new "friend", she air-quoted the word, "Do you realize how long

174

it's been since we've had a solid baritone? AND lead quality?"

Gwen leaned forward obviously having already thought about it, "I know! He could so easily pull off *Jekyll and Hyde*!"

"Oooo! *The Scarlet Pimpernel*!"

"We could return to some of the classics like... like... *New Moon*! Or *Rose Marie!*"

"*Pajama Game* would be a fun one to do."

"Oh, wouldn't he make a great Curly in *Oklahoma*?" Gwen daydreamed.

"We could shave him bald and he'd be a great Daddy Warbucks in *Annie*."

Gwen gasped, "Don't you dare!"

Evelynn suppressed a laugh, "Yeah, you're right, *Annie* has way too many scene changes... and we don't have a dog."

"But you know," Gwen grinned coyly, "We could finally do *Camelot*. He would make a perfect King Arthur."

"No... Lancelot!"

"Oh yeah..." Gwen stared off, lost in her own musical dream sequence.

"Your mother would be so proud. Finally your name-sake, live on stage!"

175

The two women giggled having the perfect leading man for every show they'd ever dreamed of producing.

"And our ticket sales!" Evelynn took the planning and dreaming stage even further. "Having Emmy- winning Nick Penn on our season ticket? I wouldn't have to spend hours and hours writing grants and searching for funding!"

Gwen snapped back to reality. "Oh... yeah... but what if... he doesn't want to let people know where he is? He did say that he was taking a break from the spotlight."

"Does our teeny, tiny, little local theatre count as a spotlight?" Evelynn blinked innocently.

Gwen shrugged.

Evelynn nodded, "But, you know, I can understand that... Maybe we can have him be a ... tree or something."

Gwen looked over at her best friend with a slight grin, "I guess I could ask... He would make a most splendid tree..."

"No harm in asking..." Evelynn smiled back. "But, if he doesn't want to, we won't push. Wouldn't want to upset our very own mailman Roy who *thinks* he's every leading man..."

Gwen couldn't help but laugh. "Hey, now don't you make fun of my Roy. He is super talented. Just not as much as his ego thinks he is. I know if we find the right role for him... "

"I don't know if the theatre could handle it. We almost lost half the cast when we put him as Conrad Birdie in *Bye Bye Birdie!* He thought he was ALL that and a bag of chips!" Evelynn snapped her finger over her head and laughed.

Gwen giggled and shook her head. "That ego... but wasn't Danni great as Kim McAfee?" Gwen smiled. "That was a good one." Gwen thought a bit more. "Maybe... if we give Roy something with a little meat to it. He might take it seriously. The talent is in there, I just know it."

Evelynn cocked her eyebrow, "If you say so. But if you produce *Death of a Salesman*, I'm pretty sure it will be more like Death of the Centre."

The two women laughed. Theatre brings out the best and the worst in people. They sat there in silence attempting to put

Roy in the parts they had just assigned to Nick.

"Yeah... nope. I think *Camelot* will have to be put on hold yet again," Gwen laughed.

"Seriously though, I totally understand about not wanting to draw attention to his hideout, but I wonder if he would be interested in teaching the kids. Maybe a summer camp or something?"

"Oh! I'm almost sure he would. He loves kids!"

"Does he now..." Evelynn teased.

"Now, don't you work him to death, Evelynn!" Gwen scolded.

"Honey, that's not even what I was thinking. A man, a handsome man at that, who loves kids, loves the theatre, loves to sing, loves his mom... is financially secure..."

"Stop..."

"Is probably a proud American..."

"Stop, Evie..."

"Seems like a perfect match for..."

"You know I don't have time for that right now."

"I was gonna say me, but if you want him... I mean, you found him first..." Evelynn teased.

"We're just friends... I don't want... He doesn't even..." Gwen stuttered.

"Oh really, because it seems exactly what you *should* want!"

"Right. I will when you will..."

"So, when are you coming to visit?" Nick spoke into his iPhone.

"Dude, you've been there for like, twelve minutes." Dave Ripke mocked him from his California end.

"Yeah, and every second of those twelve minutes you have done nothing but complain about... well, everything."

"C'mon, man, not everything... I'm just helping you stay secure in your decision to abandon your best friend."

Nick tipped his head back and laughed. He did miss his sidekick. "Maybe if you head over this way, you might actually like it."

"Okay, let's test that theory. Do you have sunny beaches?" Dave asked.

"No. Quiet, peaceful rivers..."

"So, I'm going to guess those dirty, gravelly beaches aren't covered in silicone enhanced, tanned, beauties?"

"Thankfully, no."

"Then the choices of restaurants and cuisine must be amazing."

"Ah, yes! As much catfish and fried chicken as you can eat! Good solid, down-home cookin'. You know exactly what it is you're eating and you don't spend $52 for a plate and still leave hungry!" Nick was laying it on thick trying to win the battle of City Mouse vs. Country Mouse.

"Whatever! You can't tell what you're eating because it's covered in batter... or... or... gravy!" Dave was cracking up at his own comeback.

Nick laughed, "Best darn gravy you'll find anywhere! And you can be guaranteed that there will be meat on the menu."

Dave nodded on his end, acknowledging, "Yeah, you're hard pressed to find that here. Plenty of 'pretend' meat. Sure it looks like a burger, but it's just a disguised salad." Dave chuffed.

"Exactly," Nick got serious for a moment. "Everything is just... real here. I find that... refreshing."

"Refreshing? Did you just say, 'refreshing'?" Dave was laughing. "You're right, I do need to come down there, for an intervention! We've got to get you out of there!" Nick could hear Dave ordering another drink, probably poolside. "Besides," Dave came back to the phone, "What do you have to do all night? Sit around and braid each other's hair?"

"Nope," Nick indulged and donned his thickest Southern accent, "That's when the harmonikees and banjos come out and we drink whisky out of a jug, smoke our corn pipes and spit tabacky into the fire."

"Dude... you're scaring me."

Nick laughed.

Dave continued, "I remember when you would get up at five in the morning..."

"Still do."

"And you would work all day on set and then work all night in the hotel room, editing the stuff you did all day. You can't tell me that you're not bored to tears!!"

"It has slowed down a lot, I'll give you that. But unfortunately, I can't help being a work-a-holic, so I help the folks out, and if that doesn't wear me out, I go and help out at the local theatre."

"Are you kidding me with this? The local theatre??? You're frickin Nick Penn for goodness sake!"

"I like it. It keeps me busy… and there are some really nice people that work there."

"Okay, okay, now we're talkin'. Any particular person that keeps luring you into the 'community theatre'?"

"It's not important."

"A-ha! It's a chick!! You're being hustled by a small town chick! You know she's just after your money dude… Or your fame…"

"Rip, what are you doing right now?" Nick asked shutting down the direction the conversation was going.

"Nothin', just sittin' by the pool, enjoyin' a little visual entertainment along with the perfect mo-hee-tos."

"My point exactly. You could do that same thing here."

"Dude, you don't even have a pool. Your *hotels* there probably don't even have a pool. Oh, and now that I think about it, does your little town even *have a hotel?*"

"So you'll come visit if you have a pool, is that what I'm hearing?"

"And lots of cute girls, yeah, sure..."

"Cute girls... got it. Okay. I'm on it." Nick accepted the challenge.

"Oh and don't forget my Mojitos," Dave added.

Nick laughed, "I'll put it on the list."

Max and Erin became inseparable. Every moment that Erin was not helping Miss Lisa with chores or serving the homeless, she was out in the back yard with Max. The two became fast friends. When they weren't right next to each other, Max always had an eye on her whereabouts. When she had to go inside, Max stayed close and watched for the door to open again.

Erin was content to sit for hours and make clover chains to drape Max's neck, tail, and paws with her creations. Max would stay right beside her and was equally content to be draped.

Erin talked to Max about... things. Anything and everything. He never told her to shut up or to go find something to do or that she was stupid.

Erin's fingers were buried in the fur on the nape of his neck. She mindlessly played with the thick tufts, letting it slide through her fingers as she gently tugged and released, tugged and released.

The sunshine peaked through the cloudy skies and Erin basked in it's warmth. She was draped across Max's torso.

"He hurt me, Max." She said softly, quietly, almost testing the sound of her voice. She expected Max to move away or somehow tell her to stop talking, but he lay still, watching her.

"He was supposed to love me. Brother's are supposed to love and protect their little sisters... aren't they?" Her eyes were dry as she allowed the thoughts from her yesterdays to slip back up to the surface.

184

"My Mother, not my real Mom... well, her too, I guess, said I wasn't supposed to talk about it. But it's okay to tell you, right?"

Max recognizing a question, thumped his tail and raised his big head in acknowledgement.

"He let his friends... touch me. He said that he loved me. He said that if I loved him then I would keep quiet. But I know it wasn't right. Miss Carter says if you have to keep it a secret, then it probably isn't right. After his friends were gone, he would come and sleep with me. He told me that he loved me. But he didn't care if it hurt me."

Her hands were rhythmically tugging and releasing Max's fur as she worked through her demons.

"I told my Mom... my real Mom, and she said I was a 'filthy liar'." Her voice changed to exaggerate her biological mother's words. "Then she slapped my face and said that if I was to ever say that again I'd get a lickin' from the belt.

"I dint talk no more about it. But it made me sad. It wasn't right. It wasn't right what he did to me. But he said he loved me so..."

The tears silently slipped down her cheeks as she rolled onto her side. Max raised his head, reading her movement and knowing to stay still while she adjusted her position.

"Miss Carter came and took me away from my family."

She sat up and looked at Max's face, and petted his head, "Can I tell you something else? I don't miss them. Is that wrong? I miss my Mom, my real Mom, but she hurt me too. And... and my brother scares me. When he would open my door at night... I didn't want him to come in. I didn't want him in my room." She squeezed her eyes shut to delete the memory and shook her head. "I told him that he should get out, that he wasn't supposed to be there. But he said that it's 'cause he loved me that he liked to sleep with me. But he dint like to sleep." She took a deep breath and shook her head again. "But Miss Carter says he can't ever hurt me again." She looked off into the sky, thinking, "I think that's a good thing."

She laid her head back down on her best friend's fluffy side and they both sat in silence until it was time to go inside.

She heard Miss Lisa call from the back door and waved.

"You ain't mad at me, right, Max? You'll still be my friend, won't you? And, you won't tell anybody, right? I mean, not your doggy friends. I know you won't tell Miss Lisa. But I don't want us to not be friends, okay? Ok, Max? I love you, boy. You're my best friend."

She kissed him on the nose and went inside.

Chapter Ten

"Hello, beautiful." Nick grinned, as he walked into Gwen's office.

Gwen snickered under her breath and chuffed, "Is that Hollywood-speak?"

Nick smiled easily and came to sit across from her. "Just calling it how I see it."

Gwen cocked her eyebrow and looked at his handsome face over her glasses.

"What are you working on? Can I interrupt?"

Gwen lifted her reading glasses to the top of her head, pulling her long straight hair away from her face.

"You don't often wear your hair down," Nick observed, "I like it. It's pretty."

"Thank you?" she squinted her eyes at him. "Okay, what do you want? All these compliments..."

"Can't one friend compliment another friend without wanting something in return?'

She stared at him a moment more, waiting for something to happen, but then conceded, "Yes, I guess so..." she said still eyeing him suspiciously.

"Good, cause I think you're beautiful and I've decided to tell you... a lot."

"Uh, really not necessary..."

Nick sat back in his chair. He put his hands behind his head, crossed his ankles and looked at her for a moment before he spoke, "You really don't know do you?"

A moment of panic crossed her face, "What? What don't I know?"

"That you're beautiful."

Gwen rolled her eyes and let her glasses slip back onto her face and went back to looking over her script.

"I mean it, don't people tell you that all the time?"

She glanced back up at him, "Yup. My mom, every time we talk."

"I meant..."

"Is this what you came to interrupt me with?" she only half scolded.

"Oh, uh no, actually," Nick leaned back toward her desk. "When does the adoption go through for Erin?"

Gwen sat back up and slid her glasses to the top of her head again. She looked away, checking the calendar in her mind. "One week from tomorrow. "

"Don't you have an inspection today?"

She breathed in deeply and slowly released the air, "Yes... today at 6:00."

Nick nodded and a smile crossed his face.

She couldn't help smile back as stressed as she was. "I'm pretty excited. Nervous too."

He showed his Emmy winning smile and added, "It's going to be fine. You're going to be great and Erin is going to have a home."

Gwen closed her eyes letting his words of encouragement sink in. She nodded, "I certainly hope so. I really appreciate that you... get it."

"It's all new to me, but I'm learning... I'm here for you."

She got up from her desk and leaned in to hug Nick. He stood to pull her closer to him and she allowed herself to be held. His arms were so strong and suddenly she felt so small. She felt safe there. And he smelled so good. And his arms were just the right amount of tightness. And...

Gwen gasped and stepped back. "I'm so sorry. I mean, I didn't mean to... you know... like... hang out there all day... I just..."

"Stop worrying about it. It's fine. There's more if you need another..." He opened his arms offering another round.

"Oh, uh... no, I'm good. But that was nice." She rolled her eyes at herself.. *That was nice?? I'm such an idiot.*

"So, a week from tomorrow?" Nick sat back down and dove back into business. "So, next Thursday?"

Gwen nodded, thankful for the change of subject, "If all goes well, then yes, next Thursday. If I pass the inspection, then I get to go pick her up and she can start living with me." She smiled at the thought.

She had spent a few hours every night over the last week changing her "baby" room into a perfect young lady's room. A gentle lavender covered the walls and butterflies fluttered up and around the doorframe. She bought a dainty white twin bed but left it empty. Gillian had suggested that she have Erin pick out her own sheets and bedspread explaining that it makes them feel more like it's their own. In the foster care system, so many of their choices are taken away, so Gwen heeded Gillian's advice and decided they would go on a quick shopping spree on their way home.

"Erin doesn't even know she's being adopted." Gwen stared off dreamily. "I'm going to ask her tomorrow." Gwen wasn't allowed to tell her until the final inspection. If the inspection goes as planned, she is driving to Little Rock tomorrow to talk to Erin. Gwen's stomach did a little flip flop and it brought a smile to Gwen's face.

"So, you like the idea?" Nick leaned in expectantly.

Gwen blinked back at him. "Um... yes?"

"Great! I think Saturday would work out perfectly for a pool party if that's okay with you."

"A pool party? That is a great idea!" Gwen gasped. "We could invite all of her friends from her classes!"

"Yeah, kinda like ... what I just said." Nick looked at her confused.

193

"Oh, oh, I'm sorry... my mind wandered off. I think it's a great idea."

"Did you hear the part about me barbequing?" Nick asked, raising an eyebrow.

Gwen giggled sheepishly, "No?" She laughed again, "But I think it's a wonderful addition to *my* brilliant idea." She bit her bottom lip and gave Nick a sideways apologetic glance and she was happily greeted with a return smile.

Gwen's eyes darted all about the room and Nick sat quiet knowing she was deep in "planning mode" and wouldn't hear a thing until she came up for air.

But her jubilant face started to slip away.

Nick sat up in his chair. "No, what just happened there?" All of your happiness literally just washed away."

"I can't afford a pool party." Gwen looked at him like a sad puppy. "I can't afford that!" She dropped her head but her brain was still going a hundred miles an hour. "I spent a lot of money getting her room ready and the legal fees... and the gas to go back and forth... Oh, I want to do this, but... I'd have to rent the pool, order food..."

"No... you..." Nick tried to interject, but she was already on a path.

"And I'd have to send out invitations, and I still have to get her some sheets..."

"Gwen, I can help... "

"No, absolutely not! I can't have you pay for this, it's not..."

"Gwen... Gwen...," Nick stood up and walked around her desk and took her hands in his. He effortlessly lifted her to her feet and she followed. He kept his grip on her hands as he looked into her eyes. "Gwen, you must have forgotten that one part in *your* brilliant plan where the pool party was going to be at my house."

Gwen looked at him confused. "You have a pool? At your house?" She shook her head "Of course you do, you're a ba-zillionaire."

Nick laughed, "You make it sound like such a bad thing."

"It's not, I mean, I'm happy for you, but I can't go around assuming you're going to pay for stuff just cause..."

"You're not. I offered. And no, I don't have a pool... yet."

"What? Oh, no. No, no, no.... no."

"I was planning on building one so my friend Rip would come and visit, and then I remembered Erin's big day. Gwen, I'm building it anyway. It would make me happy to have it used."

"Really? You have to bribe your friends to come and see you?"

Nick threw his head back and laughed, releasing Gwen's hands in the process. She immediately felt the loss of their warmth. "Wow, you are doing wonders for my ego today," he teased.

Gwen looked down at her shoes and smiled. When she returned his gaze she said, "Thank you, yes. We would love it if you could host Erin's Adoption party at your brand new pool." She rolled her eyes. "I can't believe I just said that."

"You won't regret it! It's going to be so fun!"

Gwen scrunched her face, "I think you're going to enjoy it more than the kids!"

"I love planning. I love creating landscapes. And my mom loves kids. She is going to bake everything under the sun, just to warn you." Nick laughed.

Gwen smiled and shrugged her shoulders, "Okay then. What should I do?"

"Invites. Invite all her friends. She's been though enough. We want to make sure she knows that she's loved and has been missed."

Gwen furrowed her brow. She reached out for his hand, "You are so thoughtful and generous and you haven't even met her."

Nick squeezed her hand in return. "If you love her, I'm sure I will too. I respect you a great deal for what you're doing."

Gwen pulled away and flopped back down in her office chair which rocked back cradling her weight. "No, don't think that, I wish it was as noble as all that but, honestly, it's also pretty selfish on my part. I wanted a family. I wanted children and I am happy that not only can I make her happy, but I can stand with some happiness too."

Nick shook his head, "Nothin' wrong with that. I think that's how families are created... and... sustained. We all need each other."

Gwen nodded. "Yeah, I think you're right."

Gwen caught herself staring into his eyes and he didn't turn away. She broke the gaze, turning away feeling heat rise in her cheeks.

Nick slapped his hand on the desk startling Gwen, "Welp, I gotta go. I have to get plans drawn up, order some greenery, buy a plane ticket for my buddy Rip..."

"You have to buy his plane ticket too? Are you sure he even likes you?" Gwen laughed.

Nick smiled and winked at her pointing his finger ... "You... you ... just... I'm gonna let that one slide. Wait till you meet him. He's a short little, crabby, shallow, sarcastic bundle of love. You're gonna love him."

Gwen raised her eyebrows and nodded, "Oh yeah, I can hardly wait."

And out the door he went.

Hey, r u home? Gwen text Nick.

Will b in about 7 min. Bringing the tractor in. What's up?

Is it all right if I stop by?
Absolutely.
Great! I'm on my way. Be there in about 15. Gwen smiled as she pulled away from her driveway and pointed her little truck toward Nick's house.

Nick was just closing the doors to the barn as Gwen made her way to the bottom of the long driveway. The sun was just beginning to lower in the sky, still giving plenty of light but also offering a brilliant display of pinks and yellows.

"Hey you," Gwen called out as she closed her truck's door.

"Hey! To what do I owe this great pleasure?" He smiled, looking over his shoulder.

"I just wanted to tell you in person... I have been approved to be Erin's legal parent!"

Nick stopped what he was doing and turned to face her. She was beaming. Her smile was so bright and it reached up to the creases in the corners of her eyes.

Nick reached out to embrace her and she gladly accepted. "That is GREAT!" He lifted her feet off the ground and spun her around. "I had no doubt in my mind!! Do you want to walk and tell me all about it? Or would you rather go inside for some lemonade or something?"

Gwen thought for just a second, "You know, a walk sounds really good. I've never been out on your parents' property before."

"You haven't?"

"No, but I must admit that I fell in love with this place from the driveway alone. What is that, like seven miles to get here?"

Nick laughed. He's known many a night when if felt like seven miles. 'It's really only three."

"Oh, well, I love it. The way it twists and turns and all those gorgeous trees, with just enough blue sky peeking through them... mmmm, breathtaking."

"Well, then, let me introduce you to the fields. I just cleared this section of hay over here to the left, so we can walk that. It leads down to a creek along the side and the back. Sometimes you might accidently find a cow or two that have drifted over to sample my Pop's hay field. " He stretched his arm out leading the way.

Nick was wearing jeans and a faded t-shirt. He wore his typical ball cap and was covered with dirt and clippings from his long day's work. She could smell the fresh cut hay with a mixture of his sweat when he hugged her.

Gwen walked along the edge of the freshly cut grass mixture and let her senses take everything in. The smell of the freshly cut hay was so sweet. She absent-mindedly reached her hands out to brush against the tops of the uncut portion. And while they walked, she told him of the inspection, how at first the two people in suits were completely silent, but the sound of the pencils on their clipboards was deafening. Then she told him about the questions. Gillian did her best to be the silent supporter, but offered assistance if she felt Gwen needed it. Which was a lot. And then she explained about that brief moment when it felt like they were scolding her and wondering if she was taking this seriously and that the life of a child hangs in the balance of their decision... she thought she had failed, and could barely breathe.

But then, she told him how after they made her sweat it out for what felt like twenty minutes, they relieved her suffering by telling her that she had passed. They both signed off on a piece of paper and handed one copy to her and kept two copies for themselves.

As she was telling her story, she hadn't realized that tears had silently slipped from her eyes and assumed that the setting sun was impairing her vision. And what she also didn't notice was that he was hanging on to every word.

They reached the back end of the field and Nick lifted some branches from her path so she could gain access. Suddenly, she really saw where she was for the first time.

The little creek was full and happily bubbling over jutting rocks, making its way down jagged, uneven paths. Its gurgling made a pleasant backdrop for taking in the view. Gwen stopped and looked all around her.

"Nick! This is remarkable! I mean... it is so peaceful and calm here. I could stay here for days!"

He came closer to where she stood to get a better look at what she was seeing.

The vines twisted and connected with tree branches making a sort of canopy, which came alive with movement every few moments. The dark green ivy wound its way up the steep slope of the opposite side of the creek ever searching for the sunshine. The rocks that lined the creek were both sharp and smooth, depending on where and how often they came in contact with the water.

"You like it?" Nick asked.

"I do. I think this is the most beautiful place I've ever seen!" Gwen gushed. "Thank you for bringing me here!"

"Just say the word and I'll put a little table and chairs out here for you to have tea."

Gwen laughed. "It would be perfect for that! It's... it's... enchanting. I bet there are fairies that fly about when you're not around."

Nick's heart skipped a beat seeing her so happy in his world. He didn't hear the caution his conscious was trying to whisper to him. She was just so beautiful.

"Gwen," Nick grabbed both of her hands and turned her toward him.

Gwen looked up at him waiting for him to speak, but he did not, and then she felt heat on her face and in her stomach and she realized that no more speaking was coming.

"I, um... do you get to come back here often?" she asked with a slight quiver in her voice.

"Gwen, I'm going to kiss you." Nick said barely above a whisper and leaning in closer.

Gwen's heart pounded in her ear and it felt like the world was moving in slow motion. Even the creek had quieted it's song. "Nick, please don't..."

She knew that deep down she probably wanted him to, but also knew that she wasn't ready for a man to feel this way about her. She had so much to do. So many jobs and hats to wear and now a child...

But before she could vocalize her fears, she had tipped her head back and received the kiss. It was soft, and warm and made her body feel like it was on fire. It was everything a kiss should be.

His right hand cradled her head at its base, while the other hand pressed the small of her back close to his body

When Nick finally pulled away and the birds chattered again, and the creek gurgled again, it only took seconds for Gwen to replace the perfect, exquisite pleasure with all the fears that were choking her.

She looked into Nick's eyes and saw nothing but tenderness there. He wanted to kiss her again. She wanted him to kiss her again, but uttered, "Nick, I... I can't..."

Her heart was pounding. She pulled away from him and fought the tangled branches to get to the open, less intimate feel of the field. "I'm sorry... I... just..."

"Gwen, are you alright? What are you sorry for?"

She stopped and turned to him, "I just can't... uh... be what you want me to be." She turned and started making her way back to the house.

"What is it that you think I want from you?"

"I don't even know, actually. I can't even imagine someone like you... even... talking to me. But I..."

"Gwen, could you stop walking, please? Just for a moment?"

She stopped and Nick took her hand in his. She attempted to pull it away, but didn't fight as he held her. She couldn't look him in the face.

"Gwen, it was just a kiss. Something I would like to do again..." His words caressed her heart and his eyes were so tender. She could feel tears stinging her eyes.

She wanted to selfishly give in to him. She wanted to melt in his embrace. He would make her feel safe... until he decided that she isn't what he wanted anymore and then he would leave. He would leave her and she would be alone again. All alone again to start over.

She turned away from him.

"I can't, Nick. I want to, I mean, but I... it's just that... I don't have time for this..."

"For what?"

"For... this." She flailed her arms between the two of them, what little space there was. "I have a full time career. That I love, by the way. And now... now..." The tears spilled from their edges, "I'm going to be a full time mom. I don't have... anything left... for... "

Nick pulled her into an embrace and she cried into his shoulder. "I am not asking you for anything that you are not wanting to give. I enjoy your company and I'd like to get to know you better." He leaned back so he could look at her face. "I like you, Gwen. I like being with you." He used his thumb to brush away a tear that slipped down her cheek.

Gwen pulled away and turned from him. "I'm sorry. I just don't have time for that anymore."

"Gwen..."

"Please don't." She held up her hand to halt his following her, and walked back to her truck, alone.

Chapter Eleven

Gwen started out early the next morning and pointed her silver Toyota Tacoma toward Little Rock. Thoughts swirled in her head and not even Josh Groban crooning to her through the speakers could quiet her thoughts.

He kissed me! How dare he!! I mean, technically, I told him not to! She battled with herself as she still flipped her phone over and pushed the Home button.

No calls. No texts.

He hasn't even tried to reach out to me. Gwen sighed heavily, missing his conversations already.

Why did he have to kiss me? And why did it have to be so amazing? And what's wrong with wanting to just be friends? Since when is that a crime in America?

She took a sip from her coffee in its Styrofoam cup and glanced at the gift package in the passenger seat.

I'm not going to mess things up this time. Priorities. I have a child now. I am adopting a child. Me... adopting a child. If she accepts me. Oh, what if she doesn't? What if she doesn't want to live with me? Then what happens? It's not like I'd MAKE her come and live with me if she didn't want to. I mean, who would do that to a child? She's been through enough.

I have to stay focused. I can't concentrate on a romantic relationship right now. I mean, it might not have turned into a relationship, but what if it did? Then where would I be? I'd fall in love! And then he'd decide that Bakersfield, Arkansas isn't good enough for him anymore. And he'd go back to his fans and his fame. But what if he didn't? What if small town life was good enough for him, which I doubt? He'd want to go out on dates! I don't have time for dates!! It's bad enough that my child has to spend hours and hours at my job with me! And what about... oh... I'm SO not ready for that.... No one has seen me naked since... I don't even want to think about that.... Really? Really brain? That's where you take things?

She hit the Home button on her phone to light it up.

No calls. No texts.

Well that just figures. Gwen sighed a very loud and very guttural sigh. *I knew it.*

Gwen pulled up in front of the little church and removed her sunglasses. The few tears that had managed to escape had smeared her make-up. She grabbed a tissue and swiped the excess black smudge away. She put a smile on her face, grabbed her brightly colored gift bag and made her way to the front door.

"Miss Gwen! Miss Gwen!!! I'm so happy to see you!" Erin ran to Gwen and wrapped her tiny little eight-year-old arms around her. "I have so much to tell you! Miss Gillian came by to see me two days... " she looked back over her shoulder at her friend Miss Lisa for confirmation, who nodded. "Yeah, two days ago! She is so nice. Oh! Oh and I want you to meet someone! He's my very bestest friend! He is so nice too and..."

Gwen laughed and bent down to Erin's level. "Honey, honey... slow down."

211

Gwen looked over at Miss Lisa, "Do you mind if we sit in there for a few moments?"

"Of course! Of course! You go right on ahead. I'll be waitin' in the kitchen for you to come on out." Shalisa folded her hands together and nodded at Gwen, giving her a quiet affirmation of love and encouragement. The entire staff had grown to love Erin and were overwhelmed with joy at what this day will mean to one sweet, precious little girl.

Gwen grabbed her hand and led her over toward one of the pews in the quiet sanctuary.

"We never get to come in here, 'cept on Sundays. This is a place you gotta be quiet." Erin whispered and pushed her glasses up with her finger.

"I know, but I have some important things to discuss with you, if you don't mind."

Erin shrugged. "I guess that's okay."

Gwen walked about half way in and slid into a pew on the right. She had Erin sit down next to and shifted her knees so she was facing her. Gwen took in a deep breath. She turned to the gift behind her and was just about to speak when she looked up and saw tears spilling from Erin's eyes.

"Oh... honey... what? What's wrong?" Gwen reached into her pocket and pulled out her mascara stained tissue and wiped Erin's tears away. "Why are you crying?"

Erin tried to convey her thoughts in a whisper, but the crying and the whispering just wasn't coming out very clear.

"Sweetie, it's okay to use your words. No one else is in here. I can't understand you. Please tell me why you are crying."

"I did something wrong? And... and... and..." she hiccupped, "...and you're not going to come and see me anymore? I try to be good. I don't know what I did wrong. Please say you'll come back Miss Gwen. I love you so much and I can be good, I promise."

The lump was so heavy in Gwen's throat that she could hardly swallow it down to speak.

"Sweetie... Sweetie... no, you have done nothing wrong. Please don't cry."

Erin looked up at her ballet teacher with both doubt and hope. Her crocodile tears still spilled even though she tried her best to contain them.

Gwen tried to wipe her cheeks dry with the wet tissue. "Erin, what I'm going to talk to you about, will hopefully make you happy. No more tears, okay?"

Erin nodded, and sniffed. She wiped her face with a dry sleeve and was ready to start from the beginning again.

"Erin... honey... "Gwen giggled as she fought for just the right words. "You know I thought of a million ways of how to say this and now that I am sitting here, I am a complete loss for words."

Erin just sat quietly and waited, still expecting the worst. Every once in a while Gwen would hear Erin's breath catching with tears ever so close to the surface.

"I... bought you a present."

Erin looked up and smiled.

Gwen pulled a small box out of the shiny metallic purple bag and handed the teal blue box to Erin.

Erin gently lifted the lid from the box and revealed a necklace with a shiny heart pendant that had two tiny diamonds embedding the outer edge.

"Erin... I would like... very much to adopt you. I would love it if you would come home with me and live with me and grow up with me and... and all the things that happen

in between. Would you be willing to maybe...
be ... uh... my daughter?"

Erin grew quiet and Gwen knew she
was taking it all in but was not sure about
which direction she was taking it.

Finally she asked, "So... you would be
my new mom?"

A smile spread across Gwen's face. "I
would, if you could be happy with that. That's
why there's two diamonds. One for you and
one for me."

"So... my mom that I have now?"

Gwen took in a deep breath, "Erin,
Mrs. Cavenaugh, your, uh, foster mom, would
no longer be a part of your life."

"She didn't want me anymore? And
my brother and sister? Carrie and Evan?
They won't be my brother and sister
anymore?"

Gwen fought hard to keep the tears at
bay but the stinging told her it would be a
losing battle. She was gathering her thoughts
to speak when Erin spoke again.

"How long will I stay with you?"

"Oh honey, that's the best part." Gwen
found her smile again, "Forever. If I adopt
you, that means you and I are family.

Forever. Even after you're grown and have a family of your own. I will forever be your Mom. Adoption means forever."

Erin was silent again.

"I ... uh... have a room all ready for you at my house. It's painted a light purple. Your favorite. And... you can decorate it however you want."

"Does it have a closet? And a dresser?'

Gwen laughed, "It does. It does indeed."

"Can I bring my clothes?"

"If you'd like. Or we can get you different ones."

"My mother would be mad if... uh... She won't be my mother any more?"

Gwen silently shook her head.

"I won't go back to her house?"

"No, honey. It'd be just you and me, kiddo."

Erin smiled. "Okay. Sure."

Gwen drew in a thankful breath, "Really?" She laughed.

"Yeah, sure, I guess so. Do I still get to go to the Centre?"

"Oh yes!" Gwen laughed, "Probably more than you'll want to."

"I'll get to see all my friends again!"

"Oh, of course! And I forgot to tell you the best part! Two days after your adoption, we are having a pool party and all of your friends are invited!"

"You have a pool?" Erin's eyes got wide.

"Well, uh, no... but a friend of mine does, and he is so excited to meet you." If I still *have* a friend with a pool, that is, Gwen thought.

"So I can invite Tereza and Emily and Brittany and Shauna and Shelbi and... Oh and Miss Jenni too? And Miss Gillian? And Ms. Betty? And Miss Danni?"

Gwen laughed and pulled her on to her lap. "Yes, my beautiful child, you may invite them all."

Erin twisted her body to wrap her arms around Gwen's neck. "I love you Miss Gwen!!!" Erin pulled back to see her ballet teacher's face in a whole new light. "Can I call you my Mom now?"

Gwen swallowed hard, "You can, if you want to.

217

Erin put her hands on both sides of Gwen's face, looking deep into her eyes. "I don't think I want to."

Gwen registered her surprise, but told herself to not say anything. This is a lot to throw on an eight-year old who is officially on her third chance of parents.

Erin ran her hand gently over Gwen's forehead to smooth the wrinkles and then turned to press her back into Gwen's chest. "My mo... um, I mean, the other one, used to make me call her Mother or sometimes Mom, but she didn't like it. I don't think she likes being a mother. I don't even know why she gots kids. She was always upset with me. She yelled a lot."

Gwen could feel the lump forming in her throat again.

"I did lots of stuff wrong."

Gwen wanted to correct her and explain that the Cavenaughs were wrong and they obviously didn't love her the way she deserved to be loved, but she could tell that the child was working through something; so instead, just held her a bit tighter as she continued talking things through.

"I think you want to be a mom." She played with the necklace chain in the palm of her hand.

And there they went. The tears spilled out and down her cheeks.

"I think you love me, cause you came to visit me. And you brought me stuff. She didn't come to see me at all. She bought me presents a lot, but it wasn't stuff I liked," her arms came up on both sides and she shrugged her shoulders emphatically, " and I even told her! She bought it anyways."

Gwen closed her eyes and kissed the top of her curls.

"Miss Gillian loves me. Miss Carter loves me too. Oh, can we invite Miss Carter to the party?"

Gwen nodded her reply, unable to speak.

"Miss Gillian's got kids and they call her Momma. And all the kids on the Walton's call their Momma, Momma. Can I call you that? Momma?"

Gwen's face was wet with her silent tears and she could only nod once again. She kissed the top of her head and managed to squeak out, "I'd like that. Very much."

Erin was bouncing off the walls. Hopping. Skipping. Chattering away.

Gwen raised her eyebrows and leaned in toward Shalisa. "Is she like this a lot?"

"Girl, yes. This is her happy. And on these days, just smile and let her jabber, 'cause on those bad days," Shalisa reached her hand toward the heavens, "It's sho gonna break your heart." She laughed and leaned into Gwen. "But, praise Jesus, you're gonna mend that lil girl's heart and she gonna be a new person. You a good woman, Miss Gwen. You good."

Gwen had brought Erin a suitcase and Erin was busily filling it with her clothes still stored in a trash bag."

"These clothes don't fit in my suitcase, Miss..." a smile spread across her face, "Momma." She giggled. "What should I do with them?

"Why don't you leave them in the bags for now, and we can put them right into your dresser when we get home."

"And the closet."

Gwen laughed, "... And the closet."

220

"Okay!"

She climbed up on top of her suitcase to keep it closed while she zipped it shut.

Shalisa had left to make copies of the signed discharge papers and handed Gwen a copy.

"Thank you, Miss Shalisa," Gwen offered her hand, "for taking such good care of her."

"You don't have to thank me!" Shalisa said in a high-pitched quick tone. But just in case, it wasn't heard, she repeated it, "You don't have to thank me." A little slower than before. "You don't have to thank... me." Gwen looked into her dark eyes and saw the beginnings of a watery sheen.

Shalisa shook her head trying to hold it together. "Lil girl. You have been such a bleeeeesssssssing to me. Such a blessing. I won't ever forget you."

She leaned down to embrace Erin. Erin happily filled her arms and accepted all the kisses. "Go on now, you got to go. Don't keep your new Momma waitin'"

"I won't!" Erin squealed. "I love you, Miss Lisa!"

"Oh girl, you know I love me some you, too."

Gwen put the suitcase and two trashbags into the back and got Erin buckled into the back seat. "You okay? Does that feel alright?"

Erin laughed. "I can do it by myself, you know. I am eight."

Gwen laughed. "Yes, I suppose you can. Just be patient with me. I've got a lot to learn. I've never been a Momma."

"Not ever?"

"Nope." Gwen climbed into the driver's seat and buckled up as well. "Not ever. You'll help me, right?"

"Oh yeah. I'm a good helper."

Erin giggled from the back seat. Gwen looked into the rearview mirror, "What's so funny?"

"Now, when I go to class, I know my hair will always be fixed right!"

Gwen laughed, "I will do my best."

They drove along in silence for only a few moments before Erin spoke up again,

"Momma, I might not get to go to the pool party."

"What? Why not? It's *for* you! It would be silly if the guest of honor doesn't show up!"

"But, I don't have a swimming suit."

"Oh, don't you worry. We're getting ready to stop by the store so you can pick out some new things for your room AND we'll get a swimming suit while we're there. How's that!"

Erin squealed from the back seat and Gwen could see her arms flapping around.

They pulled into the parking lot of the biggest Walmart either of them had ever seen and the Mother/Daughter Day of Shopping commenced!

One credit card swipe and not nearly enough bags to show for it, the two emerged in a full on shopping coma. Erin was tired. Gwen was shocked at how fast things that little girls need add up. They were both hungry so they loaded up the bags and went next door to the Cracker Barrel.

They sat across from each other and discussed their purchases.

"I can't believe we found the perfect bedspread to match your room!" Gwen beamed.

"I know!! And it has butterflies AND polka dots!!"

"Nice choice on your new swimming suit too!"

"I picked out the Merida one cause you said I look like her only with blonde hair. And I have glasses, too."

"You do! Those lil blonde curls are everywhere! I love them! We can try and get you an appointment next week to get a trim and some shampoo."

"Okay! *Brave* is one of my favorite movies."

Gwen laughed. "It must be because you have the *Brave* swimming suit, and towel. A set of sheets and even a toothbrush with Princess Merida on them!"

"And don't forget the movie!"

"Well, of course. You've got to have the movie to go along with everything else!"

"Can we watch it tonight?"

"After we get your room set up, if it's not too late, I think it would be a great idea. I have to go into work for a few hours tomorrow and I'm sure everyone will be so happy to see you."

"Oh me too! Miss Betty will be wondering where all her hugs are! She loves it when I give her hugs."

Gwen nodded, knowing all too well that Miss Betty's real paycheck were the hugs from all the children.

They continued on their way home and talked about how they were going to arrange Erin's room, how they were going to spend every day at the Centre, and how much her friends are going to like her new swimming suit… but then Erin suddenly got quiet.

Gwen would look into the mirror to see that she was okay. If she fell asleep, would that be okay? Or, should she try and keep her awake? They were really only about thirty minutes from home. Maybe a tiny nap wouldn't hurt. But while Gwen was racing through all of her brand new "mommy decisions" she heard a sniffle. She looked up to see tears pouring from Erin's face and dripping off her chin.

225

"Erin? Honey? What's wrong? What happened? Are you alright?"

Erin did not respond, but inhaled deeply and a tiny, painful sound came out of her as if someone squeezed her too hard. More tears.

"Erin. Are you hurt? Why are you crying?"

Erin's hands were in her lap, her head was down and the tears and snot flowed freely. Gwen pulled over into a gas station parking lot. She jumped out of the car and went to the passenger side. She opened the door and did a quick scan for blood or anything else outwardly that might be causing pain. The seatbelt seemed fine, she had kicked her shoes off, but no pain there...

"Erin, honey, what is it?" She grabbed a tissue and began wiping her face. "Honey, use your words. I can't help you if you don't tell me what is wrong."

Erin raised her head and looked at Gwen. She looked heartbroken. Gwen felt so helpless. "It's okay. You can talk to me."

"My... my dog."

"What? What? Can you say that again? I didn't understand you."

"My dog. I left my dog."

"A dog?" Gwen wasn't sure she heard right. "A... a stuffed dog... like a toy?"

Erin shook her head.

"What dog, sweetie. Please talk to me. I'm not going to be mad. You didn't do anything wrong, but you have to tell me. Tell me what is hurting you."

"I have a dog. He's my best friend. I meant to tell you about him but I got so excited and I forgot! His name is Max and I left him!" Huge sobs poured from her tiny frame.

"Okay, okay... you have a dog... Were we supposed to bring him with us?"

"He's my dog." It was the tiniest, saddest three words Gwen had ever heard.

"I'm sorry. I didn't ... didn't know you had a dog."

"He's going to wonder where I am. Who is going to feed him? He's waiting for me."

"Okay... uh... okay, let me think..." Gwen got a fresh tissue and wiped Erin's tears away again. "No need to cry, honey, let's figure this out, okay?"

Erin nodded and tried to slow her breathing. Gwen gave her a tissue to have her blow her nose.

"A dog. Okay. We are almost home. Let's get there and I'll call Miss Shalisa and make sure that she feeds him."

"Max."

"Max. And I'll have her tell him that we will be back to pick him up tomorrow. Okay? Is that okay?"

Erin nodded.

"Okay, no more tears, right?"

"I just love him so much... I didn't want..."

"It's okay. We'll get this figured out, alright? Let's get home and set up your room and then, apparently, we're going to make room for a dog too."

They drove toward home and for some reason, Gwen decided to take a detour. Instead of going straight into town where she lived, she turned right on a gravel road.

"Is this where we live?" Erin asked sleepily.

"No, it's on the way. It's such a pretty drive and I was going to show you where your pool party is going to be."

228

"It's back here? This IS pretty! This is the most beautiful place I ever seen!"

Gwen clenched her teeth hearing the improper speech... *Pick your battles,* she told herself, *We'll work on that another day.*

"Okay see this driveway, out your window? It's going to be down there," Gwen explained.

"Can we go see?" Erin stretched up in her seat to try and see further down the paved driveway.

"Not tonight. We already have too many things to do," Gwen laughed.

They weren't five feet past the driveway, when Gwen saw Nick's shiny black Ford coming the opposite way.

Nick slowed down as he came to her window, and Gwen did the same. It bothered her that butterflies twitched and fluttered about her insides aching to be set free.

"Well, hello!" He said as he rolled down his window. "Were you coming to see me?"

Gwen tried to look irritated but was pretty sure it came across as an upset stomach. "No, we were just taking a scenic route home."

"We?" Nick inquired.

"I picked up Erin today," she smiled. "She said that I could be her new adopted Mom."

"Hey!" Nick exclaimed, "That's awesome!" He jumped out of his truck, knowing full well that it was blocking on coming traffic... if there was any. He walked over to Gwen's window and stuck his head in. "That's great news! Are you going to introduce me?"

Gwen tried her best to give the heaviest, you're-wasting-my-time sigh, "Erin, I'd like you to meet..."

"You're on TV!" Erin shouted.

Nick gave Gwen a sideways glance and under his breath said, "*She* knows who I am."

Gwen decided not to respond. Nick made his way around to the passenger side to talk to Erin and Gwen rolled the window down for him.

"So, you're going to be living around here, huh?"

Erin smiled. "Yup! Miss Gwen was my ballet teacher and is now going to be my new Momma since my old one didn't want me any more... and but, I guess that my new Momma will also still be my ballet teacher. Right, Momma? Won't you?"

Gwen smiled and looked back over her shoulder, "I sure will." She reached her arm out to pat Erin's leg. "Erin, honey, Mr. Nick is the one who is going to host your pool party."

"You live down the long driveway?" she asked.

"I sure do."

"Can I see your house?"

Gwen interrupted, "Uh, honey, it's not polite to invite yourself places."

"I'd love to have you see my house." Nick was all smiles and it was killing Gwen. "Do you want to come over and have dinner? *My* Momma is making spaghetti, and I'm sure she would love to have company."

"Can we Momma? Can we? He invited us!"

Over the next thirty seconds, Gwen agonized over that one simple answer. She hadn't talked to Nick since "the kiss" and she really did miss his conversations. But now he was perfectly clear in letting her know that he wanted more than friendship and she just couldn't afford the extra time to develop that. No, it's better to just head home instead of leading him on. Space. That's what she needed. Space. She would get used to not texting him everyday. She would have to settle into the idea that her own personal happiness would have to wait. What if he meets someone else? Well,... then... it wasn't meant to be. Erin is more important right now.

Nick suddenly appeared back at Gwen's window. "So, whatya say? I know you can put away some cheesy garlic bread," he teased.

Gwen blushed and laughed as she looked away. Nick nudged her with his elbow, "I'm texting my mother to let her know you're coming."

Gwen looked back at Erin, "You want spaghetti for dinner tonight?"

Erin threw her arms in the air and squealed, "Yeah!"

"I guess, Mr. Penn, please add two more for dinner."

Nick winked. "I already did. Follow me guys!" He double-patted the window frame and turned back toward his truck.

Chapter Twelve

Erin unbuckled and flew out of the back seat to meet Nick. "Can I see the pool? Can we go swimming? I brought my swimming suit! It's in the back seat. It's Merida, you know, from *Brave*. I look like her 'cept I don't have red hair. I have blonde hair. I gotta towel too."

Gwen came over and put her hands on her shoulders. "I don't think the pool is ready, sweetie."

Erin looked up at her like that was the dumbest answer ever. How can you have a pool party if the pool isn't ready?

"I'm afraid she's right," Nick stepped in. "I can show you where the pool is going to be, but they haven't built it yet."

He reached out his hand and Erin gladly accepted it and they started toward the back of the house.

Gwen tagged along behind and rolled her eyes. Ugh! Why does he have to be so perfect?

They walked around to the backyard and Loraine came out the back door. She was wiping her hands with a dish towel and tossed it over her shoulder as she leaned over the railing of the cedar deck. "I thought I heard voices.

"Hey Loraine! Your son kidnapped us out on the road."

"Yeah, not surprised. Thinks he's Robin Hood." She threw her head back and laughed at her own joke. "I'm so glad you could join us for dinner. It will be nice to have a little estrogen around the table."

"I couldn't turn down your cooking," Gwen cooed.

She flapped her dishtowel at Gwen and happily accepted the compliment. "I'm so glad that you and Nick have become such good friends."

Gwen unconsciously looked down the path she was on only the day before practically running away from the nicest, most handsome, thoughtful…

"And it's about time that he met someone that doesn't turn to mush because of that smile. He's not all that," Loraine teased, "I changed those diapers."

Gwen was brought out of her reverie, when Loraine laughed. Such a sweet laugh. She genuinely loved her boys, and taught them to be very down to earth. Nick may have been an Emmy-winning super star in California but here on the farm, he was Nicholas Adam Penn, third son of Curt and Loraine Penn and not too good for an honest day's work.

They both looked out into the vastness of the "back yard" and watched Nick measure out the size of the pool with long steps and Erin doing her best to mirror his every move.

"He's so good with kids." Loraine smiled with fondness.

"How has he not had any of his own?" Gwen asked.

Loraine sighed, "I guess it just wasn't right." She shrugged. "He was with that other gal long enough, but, I don't know, they just didn't fit right. I don't think she wanted kids at all. We only met her the once, and we had to go out there to do it."

235

Gwen furrowed her brow, "Only once? It was what, eight years?"

Loraine shrugged again. "She never wanted to come out here and it broke my heart because Nicholas loves it here so."

Gwen nodded, "You can tell."

"He's a good boy. You two make a good match."

Gwen's shoulders tightened and she chuffed, "Oh... oh no... See that adorable little shadow behind your son? I am adopting her this Thursday. She is going to be my everything along with the theatre. And you already know how much time I spend there." Gwen chuffed again, "I don't ... I don't have time for anything ... or anyone else in my life right now. Too many changes as it is." She chattered nervously.

Loraine just nodded and smiled knowing full well that she was standing next to the woman who would eventually be her daughter-in-law.

Loraine and Erin were playing Go Fish while Nick and Gwen cleaned up after dinner. Curt found an excuse to check the baler to make sure drying the dishes wasn't assigned to him.

"I missed talking to you today," Nick spoke in low tones.

Gwen turned away and focused more intensely on her plates and silverware.

"I was at least hoping for a text to let me know how it went."

Gwen raised her eyebrows and nonchalantly responded, "Well, you found out another way. Live and in person. Erin was more than happy to fill you in on all the details."

"You know what I mean." Nick scooped up the forks from the rinse water and dried them. Gwen stayed quiet. "Well, how was your first day?"

Gwen looked up at his face and remembered it being so close to hers only hours before. He was looking at her so intensely, or so she thought. She felt the stinging in her eyes feeling that tears were close by. She wanted him to kiss her again, but knew that if he did, she would fall in love with him and ruin everything.

She turned back to her sudsy water, "It was... good. It was good. We are going to have to learn each other's languages as Gillian puts it... there were a few tears... but... I think, we're uh... going to be okay."

Nick nudged her with his elbow sensing that if he went in for the hug she would probably shut down. "That's good! It's great! It'll happen, don't rush it. Let her take her time."

Gwen looked up at him and furrowed her brow. "How do you do that?" she asked. "You always know the right thing to say. If I didn't know any better, I'd think that you had adopted a child!"

He couldn't tell if she was being sarcastic or sincere, so, to play it safe, he used his million-dollar smile as a get-out-of-answering card.

Nick walked them to their truck after Erin hugged everyone at least twice and Gwen passed out a couple herself.

"So, text ya tomorrow?"

Gwen looked down at the ground, "I don't know, Nick. I kinda have a lot on my plate right now."

"Wouldn't it be easier to have someone to talk to? We could all use a little help."

She uncomfortably shrugged her shoulder but couldn't bring her eyes up to his.

Erin tugged on her arm, "Can we gooooo?"

"I got this," Nick gallantly stepped across Gwen and picked up Erin and launched her into the air. "You've had a busy day, haven't you? Let's get you in the car."

"Uh, she can do her own seatbelt, you know. She is eight." Gwen teased.

Erin giggled. "I am eight, you know."

"Oh, my apologies, princess."

"It's okay. You can help me if you want to."

"I would love to. I'm a good helper. I... am a gooood helper." He looked past Erin to Gwen hoping she was paying attention. She gave him a sideways glance, but a smile accompanied it, so he knew she was picking up on his clever and so very subtle hints.

He returned to Gwen's window and folded his arms on the window. "Thanks for coming to dinner. My mom loves company."

"We enjoyed it, didn't we, Erin?" She looked back and saw that Erin's eyelids had grown heavy. She was barely hanging on. She laughed, "Just take that as a yes."

Her eyes met Nick's, but then she quickly darted them away looking at her fingers trace the bottom inside edge of the steering wheel.

"We can't be friends either?" Nick asked.

"I would love to be your friend, Nick. It's just that..."

"Listen, I don't want anything more from you than you can give."

Gwen lifted her eyes to his, wanting to believe it was true. They had grown so close in the last month that she hated the thought of having to lose everything. But can she just be friends with Nick Penn?

"Really?"

"Yes, of course. I've got a life of my own, plus, I've got a lot of baggage that I need to sort out. I'm not looking to jump into a relationship right now."

"Yeah, but I thought..." Gwen looked away again.

"Look," Nick turned her to face him with a finger to her chin, "I'm not going to lie. I really think I felt something between us, but, don't forget, this is a whole new life for me too. I have a lot of adjusting to do on my own."

Gwen turned away from him, but was listening. She decided that she could be friends, but that was it. No hugging, no kissing... just... friends.

"If you'd be willing to be my friend, I would be so grateful."

Gwen smiled, thankful for his honesty.

"Okay." She said smiling. "We can."

"Great. So, I'll talk to you later. Let me know how the first night goes."

They both looked back at the sleeping child.

"I think it's off to a good start." Gwen smiled.

"You want me to follow you and carry her inside?" Nick offered.

Gwen cocked her eyebrow, "I have to figure out how to do this on my own, Nick."

He retreated from the window hands up in front of him. "Okay, okay, just trying to be friendly."

Gwen laughed, "I think I can handle it."

Chapter Thirteen

Guinevere came into the Fine Arts Centre's main office and flopped down in the office chair beside Betty's desk. She was sprawled out with her head back when Betty commented sarcastically, "Such the prima donna"

Gwen opened her eyes long enough to peek at Betty's smiling face, and then she extended her graceful toes to the floor. "There, my toes are pointed, better?"

"Oh yes dear, much!"

Gillian strolled in after all of her students were claimed by their parents, "Hey you!" she called out to Gwen, "I haven't seen you since you got Erin! Congratulations, by the way! How's everything going?"

Evelynn, standing at the printer in the office, gave Gwen a sideways glance wondering just how much she was going to share with Gillian. They had been on the phone every day. She knew there was a lot to tell.

Gwen sat up straighter in the chair. "It's been... a learning curve." She nodded.

Gillian laughed to herself knowing all to well, having at any given time, at least four foster children under her roof. "I remember when I first brought Allie home. It was so hard. Two humans literally thrown together; both having baggage and both needing each other and desperately wanting things to work out. I read her file. So, so sad. She would cry in her sleep for, like the first few months I would say."

Evelynn finished at the printer and joined the ladies in the conversation. "I seem to remember that," she nodded. Evelynn sat in an office chair across from Gwen.

Gwen turned slightly to see Gillian who was standing just behind her right shoulder. "Yes, that's kind of what we're going through. Although," Gwen paused putting her thoughts together, "while sometimes she wakes up from nightmares, she has trouble communicating. So she just cries instead. It's like she's forgotten how to use words."

244

"Oh, that's so sad. That sometimes happens, especially when there has been abuse in their history," Gillian commented.

Gwen nodded. "I'm not sure how much and to what extent, but I do know that it was within the family."

"Did Susan not give you a copy of her file to read?"

"She did, but I didn't really... want to ... read it? If that makes sense? I didn't want to "pre-judge" Erin, based on what her file said. Susan did say, that I am not to use any kind of spanking or physical reprimands because she was... apparently punished with uh... unnecessary means." Gillian shook her head and rubbed her forehead.

"Was Susan able to give you any other advice?" Betty asked.

"She did, some. She did say that there were going to be crying jags and that I should use phrases like, 'use your words', 'let me help you'... I feel so... stupid some times."

Gillian closed the gap between them and placed her hands on Gwen's shoulders. "It will get easier. You're both just learning. I'll keep you both in my prayers."

A tear slipped from Gwen's eye and she quickly wiped it away. "I know. I know. And thank you, we need that. I think God gets tired of hearing from me. But, like, last night, or wait... let me back up." Gwen wiped under both her eyes again. "There is this dog. His name is Max and apparently Erin befriended him at the church. She wanted to bring him home with her so badly, and... and I wouldn't have minded, but by the time we got the chance to call the church about Max, they said that he was gone. They didn't know where he came from or where he went, but it was almost as if he was there for Erin just to help her though that transition. So, I can understand how important he is to her. But," she sighed heavily, "I can't find him. I've called everyone I can think of and no one has seen him. But she cries for him every day. It's the most heart-wrenching thing, honestly."

"Maybe we can get her a puppy," Betty suggested. All three women looked at her sternly. Her eyes got wide and she put on her best face of innocence and shrugged. "It's a Grandma thing, I can't help it."

"In fairness to you, Betty, it has crossed my mind. But I just don't think I can handle a puppy on top of everything else."

"Right, she can't even handle a boyfriend."

Gwen gasped in exaggerated shock that she was so utterly betrayed in front of these perfect strangers.

"What's this? Is there a suitor we don't know about?" Gillian jumped in.

"Well, if you don't know about him, you must be living in a cave," Evelynn teased.

"Who is it?" Betty came right out and asked.

"Nick Penn!"

"Loraine's boy?" Betty clarified.

"The very one," Evelynn laughed. "I mean, you don't think he has better things to do than to paint the set? And only when Lady Guinevere happens to be painting the set?"

Gwen felt the heat rise on her cheeks as she covered her face with her fingers.

"Oh, he is so handsome... and that voice! How have we not snagged him for a leading role yet," Gillian chimed in.

"Oh believe me, she's working on it! Don't let her fool you!" Gwen came to her own defense.

As if a light bulb came on over Gillian's head, "Is that why he's throwing Erin her very own pool party?"

Evelynn couldn't resist, "Not only is he throwing it, he's having a pool- an in ground pool- built just for the occasion!"

Gwen was laughing and turning every shade of red, "No he's not... he's building it for his friend."

"Oh honey, marry that man! When's the wedding?" Betty giggled.

"She has bound him to friendship." You could hear the collective gasp from the other two women, and Evelynn nodded. "Right?? This man wants to be with her all the time! And... and it's not like he's ugly or anything. He's not even annoying!"

"Sounds like you should marry him!" Gwen teased back.

"Ya know..." Evelynn pointed at her best friend as if she was considering it.

"Yes, he's pretty amazing, and yes, we have a lot of fun together, but that's totally different than raising a family. *I* decided on

248

this adoption before I even knew Nick, so it's not really fair to tack that on to someone's life unexpectedly. C'mon guys, you can see my point, right? I just don't have time to build a relationship with a man right now."

"I don't care how much time I didn't have," Betty interjected, "I'd make time for that man. Any man that shows, not just says, but shows so completely that he is in love with you, I'd definitely make time for."

"And he apparently likes Erin, I mean he hasn't shied away." Gillian added.

"Yeah, that's because we're just friends," Gwen attempted to defend herself. I have a full time job here, I have a full time job raising a tiny person that I don't even know. I don't have time for someone else. It'll just ruin everything."

"Do you not have feelings for him?" Betty pried.

Gwen furrowed her brow and couldn't find words.

"That's true, Mom," Gillian chimed in. "If she doesn't think she could love him back, it's better not to encourage it."

"She has feelings for him, "Evelynn clarified. "Haven't you guys seen them together?"

"But the theatre..."

"Why not give it a chance? It's not like you have to get married tomorrow or anything," Gillian offered.

"My thoughts exactly." Evelynn crossed her arms in victory.

"Really? You have no room to talk. The theatre is your life too." Gwen tried to salvage her ground. "You don't go on dates."

"I've been on dates!" It was Evelynn's turn to be on the defensive.

"When? When in the last year have you been on a date?" Gwen challenged like only best friends can.

"I once went out with Dr. Dower."

"Eugene?" Gwen scoffed, "You're going to count Eugene Dower?"

"Uh, that's Dr. Eugene Dower."

The women were all laughing and Gwen really did feel better in the company of her friends... even being teased. God had put her in the right place at the right time and her life was slowly becoming everything she had hoped... well, mostly.

I just need to remember that you're in control, God. You order my steps. And this time I'm making sure not to let anyone interfere with the amazing gift of motherhood that you have given me.

"Ladies, as much as I hate to break this up, your next classes are arriving." Betty, always the theatre mom.

A group sigh was heard in the office as the ladies adjusted their skirts and shoes and put on their best teacher face.

Gillian leaned in and quietly asked, "Dr. Dower the dentist? You went out with him?"

Evelynn rolled her eyes and spoke exasperatedly, "Yeeesss..."

Gillian looked at her to make sure she heard correctly.

"And now you know why it was only one date." The ladies laughed and went out to greet their students.

"Miss Susan! Miss Susan!!" Erin squealed from the front door. She opened the screen door and let Susan Carter enter the living room. "Wanna come and see my room?"

"Of course I do." Susan leaned down and hugged Erin who was still dressed in her ballet clothes.

"See my pretty ballet bun? My Momma did it. I had ballet class. Do you like my leotard?"

"I do. I do. You look just like a dancer." Erin giggled, "I am a dancer!"

"Erin, honey, let Miss Susan get in the door." Gwen walked over to greet the worn out social worker with a hug. "Can I take your bag?"

Susan handed her briefcase over to Gwen and followed Erin to her room. Gwen took the briefcase to the kitchen table and went to the fridge to grab some lemonade.

She could hear the animated conversation from down the hall and could only imagine what Erin was chatting about. And poor Susan, still in her business clothes.

The two emerged from the bedroom and Erin tugged Susan toward the back door.

"And see? See? There's my swing set! They just built it yesterday!! I can climb on it

252

and swing. It has a slide and a tunnel!! It's that yellow thing in the middle. That's a tunnel. Do you want me to take you out there? Or... or ... you can stay on the porch and watch me. That's what Momma does. She doesn't swing with me. She's too big."

"That's a great idea," Susan said, "You can go swing and your Mom and I can sit and talk on the back porch." She looked back over her shoulder at Gwen. "Is that okay with you?"

"Way ahead of you," Gwen smiled, as she walked toward the back door with a tray of glasses full of lemonade.

Erin jumped down the three steps off the back deck and ran toward her swing set, while Susan and Gwen sat in the lawn chairs around the umbrella-shaded table.

"Thank you so much for coming out this evening. I really do appreciate it," Gwen said, sitting. She still wore her ballet attire as well. "We rushed home today."

"It's no problem. I do my best to accommodate my parents. I understand you have to work. My job has never been one of those fancy nine to five things."

Gwen laughed, "I completely

253

understand! Who does such a thing?"

Susan stretched out her back as she tried to get comfortable.

"Are you alright? Do you need a pillow or anything?"

"No, no, I'm alright. I had those surgeries and sometimes they still haunt me."

Gwen nodded, "Please let me know if you need anything."

"I am fine, really." Susan smiled. "So, tell me, how are things going for you? Erin looks good. Happy."

Gwen smiled. It was a genuine smile. "I think she is. We are starting to get a rhythm, but it's only been a few days."

"That's good. Is she excited about the adoption day?"

Gwen laughed, "I honestly think she's more excited about the pool party!"

Susan nodded but then added, "About that, is there someone... that is, are you seeing anyone right now, because we would have to ..."

"No. uh...no. I'm not involved with anyone." Gwen was quick to answer.

"We just have to make sure that Erin's home life is safe and..."

"It's safe. "

Susan tried to hide her giggle and reached out to touch Gwen's hand. "It's okay if you are, but I would just need to vet him and make sure there is no criminal history."

"Oh." Gwen let out a breath. "I am not seeing anyone. No boyfriends here." She let out a nervous laugh.

"So, Nick Penn..."

"We are just friends. I mean, he's never even been to this house. And yes, the pool party is at his house, or I guess it's his parents' house, and there's going to be lots of people around... He's very nice. He would never... I wouldn't do anything to mess up this adoption."

"He seems like a very nice man. I've seen a few episodes of his television show." Gwen laughed. "I haven't seen any. He teases me about it all the time." Gwen furrowed her brow. "Well, we do spend a lot of time with him at the theatre. But..."

"It's no big deal, but it's better to cover all the bases. I'm sure he wouldn't mind."

Gwen nodded.

"How does Erin behave around Mr. Penn?"

Gwen glanced back over her shoulder to see Erin climbing up her rope ladder to get to the upper deck of the play set. "She loves him. She loves being around him. And he is so patient with her. That swing set... from him." Gwen rolled her eyes.

Susan smiled but is always wary. They talked a bit more about what to expect at the adoption hearing and went over a few other minor details and Susan changed the subject.

She paused and tapped her finger on the table. "I need to tell you something, but I don't want you to be alarmed. It has nothing to do with the adoption. That is good to go, but it is still some information that you need to be aware of. I know you chose not to read Erin's file and I had hoped it would be a long time before we had to discuss this, but..."

Gwen took in a deep breath, preparing for the worst. "Go ahead... I can... I mean... I'm ready."

"Erin was... Susan stopped and shook her head. "Her situation was a mess. There was physical abuse by her mother. There were different 'boyfriends' in and out of the home. But, from what we gather, her brother

Beau did the sexual abuse. We believe that because of the general abuse in the household, that he perpetuated what was... normal to him."

Gwen stiffened and leaned back away from Susan, not as ready as she thought.

Susan held up her hand, "I'm not... I'm not going to bore you with the details, but you need to know that when Erin was taken from the home," Susan looked down and swallowed. This never got easy. "She was... severely... " Susan kept things simple and vague, "mentally and physically abused."

Susan looked away but covered Gwen's hands with her own. "When she was interviewed, she... would barely speak. But they finally worked with her to find out that her brother was the main abuser."

Gwen pulled her hand from under Susan's and covered her mouth. Her heart was breaking with every word. She looked over at the play set and saw Erin swinging and singing as if she had never known a hardship in her life.

"The boy, Beau," Susan continued, because she must, "was sent away to the Juvenile Sex Offender Treatment Program.

Their job is more to rehabilitate rather than to punish."

Gwen nodded, understanding.

"He is scheduled to be released sometime this year." Susan let the weight of her words settle in.

"Do... do I need to be worried?"

Susan shook her head, "Erin's files are sealed. But I am required to tell you."

"Is there anything we need to do?"

Again Susan shook her head. "I am hoping that nothing further will be mentioned on this subject. But I do have to follow through, since, technically, at this moment, Erin is still in the foster care system.

"Gwen nodded. "Okay." Gwen looked again out to the yard and had a new-found respect for the child. How strong this child is. What purpose God must have for her.

Susan smiled at her. "If you have any questions or need to talk about anything, don't you hesitate to call me. I am all about keeping my families happy and growing. Erin will blossom with you. I can tell."

Gwen held her hand and smiled, thankful for the encouragement.

"I need to be getting on. I have one

258

more stop before I can call it a night," Susan said as she stood up from the table.

Gwen called Erin in from the yard to say her goodbyes.

Erin jumped from the swing and ran around the slide back toward the deck. In mid-run, she added a cartwheel for good measure.

Susan laughed, "You've got your hands full with this one."

"I do." Gwen joined in the laughter. "She is going all day long, until she hits her pillow and then she is out cold!"

Erin jumped up the three steps of the deck, spun in a circle and landed in a hug around Gwen's legs.

"Aw, honey, you got mud on your tights." Gwen crouched down in front of her and tried to wipe the dirt away.

Erin started to cry. She looked from Gwen to Susan suddenly in a state of panic. "I'm sorry. Please don't send me away. I didn't mean to."

Gwen looked up at Susan who stepped back and watched. "I'm not mad, honey. We just have to remember to have you change clothes if you're going to go and play outside.

I didn't even think about it."

Erin couldn't stop crying.

"Honey, it's okay." Gwen pulled her down onto her lap. "We are not ever going to be apart." She took Erin's glasses off her and wiped the tears from them with her shirt then slipped them back on her face. "I know the adoption is Thursday, but as far as I'm concerned, you are already my daughter. I am never going to let you go. We are a family. Forever, honey. Do you understand?"

"You still love me?"

"Of course I do. Nothing you could do could make me stop loving you."

Erin threw her arms around Gwen's neck. Gwen looked up at Susan again.

Susan smiled and leaned over to stroke Erin's back.

"You've got a good Mom here, honey. She's not going to leave you."

Erin sat back up and looked at Gwen's face as if she could read the truth in her eyes. Gwen took the opportunity to sneak in a quick kiss on Erin's nose, which brought a giggle from the child, so Gwen did it again.

Soon, Erin's whole face was covered in tiny kisses and the tears were forgotten.

"Okay, you silly girl, Miss Carter has to leave. Hop up so you can give her a hug goodbye."

Erin did as she was told and wrapped her tiny arms around Susan's waist. "I love you. Thank you for coming to see me and my new room."

Susan leaned over and tipped her chin up. "You are welcome. It makes me happy to see your beautiful smile. Can you walk me to the door?"

"Yup!"

They walked inside and Susan grabbed her briefcase and the outstretched hand of one happy eight-year old and turned back to Gwen. "I'll see you Thursday!"
Gwen smiled and nodded.

Chapter Fourteen

"You said there would be hot girls," Dave Ripke whined at his best friend while standing on the deck of the only-finished-yesterday pool.

"Buddy, it's ninety-three degrees, so I'm sure they are plenty hot, and you were not age-specific. You said 'cute girls'. I just happened to have access to 48 giggling, squealing, high-pitched screaming girls that are too darn cute. But, you have your pool and, I brought you a Mojito. Don't give it to the children." Nick handed him a fancy glass complete with a paper umbrella.

"Dude, I don't even know you right now."

"Yes you do, you just don't remember. It means a lot to me that you're here." He slapped him on the shoulder, "It means a lot."

"Yeah, yeah." Dave had to raise his arm to keep a child from running into his drink. "So where's this girl,... this adult female that you are so enamored with."

"Oh, Gwen. She's right down there at the bottom of the stairs."

Dave was staring at Gwen, Gillian and Evelynn as they were trying to slip floaties over Erin's arms. "Oh, dude, she is gorgeous!"

Nick furrowed his brow, "I know that, but... wait, what?"

"Dude you have to introduce me."

"I was intending on it, but..."

"C'mon, you said she wasn't interested in you 'like that'" he air-quoted the words. "But wait till she gets a load of the Rip!" He licked his fingertips and smoothed the hair down behind his ears.

Nick rolled his eyes and took off to catch up with his friend before he embarrassed himself.

Dave sucked in his gut and started to saunter over in their direction. "Ladies, you are looking ravishing today, may I say?" Dave cut right into the center of the coven of women. "Scoot over, kid." He exaggeratedly bumped Erin with his hip and stared directly up into Evelynn's eyes. He was about four inches shorter than her, but he was undeterred. He reached out for her hand and pressed the back of it to his lips. "I don't think we've met, my name is Dave Ripke. I'm Nick Penn's best friend. He couldn't have made it anywhere without me. Can I get you a drink?"

"Uh, sorry," Nick went to stand behind Gwen, "Nick, you blockhead, this is Evelynn. She's the executive director at the Fine Arts Centre. This is Gillian who also works there..."

Dave turned and nodded at Gillian, but kept a hold of Evelynn's hand.

"And this is my friend Guinevere, uh Gwen."

Dave dropped Evelynn's hand begrudgingly and turned 180 degrees to greet Gwen. "I've heard so much about you. It's nice to finally meet you."

"And you as well. I know Nick is really happy that you were able to come out and visit our tiny little town. It's no California, but it..."

"Yes, yes it is," Dave hurried her along, "It was nice to meet you, but if you'll excuse me," he turned back around to face Evelynn, "Would you care to grab a drink with me?

Apparently I have the only alcoholic beverage in the entire county, but I've heard there some pretty potent root beer on the patio."

All eyes were on Evelynn, anxiously awaiting her answer. Rip added to his invitation, "I look so much better 'under the influence'." He air-quoted the words. "Did I also mention that in addition to my charm, I am quite hilarious." He shifted sideways and thrust his elbow toward Evelynn, not taking 'no' for an answer.

"I... I would love to." Evelynn replied, and linked her arm with his.

Gillian looked up at Nick, "He's not a doctor is he?"

Gwen laughed and answered for him, "Oh, no, he was Nick's camera man on his show and they've been friends for years."

"Aw, you do listen." Nick teased her.

"I'm sorry, what? Did you say something?"

He grabbed her and picked her up off the ground while she squealed like one of the little girls. "You're goin' in!"

"No, Nick noooo!!" She squirmed and fought, but it barely affected Nick's intensions. He flipped her around to hold her

266

like a baby and took her to the edge of the pool… He extended his arms ready to drop her, when the tiny hands of Erin pushed them both in.

They both came up from the water and laughed and looked over to see Erin doubled over with laughter on the side of the pool.

"That does it! Come here you!" Nick reached out of the pool and grabbed Erin and pulled her in the water too. She giggled with delight as he tossed her up in the air and braced her fall, just enough so she never went completely under water.

That was apparently the invitation for all forty plus little girls to jump in too.

Erin reached her arms around Nick's neck and hugged him. "This has been the best day ever! I love you!"

Nick hugged her back, "I love you too, honey."

And while this would normally be the greatest time in Gwen's life too, because in that instant, it felt like a real live family, she could instantly feel the bricks being stacked up that much higher around her heart. She backed away from the scene and the water fight. Her heart was not filled with joy, but with regret for allowing Erin to get so close with Nick. Now it's going to break her heart too. *I knew I should have stayed away*, she thought.

The party continued on for a few more hours, complete with cake and ice cream and as the parents started coming to retrieve their kids, Nick happily obliged them with photos.

The guests were finally all gone and Evelynn and Dave were picking up trash left on the tables.

Gwen was grabbing leftover plastic cups that were all around the deck of the pool when Nick came up and took her hand.

She looked up at him and smiled. She couldn't help it. She loved having those blue eyes stare down at her.

"You look pretty tired," he said barely above a whisper.

"I am. This party was so great. Thank you, Nick. I really mean it. And that barbeque! It was amazing!"

He pulled her into an embrace and she folded into it.

"You liked that, huh?"

Before they realized it, they were swaying back and forth swaying to music no one else could hear.

"You made Erin feel so special."

"I enjoyed it. I was happy to do it."

"Gwen," Gillian called out, "I'm going to take Erin inside to get some dry clothes on her."

Nick dipped her back, and Gwen extended her leg beautifully, so she could give Gillian an upside-down thumb's up.

When he lifted her back up and pressed her against his chest she obliged but insisted on looking past him.

"What has your attention?" Nick asked still swaying.

"Evelynn and Rip sure seem to be getting along." Gwen giggled under her breath.

Nick looked behind him at the two of them laughing and collecting trash. "I told you, he's a pretty funny guy when he wants to be"

269

"Should I be worried?" Gwen leaned back and looked at Nick's face.

"I'll vouch for him. He's harmless... mostly."

Dave picked up a cup and accidently spilled its contents all down Evelynn's leg. Gwen couldn't hear what they were saying but could tell that he was apologizing profusely and trying to find a delicate way to wipe the sticky soda from her leg.

Gwen couldn't help but laugh and was a little bit shocked that Evelynn didn't get upset. She was actually laughing!

Nick laughed, "I did say, mostly..."

He pushed Gwen out away from him and spun her under his one arm.

Nick pulled her back against him again and she lay her head on his chest smiling as he rocked her slowly in his arms.

They were quiet... swaying. Gwen was starting to relax and give in to the good feeling of strong arms holding her so securely, but then she felt the lightest, softest kiss on the back of her neck. Her breath drew in short, but she didn't move. Another kiss and then another. The sweetest, most tender kisses. She closed her eyes and let the shivers run up and down her spine. She could feel his arms tighten around her as he moved her hair to the side. Her breath caught but she didn't want to move. His touch felt so... so... right.

He kissed her neck and tipped her head towards his face. Gwen melted into his touch. He kissed the outline of her jaw and tipped her head back slightly and then tenderly but deeply kissed her mouth.

She was caught up in the kiss. His arms around her, she squeezed him tighter around his waist taking in the intensity of the kiss. It was amazing. She kissed him back with equal intensity until...

Her alarm went off in her head. She tried to pull away, but he silenced her with his lips. Her body suddenly went rigid and she abruptly pulled away. Her heart was pounding; her pulse was racing; her lungs were heaving.

She stepped back a couple paces to put some space between them. He was just as breathless as she was. She could see passion in his eyes and could only imagine that hers looked the same.

"No, Nick... we can't." Her arms were outstretched in front of her keeping him at a distance.

"But why can't we?" He was reaching out for her again. He grabbed her hand and tried to pull her close attempting to salvage the tender moment. She pulled away.

"I told you... I can't... I don't..."

"I know, you said you don't have time, but couldn't we..."

"You said you understood!" The tenderness was gone, and panic engulfed her. "You said you didn't want anything more than friendship from me." Her eyes pleaded with him to understand.

"I know I said that, but then... I..."

"You lied to me, Nick! You told me that we were fine! Friends were just fine!"

"I didn't mean to." Nick took a step back and ran his fingers through his hair. He looked down to the newly polished wood of the deck. His fingers held his hair back from his face as he looked over at Gwen again. He looked ashamed. "I lied to myself, Gwen. I thought I could keep it the way you wanted. I'm sorry. I care about you, Gwen. Can't you see that?"

"No, I don't see that. You're going to get me thinking that I can have more and then you're going to leave me! You're going to leave me and Erin! And I don't have... have... time." She burst into tears and her whole body shook with pain.

He moved to her and stroked her hair and the sides of her face with both hands, "Honey, I'm so sorry. Who did this to you? Who broke you?" He lowered his hands to her shoulders and gently wrapped his arms around her. "C'mere... Shhh.., it's okay. We can figure this thing out. I know you care for me... and..."

She pushed away from his embrace once again. "No. I don't, Nick Penn. I felt friendship for you. That is all. You... you... you just think... cause you're famous, you can have anyone you want." She had to turn away from him before he could read her expression. He would see instantly that it was the fear talking and that she didn't mean a word she was saying.

"Gwen..."

"I'm sorry. We have to go." She turned away from him and Gillian, who was standing on the lawn with Erin waiting for the right time to interrupt, saw that it was now. She nudged Erin toward Gwen's outstretched hand.

Erin held onto her Momma but looked back over her shoulder at Nick with tears in her eyes and waved.

Gillian, Dave, Evelynn and Loraine all stood silently not knowing what to say that could possible help the situation.

Evelynn spoke silently to Dave, "I guess I'd better go, too. It was really nice meeting you."

"Hey uh... can I call you?"

Evelynn felt a flutter in her stomach, "Yes, please do... " She looked away and blushed slightly at her quick answer, " I uh, meant... um, could you let me know how things go over here?" She looked up to the deck as Nick dropped into a chair and put his face in his hands.

"Yeah sure, I can do that. Uh, you can keep me posted about your end of things too."

"Okay. I'm sorry. I really should go..." She touched his arm and he reached out to grab her hand. She smiled at him and then turned to leave.

Gwen leaned on one arm with her hand squishing her face, with a perfectly good take-out Cobb salad in front of her.

Evelynn sat across from her eating her pressed turkey sandwich waiting for some kind of conversation to happen.

Ever since the "kiss" Gwen had been moping around the theatre unless she was with her class or with Erin.

Evelynn loved seeing those two together. It's like Erin was surrounded in sunshine and it affected everyone she met. Gwen was another person when she wore her "Momma hat". She was happy. But in between times, she was missing Nick Penn, but would refuse to admit it.

The once familiar "clang clang" of Gwen's phone sounded off. She looked over at it, Evelynn could see the wheels spinning, but she turned it face down and went back to picking at her salad.

"Aren't you going to read it? Evelynn asked.

Gwen just shrugged.

"How long is this going to go on? It's been three days, Gwen. Don't you think you're being a little childish? It was a kiss. A perfectly natural thing to have happened. You two are very close..."

"He said it wasn't like that. He said he could be my friend." Gwen finally sputtered out. "I've already explained it to you."

"You did, but don't you think it's been long enough? Can't you forgive him?"

Gwen looked away, "I feel... betrayed. I trusted that we could keep things at a friendship level."

"Honey, are you sure betrayed is the word you're looking for? And not, maybe, scared? Because if you were going to be honest with yourself, I don't think you really wanted to keep it at a friendship level. I saw that kiss."

Gwen glared across the table and then rolled her eyes.

"I'm your best friend. I'm not going to tip toe around you. Someone has to say the hard things, and this time it has to be me."

"Maybe, but must you enjoy it so much?"

"My sweet Guinevere, this is not pleasurable to me. I can see love waiting for you and you are pushing it away."

"I don't want it. I don't need it, right now."

It was Evelynn's turn to shrug. "Okay, but eventually he's going to stop trying. Are you really ready to let that happen?"

Evelynn got up from her chair and went around the desk to kiss Gwen on the head. "I love you, you stubborn girl."

Gwen frowned at her and went back to picking at her salad.

Evelynn spoke while she cleaned up her Styrofoam to-go containers, "You need to decide what you're going to do about that bowl of lettuce in front of you. You have a class coming in twenty minutes. I'm going to be over in the theatre. Dave has a suggestion for our lighting system. Says it will cut our bills in half!" she smirked. "I'm all over that!"

Gwen nodded, not really hearing, but shoved a forkful of greens in her mouth.

When Evelynn left her office, Gwen flipped her phone back over and hit the home button, lighting up the screen.

Text Message:

Nick Penn

She sighed and coded in her access. The message read:

How's Erin? Is she the best daughter ever? I know she is.

Gwen, I miss talking to you. I miss being with you. I wish you would forgive me. I don't know what to say.

"I don't know what to say either." Gwen said out loud to no one.

Chapter Fifteen

Gwen sat in a circle on the floor with fourteen teenagers in her theatre arts summer camp . She happened to glance up at the closed door to the classroom and could have sworn she saw Nick walk by. Shaking it off, she continued with her class.

"Great job, Shameka and Janet. Improv can be tricky but you want to work with your partner not against. So, pretty much, no matter what they say, the answer is 'yes' and you just roll with it to see where it takes you."

Gwen furrowed her brow. Did she see Nick again?

"Okay, who's next? Pam? Aaaand... Dionne."

Just then the classroom door opened. Nick stuck his head in, making no eye contact, not saying a word, but reached in, grabbed the trashcan and disappeared again. Everyone paused and watched the door.

279

Moments later, Nick appeared again with the empty trash bin. He set it down as quietly as possibly. He lifted his head, smiled and nodded an apology for interrupting.

"Miss Gwen, was that Nick Penn?"

"It was! He's that guy on tv!"

"No it wasn't, stupid, why would Nick Penn be cleaning out the trashcans?"

"Don't say 'stupid'." Gwen absent-mindedly scolded, trying to figure out the appearance of Nick Penn herself.

"Maybe he's doing a new episode! Maybe he traded places with someone who works here!"

"Ms. Gwen, are we going to be on tv?" Janet asked excitedly.

"Uh, no, Janet. Sorry, honey, no such luck."

"So was that Nick Penn?"

Gwen calmly responded, "I'm not sure, but I will do some digging during the lunch break, how's that?"

"Do you think he'd give us an autograph?"

The room bustled with noise and energy.

"Okay, okay... if you want the janitor's autograph, I'll see what I can do," Gwen laughed. "But in the meantime... I think Pam and Dionne have a skit to work through." And calm was once more restored to the classroom.

Gwen burst into Evelynn's office. Evelynn scrunched her eyes closed and waited for the verbal blast.

Silence.

Evelynn eventually opened one eye to see Gwen standing on the other side of the desk with her hands on her hips. Her hair was in a messy bun piled on top of her head. She wore the Bakersfield' Summer Camp t-shirt and dance pants.

Gwen patiently raised her eyebrows and asked, "Could you maybe tell me why Nick Penn came into my classroom today to empty my trash?"

"Don't be mad..." Evelynn implored.

"Why would I be mad?"

"Because I just hired him."

The words hovered around Gwen's lips before she could add sound. "Um, what?"

281

"I hired Nick to do some maintenance work around the Centre and the theatre. He and Dave were on the roof cleaning the air conditioning units or something or other. I would have never thought of that..."

Gwen closed her eyes trying to remain calm. "Why? You know I'm trying to do the right thing here..."

"Well, we needed some help and..."

Gwen flopped into the chair, "But why him, Evie? Why Nick Penn?"

Evelynn looked down and the guilt surfaced. "He made me an offer I couldn't refuse."

Gwen looked at her and raised her eyebrows expectantly waiting for her to continue.

"He only wants minimum wage, and Dave will be volunteering on whatever project Nick will work on. He said that he didn't need the money, but said he wanted to be taken seriously, but... oh... and," Evelynn muttered a complete sentence of something under her breath looking everywhere but at Gwen.

"I'm sorry? What was that last part? I couldn't quite understand that."

Evelynn sighed, "A...um, large, anonymous donation was made to the Centre."

Gwen looked blankly at the Executive Director of the Bakersfield Fine Arts Centre. "You sold your soul to Nick Penn."

Evelynn dropped her head and giggled. "I did. I sold my soul to Nick Penn."

"So, he gave you money so you could pay his salary?" she asked unimpressed.

Evelynn looked squarely at Gwen, "And. THEN. Some."

Gwen sighed and looked about the room trying to sort out the emotions rushing through her.

"It's kinda sweet," Evelynn offered.

Gwen just blankly stared at her friend, at a loss for words.

Evelynn cleared her throat. "Uh... I mean... what a jerk! Who does he think he is helping out a non-profit, local theatre?" Evelynn didn't wait for an answer but shook her head. "Some people."

The corners of Gwen's lips lifted slightly. She swallowed the lump that was forming in her throat but still said nothing.

Evelynn knew Nick's ulterior motive and loved the idea, but just at this moment, she was feeling a little guilty for playing her part. "You okay?"

Gwen nodded, but her expression was sad... confused. She sighed again and silently went back to her classroom.

That whole week, every time Gwen turned around, she was practically running into Nick. He was cleaning, or sweeping or painting or moving things from one room to another.

The kids would whisper and try to look out the windows as the rumors of the famous tv actor were beginning to spread.

"Evie. You have to do something." Gwen finally caught Evelynn in the hallway at a lunch break. The kids were all playing and eating lunch outside while the adults took a moment to revel in the quiet.

"What's up?"Evelynn asked.

"Nick Penn. He is everywhere. The kids are going nuts."

"He's working, Gwen." Evelynn was beginning to tire of the Gwen and Nick drama when it was so evident to everyone but Gwen that they belonged together.

"I know. But it's not like he's just some random guy. It's distracting."

Evelynn sighed. "Okay. I understand. I'll talk to him." She started to walk away. "Unless you want to…"

"Nope. I'm good." Gwen walked in the opposite direction.

Monday morning. The beginning of a new set of summer camps and Gwen was starting to feel the weight of non-stop teaching in her lower back. She and Erin have been running from morning till late evening. Erin was completely unfazed. She was ready to go first thing in the morning and stayed happy most of the day. And even when they went home for the evening, she was still not ready for bed. She would think of a hundred and one things she needed to do before she would unwillingly go to bed.

And lately, she's been asking that Gwen keep her door open, as well. Gwen thought nothing of it but was so completely worn out by the time she hit her own bed that she was grateful when Erin finally conceded to go to sleep.

This morning when they walked into Gwen's office, she found a package waiting for her on her desk.

A sticky note attached to the cardboard box read, "It's watermelon season, your favorite."

She looked over at Erin with a smirk. "Did you know anything about this?"

"No, what is it?" she asked with a leftover yawn.

Gwen shrugged, "I don't know. Let's see!" She gingerly opened the box and found a small white Styrofoam cooler, a bottle of wine, some muffins, and some orange juice. Gwen couldn't help but smile.

She pulled out the cooler and opened it. It was filled to the brim with chunked watermelon. Gwen smiled and touched her cheek, taken aback at the kindest of gestures. She remembered telling Nick how she loved watermelon; that she could probably live on it, but hated cutting it up. And here were at least two watermelons all neatly chunked and ready to eat.

She took the top piece and put it in her mouth. She closed her eyes, enjoying the sweet flavor of the decadent fruit.

"Watermelon!" Her reverie was halted at the thought that now she had to share with her child. *So much for selfish pleasures...* she thought.

She ate another piece as she retrieved the other goodies from the box. A note was on the muffins and orange juice for Erin.

"Here, sweetie, these must be for you." She handed the treats over and Erin looked at the bright orange sticky note.

Erin, have a great day at your summer camps! I know how much you like chocolate chips, so Miss Loraine put them in some muffins for you.

The orange juice had a note too.

Erin, I almost forgot. Here's some orange juice for you, too! See you later! Love, your friend, Nick

Gwen pulled out the bottle of wine. It was a watermelon-flavored Moscoto. It's note read: *This is for AFTER the camp. Don't get it confused with the orange juice, (as much as you might want to!)*

Gwen couldn't stop smiling. How sweet. *How... incredibly sweet,* she thought.

Gwen looked up and saw that Erin was working her way through the center of one of her homemade muffins. She had chocolate lining the edges of her mouth. Gwen laughed. "Okay, little piggy. Finish that up and go wipe your chocolatey face! We have to get the classrooms set up."

But just one more bite of watermelon first... she went to put the lid back on the cooler, ... okay, maybe two.

Nick did his best to stay away from students and their families so as not to be an unwelcome distraction. He found plenty of work to do to keep busy elsewhere.

"As competent as these women are at running this huge place," he would tell Dave, "they need a 'man's touch'. There's so much stuff that needs some upkeep that they probably don't even know about." He and Dave painted, sorted and cleaned out the workshop, cleaned out gutters, and updated or repaired expired equipment. Dave used his experience to rewire and update the lights and sound systems and tidied up all of the loose wires that hung dangerously everywhere.

"Yeah, " Dave added. "No wonder they practically live here. I can see how it can get overwhelming, real fast."

"But Momma... you said..." Erin whined as the hours began to drain her.

"I know, honey, but I forgot that I have to set up all of the art projects for the art fair tomorrow. You want all the parents to be able to see everyone's work, don't you?"

"Yeah, but..."

"I'm sorry, honey. I can order some pizza for dinner."

Erin flopped on a bench in the hallway, "We had pizza already..."

Nick came down the hallway with his hands up defensively in front of him. "Can I help?"

Both Erin and Gwen looked over at him and he could see they were exhausted.

Erin lifelessly stood up from her bench and walked over to Nick and dropped her head on his stomach.

Nick laughed and stroked her back, "Tough day, kiddo?"

"Yeah, tough week. It's hard being Momma's daughter."

Gwen took in a deep breath, feeling defeated.

"How about this... Guinevere, would you mind if I take Erin home with me while you do whatever it is you have to do here? You can come by and pick her up when you get finished... or, better yet. Why don't you shoot me a text when you are ready and I'll bring her back in?"

"Oh Nick, I wouldn't want to put you..."

"I'm offering. It will give you plenty of time to get the art display up."

"Please, Momma?"

Gwen sighed and rubbed the back of her neck unconsciously. She looked over at Nick gratefully. "If you're sure...?"

"I am. We'll have a great time. Maybe we can get a few laps in the pool."

The life returned to Erin, "Yeah!"

Gwen couldn't help but smile. "Thank you, Nick... really. I guess my old life has some adjusting to do."

Nick smiled at her, a warm, sincere smile. "You'll get the hang of it. I'm happy to help." He looked down at the child. "Well? You ready to go?"

"Wait! I have to get my bag from Momma's office! Wait for me, kay?"

"I'll be right here." Nick gave her a high-five and off she ran down the hallway.

"Did you want me to help carry the projects down to the lobby?" Nick offered.

As much as she wanted to say no, "Could you?"

"Absolutely."

They walked down the hallway carrying boxes in silence. When they reached the theatre's auditorium, she was thankful to see that easels and the tables were already set up. She looked over at Nick, "You?"

He shrugged. "You did offer me a job... I just... took a while to accept it."

Gwen tiredly gave up a laugh and nodded. "Thank you."

She wanted to flop her head against him knowing that he would catch her the way that Erin so comfortably did. *No, it's better this way.*

He wanted so much to reach out and comfort her. He could see that she was emotionally and physically drained. He knew that if he could just prove to her...

"I really appreciate you taking Erin. She will love a home cooked meal. I honestly don't remember summer camps being so overwhelming before." She tried to make conversation while pulling items from the boxes.

"Well, you weren't a mother last year. That changes everything."

She nodded. "It does."

"She's worth it. You'll figure things out and be back to your old self again in no time."

My old self, being alone, is what you're saying, Gwen thought. Well, you're right. I'll just keep my distance so you won't catch me off guard.

"Well, I'd better get back to my spot in the hallway before she finds out."

Gwen laughed. "I think you'll be alright. She gets distracted easily. You might have to go and find her."

"I'll do that. I know Mom's waiting for me to get home." Nick started to turn away but added, "You wouldn't want..."

"No thanks," she lifted up a paper mache lion... or horse... or dog? "Duty calls."

Nick nodded, "Okay, I'll wait for your text."

"Um... Nick?" Gwen called out. He stopped and turned back around to face her. Her heart pounded in her chest as he waited for her to speak. Say something!!

"Thank you... for everything. I mean... the uh... gift the other day, too... and for... uh..."

Nick dropped his head breaking eye contact and smiled half-heartedly. "It's no problem."

The Art Fair was a success and Gwen was sitting on the floor in her dress trying to build up the energy to clean up the remnants of the day.

Nick poked his head around the corner, "Is everyone gone?"

Gwen looked up and smiled at him. "Yeeeessss... Yes they are."

He stepped into the lobby and looked over the disheveled lobby space. Scattered bits and pieces of artwork that weren't claimed, cups, napkins and toothpicks littered the tables.

Nick lifted his ball cap from his head, scratched his head and neck and then flopped it back in place. "Well, it did look nice in here. You did a great job getting everything set up."

Gwen had closed her eyes but smiled, "Thank you. I try. I want it to be special for the kids."

"Speaking of... where's Little Bit?"

"She went home with Stephanie. Her mom is going to bring her to church in the morning, and I'll pick her up there." She absent-mindedly rubbed her face before dropping her hand back in her lap.

Nick sat down at Gwen's feet and picked one up in his hands and started rubbing it.

"Oh, you don't have to do that," Gwen half-hearted argued. "Dancers have gross feet."

Nick laughed. "I won't look." He massaged her foot a moment more before

294

speaking again. "Can I talk to you about Erin?"

Gwen's eyes shot open and she sat straight up. "What's wrong? Has something happened?"

Nick raised one hand still cupping her ankle with the other, "No, no... nothing happened, I don't think. But I didn't get a chance to talk to you last night when I dropped her off. Relax, relax..." He switched feet and started massaging the other foot.

Gwen leaned back against the wall, "You just keep doing that and I'll be so relaxed, you could do whatever you wanted..."

Nick raised his eyebrow, "Really..."

Gwen opened her eyes and pulled her feet back from Nick's grasp, laughing, "I didn't mean that..." She looked down blushing. She tucked her legs into her long dress and leaned back against the wall again. "Tell me about Erin. Did you guys have a good time?" she asked smiling.

"Oh, she's a great kid. A really great kid. I barely got any time with her. My mom and dad kept her away from me most of the night. And if there was any kind of sugar buzz… that was not me."

Gwen laughed. "No, she was out. She didn't even make it home before crashing."

"Good." He paused and just looked at Gwen lounging in a formal dress, sitting on the floor, completely exhausted and still the most beautiful woman he's ever seen.

Gwen opened one eye to make sure he was still there. "You okay?" she asked.

"Oh, yeah… yeah… about Erin. Last night as we were coming back to meet you, she mentioned something about the Bogey Man."

Gwen opened her eyes and furrowed her brow.

Nick continued, "Yeah, that's what I thought." Acknowledging her face as a response. "She said that she knows who the Bogey Man is. He comes to her house."

"What? That's creepy." Gwen sat up and rested her elbows on her crossed legs.

"I know. I'd never heard her talk like that. I asked what he does and she said nothing. He stays outside."

Gwen shook her head slowly trying to think of something that might have happened recently, but was coming up empty. "I don't know ... why..." Gwen furrowed her brow again, deep in thought. "She has had a few more nightmares these last couple weeks. I wonder if she's remembering things, or... if something has triggered them... She hasn't said anything to me. I just thought she was overly tired."

"I asked her if she was afraid of the Bogey Man, and she said she was. I told her that I'd never let him get her. She asked, 'Well, what if he did?' I told her that I'd take her right back and beat him up. That got a smile out of her, not the laugh I was going for, be she seemed to accept that answer."

Gwen reached forward and touched Nick's hand. "Thank you for that. Thank you for making her feel safe." She squeezed his hand.

"I meant it." He looked at her intently letting her know that he was sincere.

Gwen smiled, "I know. I am grateful for that."

Her hand lingered on his until he pulled away and stood up. "So... do you want help putting the lobby back together?" Nick asked cautiously.

"Heck yeah, that's why we pay you the big bucks." Gwen winked at Nick to let him know she was teasing.

"Well, okay, but I'm not doing it alone. You don't pay me that much." Nick laughed and reached his hand down for Gwen to grab.

Gwen whimpered but took his hand. He effortlessly helped her to her feet.

"Do you mind if I get out of this dress first?" She bent over and picked up the heels she'd discarded earlier.

"Not at all. Do you need help with that too?" He gave her a full smile and a wink.

"Uh, no thank you, Mr. Penn. I can manage." She smiled coyly at him.

"I'm just here to help. My contract was a little vague on my job duties, so... you know... thought I'd ask."

Gwen turned to face him and curtsied, "You are too kind. Willing to go above and beyond, I like that. I'll put in a good word with the boss."

Nick laughed.

At the end of summer, Nick gave an exclusive four-hour "Evening with Nick Penn" for the students that participated in the summer camps. Gwen had been avoiding him all week. He felt like he would take two steps forward and then have to take three steps back. But he had promised Evelynn that he would do this for the kids and was actually looking forward to it.

He talked about celebrity life, the trials and tribulations of making it big. He answered questions, gave advice and was available for photos. Tons of photos.

"What's the best piece of advice you can give?"

"I would say, hands down, finish school. Always have a back-up plan. This business is vicious and you may be on top one day, and literally on the very bottom the next. I have been very fortunate, but it wasn't easy. My degree is in English Literature. I was going to be an English professor. Get your education!"

"What are you going to do next?"

Nick's eyes shot over toward where Gwen was standing. He shook his head from side to side, "I'm not really sure. We will have to see what comes my way."

"Are you a triple threat?"

Nick laughed, "Can I act, sing and dance? Is that the question?" He took a moment to think. "I got in the business to sing. I love to sing." He glanced over at Gwen who was standing on the edge of the auditorium. She had her arms folded across her chest, but she was listening. "I guess I can act. I've been in plenty of musicals. Did an episode on a soap opera. Didn't care for that much. But for *Real People, Real Lives*, that was just me, being me." He laughed, "Maybe I should round out my resume since I'm out of work. Do you think I should take lessons from Miss Gwen?"

The audience clapped and screeched and whistled. Gwen merely rolled her eyes and disappeared from the theatre.

"Sing for us, Nick!" someone in the audience shouted.

Nick laughed and lifted his hands up, "I'm not sure we have time for that."

"Yeah, c'mon! Sing something!" The audience clapped and encouraged.

Gwen suddenly appeared from the right side of the stage and raised her hand to quiet everyone back down.

"What are you guys shouting about?" she called out. "Do you not know how much talent there is right here in this very theatre?"

The audience roared and applauded. Evelynn, however, had no idea where this impromptu appearance by her moody best friend was going and stood by waiting to interrupt.

"Do you think you have to be on television to be talented?" Gwen asked the audience. Evelynn covered her eyes.

"Nick Penn is just a man! You guys think he's so great just cause he had his own tv show, is on television commercials..." Gwen looked over her shoulder at Nick who stood pensively wondering how bad this was going to turn out, "...and radio commercials."

It was like the person in the office who never gets drunk finally decides to drink and tell everyone what they have been hiding inside for years.

"He can't even dance!" Gwen threw in. The audience laughed and clapped.

Then all of a sudden, Gwen broke into the song from *Annie Get Your Gun*, *Anything You Can Do, I Can Do Better.*

She only had to wait a half a second before Nick jumped right in on the impromptu cue, "*No you can't!*"

They sang the entire duet and played it up to the hilt. They were laughing, the audience was laughing and Evelynn jumped on the piano to offer some background music.

The final notes of the song were barely able to come out because the actors were laughing so hard. But they finished strong and hugged on stage as the audience roared in praise.

They bowed and Gwen stepped back and motioned to her partner, "Nick Penn, everybody!"

Nick, too, stepped up, bowed for the audience and then motioned to the Centre's new favorite teacher, "Your very own, Guinevere Collins!

They held hands and took another bow. She blew a kiss to Nick and exited the stage.

At the end of the presentation and questions, Evelynn got on stage next to Nick and thanked him and gave him a huge hug. Nick exited the stage and the audience got antsy. "Don't worry, Nick will be in the lobby before you go, but I have one more surprise for you. I know you've seen this guy around."

Evelynn gestured to Dave Ripke to join her on stage. "This is Dave Ripke. He was Mr. Penn's cameraman when he was on the *Real People, Real Lives* set. He is visiting Bakersfield, and he made it a point to capture a little of what our summer camps are all about here. Take a peek at what he made for you!" She nodded to the crew in the tech booth to lower the lights and white screen and begin a video.

The kids laughed and squealed and pointed at the clips seamlessly blended together to show a perfect collection of all the kids and all the various camps that were offered the past six weeks.

The kids loved it. And Nick Penn made sure each and every child got a copy to take home.

Gwen, in the meantime, went back to her office and cried.

The camps were over. The theatre was dark and all the children were gone. Gwen decided to put the workroom back into some kind of order before she headed home. They had the Bakersfield Summer Fair coming up, in which the classes from the camps and some classes of the regular school year were invited to perform.

She was pretty sure that the float they used every year in the parade would need a fresh coat of paint... *That can wait until tomorrow,* she told herself.

Gwen walked into the workroom and flipped on the overhead light. The room was practically spotless. The floors were cleared of sawdust, debris, trash and leftover flats. There were new shelves with bins hiding away all of the tools and extension cords. There was even storage for the nuts, bolts, screws and nails. Gwen was afraid to step in any further because she might disrupt something.

"How am I supposed to find anything in here!" she yelled into the empty room. Her frustrations had reached their limit. "Everywhere I go, Nick Penn is there! What are you trying to do me?" she called out to the heavens.

I'm trying to stay away from Nick. I'm trying to focus on being a good mother. I know that having it all is too much to ask. But couldn't you make me hate him? Maybe just a little? Lord, I love being with him. But I don't want to get hurt again. I don't think I could take it.

She sank to the floor at the edge of the room; her heart breaking and she couldn't even see that she was the cause.

"Am I interrupting?" Nick's deep voice came from behind her.

She lifted her head slightly in response, but said nothing.

"I... uh, just finished this room up this morning. I hope it helps." He looked down at Gwen slumped over on the floor and wanted so badly to pick her up and hold her in his arms and love away her sadness. Both of their sadness.

"I think I've pretty much got you ladies all caught up with the maintenance that might have been holding you back." He paused, inviting a response... a thank you, a scolding, a... a... something. He took in a deep breath and filled up the silence, "You are one of the hardest working women I've ever met. I don't know where you find your continued strength. Inside and out." He nervously chuffed. "You are amazing."

A tear slipped down her cheek. She wanted to stand and face him and let him wrap his strong protective arms around her and give in to all the weaknesses she felt knowing that he would protect her... for a time. And then he would leave.

"I... believe my work here is done. You ladies really don't need me here anymore, so... I... turned in my notice."

Gwen flinched at his words. She turned her head slightly, so he knew she was at least listening. She wanted so badly to protest his leaving, but deep inside, she knew that this was going to happen anyway. Better now than later before she admitted her feelings for him.

She could feel him move closer to her and when he crouched down behind her she stiffened but remained silent.

"I... don't know what else to say... or... or do. I know you're scared...or... too hurt... I can feel it when I'm around you." Nick took

306

in a deep breath and continued, "I don't know if you think that I am some famous guy that goes around trying to woo and buy my way into women's hearts for sport, or... what... but... I'm not. I thought you felt the same for me. I could be wrong. But I am asking you to give me a chance. We don't ever talk about how you have been hurt in the past, but it's not fair to judge me the same as someone else. Just... a chance." He shifted his weight and reached out to stroke her long hair but changed his mind. "Being so close to you and not being able to love you... is torture for me. So, I am giving you the space that you have requested. Say 'yes' to me Gwen." He stood up and let out a sigh, "This is the last time I will ask. I'm not that guy, Guinevere. I'll leave you alone... I hope... you... come to me."

She heard his footsteps put distance between them. She squeezed her eyes shut trying to keep the pain down deep, but she couldn't stop the tears.

Chapter Sixteen

Storm clouds were forming over the theatre. Gwen, Dave and Evelynn pulled in the flats that they were painting outside into the back of the theatre.

Dave bumped against Evelynn's hip causing a waterfall of giggles. Their dancing about was causing the back half of the eight-foot panel to jerk one way and another, which provoked a scowl from Gwen who was holding up the front half. This caused quiet giggling and scolding of each other from the back half.

There was a lot of flirting going on, but as usual, Gwen was preoccupied with other thoughts and didn't even notice.

The thunder cracked fiercely as they slid the wide barn door closed.

"Looks like there's going to be some serious lightning. We'd better get these stage lights and the computers unplugged," Evelynn was saying.

"I'll go to the loft and get everything there," Gwen said.

"Hey, we're going to go to the Chicken Depot and grab some dinner, do you want to go?"

"Nah. You guys go ahead."

Gwen went up to the balcony and to the sound room, gingerly stepping over cords and empty water bottles. "I really need to talk to them about that," Gwen rolled her eyes and picked them up as she went.

She waited for Evelynn and Dave to get off the stage before she turned off the lights. She took just a moment to notice that Evelynn is always smiling when she is with Dave. She would have thought his sense of humor to be the total opposite of hers.

"At least somebody's happy..."she mumbled under her breath. A moment later she shook her head, "I'm not unhappy, Lord, I don't know why I said that. We all have to make sacrifices, and I guess I sacrificed a husband for a child. I get it. I'm okay with that... " The words came out of her mouth and even though she spoke them, she hoped God couldn't hear her fib.

Nick jumped off the tractor just outside of the barn. He knew Dave was at the theatre helping with the lighting and he really wanted to be there too. But, now is not the time. She needs space. She needs to understand that he's not going anywhere. "Not my time, but in Your time," he whispered to himself.

The lightning cracked overhead and not even a couple seconds later, the thunder responded.

Nick quickened his pace to get the farm equipment inside the barn before the rain hit.

He pulled his phone from his back pocket and clicked it to life. No messages. He noted the time and looked up at the sky hoping his parents would get home before it got too bad.

Gwen walked to the office where Betty and Erin were playing dominos. She stopped to hear their conversation before they heard her arrive.

Erin was saying, "He's really nice, and I love him. He would take care of me and he would listen to me when I had stuff to say. He loves me. He's my best friend."

"I'm so glad that you have a best friend, Erin. I'm sure he's okay. Maybe you'll find a new best friend."

"Like Mr. Nick? He's my friend too. I wish you were at my pool party. It was fun. But then Momma got mad and we had to go. She was crying. I was crying too 'cause I didn't get to say goodbye to my friend and I didn't get to hug everyone. It made me sad."

"Well, "Betty offered, "you can give them two hugs next time you see them." She smiled.

"Yeah! That's a good idea. I can give Miss Gill two hugs and Mr. Nick two hugs... but Momma says we prolly won't see him as much any more 'cause he's real busy with the farm and helping his dad and stuff."

"Oh she did, did she?" Betty asked again looking up and seeing Gwen leaning in the doorway.

"Yeah, my Momma works a lot. And since Mr. Nick isn't working at the Centre any more, we won't see him much. She says that she's gonna be busy too cause the Fair is coming and she has to get ready for the new classes and the next play and stuff. I help her a lot, too. Hey, it's like I work here too! 'Cept I get to take the classes an Momma gets to teach 'em!" Erin giggled.

"Erin sweetie, can you please go and get your things, it's about time for us to head home." Gwen came into the room and kissed the top of Erin's head.

"Hi Momma! We were playing dominos!"

"I see. I see. But there's a big storm coming and we don't want to get stuck here. Go on now, I'll help Miss Betty put the dominos away."

"Okay Momma!"

Erin skipped from the office and down the hall to the student lounge.

"Thank you so much for keeping an eye on her." Gwen stretched and yawned.

313

"I'm happy too. She is just the sweetest thing. I don't know how anyone could say a bad word about her. I don't mean to speak ill of others, but that Mary Ann Cavanaugh sure has something seriously wrong with her."

Gwen nodded, "I know! I saw her at the bank the other day, and she looked right through me. I heard that she fought right up until the day that the judge signed the papers to have Erin committed. And then, since that tactic didn't work, she wanted the judge to refuse her living in Bakersfield! Said it would upset *her* children!"

Betty just shook her head, "I don't understand the way people think sometimes. I really don't."

"I know." Gwen rubbed her forehead. "But, if it hadn't happened, I wouldn't have a daughter right now."

"Your lips to God's ears. He does work in mysterious ways."

"I never would have thought I'd be a single mom either, but we'll manage. What's that saying? He only gives us what He feels we can handle?" Gwen was mindless picking up domino pieces and stacking them in the box, not really giving much thought to what she was saying.

Betty sighed.

"What's wrong?"

Betty could only shake her head. She paused for a moment but couldn't hold her tongue and stilled Gwen's busy hands by placing hers on top. "God is trying to bless you and you are getting in His way."

Gwen furrowed her brow, confused.

Betty tried another route. "He wants to give you your heart's desires but you have to let Him."

"I am! I am so thankful for Erin! I don't take that for granted at all."

"I know sweetie, I know. I'm not saying that. You have been hurt. I know and you are still healing. But, you have to let go of that past hurt so He can replace it with happiness."

Gwen just shook her head, but still wasn't understanding what Betty was trying to tell her.

"Tony is the love of my life. But my story is paved with sadness because of the choices I made and I didn't trust Him to know what was best for me. I had to wait twenty-

315

two years before I could be rejoined with my soul mate. Don't let too much time pass by, before you give your heart over to love. Go tell Nick that you love him and that you will make time for him if he is willing to fit into your and Erin's life."

"But I don't..."

"Yes, honey, you do. The two of you fit together like a hand and glove and you would make a perfect... little... family."

"But... what if..."

Betty interrupted, "Honey. Everything we do is a 'what if'. What if I get my hair cut and I don't like it. What if we offer this new class and no one signs up? What if I paint this room and I don't like the color? What if I try this restaurant and it stinks? " Betty took in a deep breath before she continued. "You have to take a chance. Nick has given you plenty of time to see his character. To see his integrity. To see how he sincerely feels about you and your daughter. Love can't grow until you let it into your heart."

"I DID let it into my heart and he LEFT me!"

"And you are still here. Your heart can heal and love again."

"I just don't want to hurt anymore."

"But you're hurting now, aren't you? Forcing yourself to be without him seems like it's hurting you just as much." Betty wrapped her arm around Gwen's back and rested her head on Gwen's shoulder. "You aren't protecting your heart. You are causing the hurt it feels. I'm sorry, honey. No one can promise you that life won't hurt. It's full of hurt. But it is also filled with such joy. You can't really embrace all the beauty until you've witnessed some darkness. That's why we have rainbows. Always move toward the sunshine. It's where He's wanting you to go."

"But... I just don't know..."

"If you say so. I'm not trying to pressure you. It seems like the girls and maybe even Nick are giving you enough of that, but I speak from experience, those years I was without my true love were... okay, I have some good memories, but nothing compares to the years that I have been with him. I got a second chance. And I am sad and maybe even a little bit greedy that I didn't have more." Betty patted her back and reached down and grabbed her bag. She kissed Gwen on the head, "Don't forget to

317

turn out the Student Lounge light." She paused at the door, "Your heart knows, honey. You just have to listen. It's trying to tell you something."

Gwen looked back over her shoulder at Betty. She nodded and smiled and without words promised to heed her advice. "Be safe driving home. Would you please shoot me a text when you get there?"

"I can do that for you," Betty called out from the hallway.

"Bye Miss Betty! I'll see you tomorrow!" Erin hugged Betty on her way out.

"Okay Momma, I'm ready."

"Did you turn out the light when you left?"

Erin dropped her head back and suddenly her bag was the heaviest thing in the world as it hit the floor. "Uuuggghhh... I forgoooot."

"Go do it."

In a few moments she was back and with just enough time for Gwen to gather her things as well.

"Um... Erin... would you want to stop by and visit Miss Loraine and Mr. Curt on our way home?"

"And Mr. Nick too?" Erin jumped up and spun in a circle.

"Yeeeessss, I guess so..." Gwen feigned exasperation.

Nick sat in the dark at his house for an hour. He tried to stay calm and not worry, but his parents should have been home by now.

The storm wailed and thrashed outside the house. Tree limbs were scattered across the front yard. Leaves covered the pool in the back yard.

He tried to use his cell phone but was not getting any reception.

Nick paced from the living room looking out the front window, to the kitchen, looking out the back window.

He felt helpless. He needed to be doing something, but what?

Finally he could stand it no more. He grabbed his keys and went out to his truck.

He drove slowly up to the top of his driveway and his phone started going off. The sound of a xylophone scale alerted him to a message. Then another. Then another.

He put his truck in park and prayed that the messages would come through.

The first one was from his father: "This storm is lookin' nasty, son, be sure and pull the tractor all the way in the barn and your Mom is worried about her plants on the deck". Curt laughed, "Could you see if there's anything we can do with them. You know how she loves her plants. Okay, so, we'll be takin' it slow. Not to worry. Love you, son."

Nick rolled his eyes. Tractor in the barn. Check. Plants... not so good. I'll get new ones tomorrow. He laughed.

The second one from his mother: It sounded like she was out of breath, "Nicolas... there was a deer... for... forgive her." She paused. "I love you, my beautiful boy. I love you so much... I have to call your brother."

Nick's head was spinning. "What is she talking about?" He hit the callback button. It went to voicemail, "Hey Ma, what

320

do I have to forgive the deer for?" he laughed. "And, let me just tell you now, you're not going to be happy with your yard. But we'll fix it. The power's out at the house and cell phone usage is... iffy. Love you too, Mom. See you soon."

Third message: "This message is for Nick Penn. You are the emergency contact for Curt and Loraine Penn. Please come to Bakersfield Hospital as soon as you get this message. There has been an accident."

Nick felt pin pricks on his skin and his heart rate skyrocketed. He could feel it pounding in his chest. His mouth went dry as he was trying to think of what to do. For what felt like hours he struggled, remembering how to put the car back into drive.

He wanted to tear down the road to get to the hospital as fast as he could, but the rain was delaying his travel. Water stood in puddles on the road and his tires rebelled every time he tried to speed through one.

Nick tried to accelerate but his front tire hit one of the puddles and caused him to skid. His truck fish-tailed and spun out.

Nick's truck stopped sideways on the road within inches of hitting a fallen branch.

He jumped from the truck and drug the branch off to the side and sent up a grateful prayer for his safety then added, "Please, Lord, let them be okay..." He prayed as he worked.

Completely drenched and filthy, he climbed in his truck and tried to call his mother again. Voice mail. He tried his father. Voice mail. His thumb hovered over Gwen's name... He wanted to talk to her so bad... Would she reject him? Would she set things aside long enough to get to the hospital first? Is she all right in this storm? Is Erin afraid of storms? His heart pounded in his chest. He wanted to be near her. He could use some support right now. He took a chance and dropped his thumb down activating the call. Voice mail.

Nick felt suddenly so alone. He slammed his hands on the steering wheel, once, twice.... three times trying to gather his composure.

"Okay," he said out loud. "Let me get to the hospital. I have no idea what has happened. It could be nothing." He took in a deep cleansing breath and nodded to himself. He started the truck and calmly proceeded on his route to the hospital.

Nick burst through the hospital doors and stopped to gather his bearings and figure out where he needed to go. He heard his name called. When he turned to look, Gwen was coming from the waiting room. She was wet from the rain and her arm was bandaged but Nick could see blood seeping through. She walked with a limp but otherwise seemed to be okay.

He ran to her and put his hands on both sides of her head and kissed her forehead. He stepped back to assess again and pulled her close to him. "Gwen... oh, Gwen. He kissed her forehead again. "Are you okay? Why are you here? What happened to you?"

She nodded and opened her mouth to speak but Nick continued.

"Oh, I'm so glad," he exhaled. "Erin? Is she okay? Is she with you?"

Gwen nodded again and looked to the large double doors. "She's back there getting checked out."

"You're limping..."

"They just x-rayed it... and I..."

He embraced her again, "Oh, you should be sitting..."

"Nick," Gwen looked up at him with tears in her eyes, "I'm so sorry." She dropped her head down and started to cry.

Nick lifted her face to his, "What is it? What's happened?"

"I... there was an accident... this... this deer ran out in front of my truck and... I'm so sorry.... I..."

Every inch of Nick's skin prickled. He swallowed hard trying to move the lump in his throat. Nick couldn't move for a moment remembering why he was summoned to the hospital in the first place. He walked past Gwen and stood at the information desk. "Excuse me...,"he said as calmly as he could muster. "Excuse me, I'm Nick Penn. I received a call about my parents."

A nurse came around the corner and put her hand on his forearm. "Yes, Mr. Penn, if you could come with me..."

Nick looked back at Gwen and saw the tears in her eyes. He turned away from her and focused on the double doors he was walking toward. He could feel his vision beginning to blur with his own tears.

Gwen sat in the lobby holding herself, trying to keep the chills at bay. The shock from the accident was beginning to wear off and each and every ache and pain was beginning to make itself known.

A steady stream of tears ran down Gwen's face. She tried not to think about the accident but it wouldn't stop replaying over and over and over in her mind as if to punish her. The weight of her guilt was already enough to suffocate her.

The deer jumped from out of nowhere. She slammed on the brakes trying to avoid impact, but when she did, the truck spun out of control. She tried to tap the break but accidently hit the accelerator pedal. The truck pulled out of its spin and directly into the front corner of a navy blue sedan. Gwen's head hit the steering wheel before the airbag had a chance to inflate. An explosion of glass seemed suspended in the air as if everything was suddenly in slow motion.

Her seatbelt dug into her skin. Her left arm was dotted with glass shards and she was bleeding. Her right foot was screaming out in pain and she could feel it swelling without even looking down.

There was an eerie silence surrounding the two tangled vehicles. Gwen fought against her own body to turn to look in the back seat. "Erin? Honey? Are you alright?"

Erin's body was slumped over her seat belt. Her window was shattered and pieces of glass covered Erin's body. "Erin!" Gwen yelled, "Erin! Can you hear me?"

Gwen tried to open her door. It was stuck. She used her left foot to kick it open.

When the door swung open. She could see down inside the passenger seat of the other vehicle.

Gwen gasped in horror as Loraine Penn lay silent in the passenger seat. A piece of metal pierced her chest. Her eyes were closed and she held her cell phone in her hand. "Loraine! Loraine!" Gwen slid down from her seat and banged on the window. "Oh no...No!" Gwen cried out. "Loraine!! Can you hear me?" So much blood. It dripped from the door frame onto the wet ground. Even though the rain had not let up, a pool of thick red blood began to form a puddle at Gwen's feet. Gwen's voice became a whisper, "Please hear me. Please be okay." She tried to open her door but it wouldn't budge.

She hobbled around to the driver's side to see Curt pressed against the back of his seat and the inflated airbag holding him in place. The right side of his face was bleeding and he was still.

Gwen opened his door, and put her fingers to his neck to find a pulse. His heart was beating. "Curt... Curt, can you hear me?" She pushed the airbag away to keep it from suffocating him in case his head fell forward. "Curt! Hang on, I'm calling 911." She limped back to her truck to find her phone.

"Erin! Oh, honey! Are you okay?" She ran to the passenger side of the truck and opened the back door. Glass fell from every direction. The right side of Erin's head was bleeding. "Oh... Oh... Oh God, please...." She felt under her chin for a pulse. "Thank God..." She reached past Erin and grabbed her dance bag. She pulled out a towel and a pair of tights and tied the towel to Erin's head to stop the bleeding.

Blood was dripping down Gwen's arm and hand, but she barely noticed. Rain was pelting her and it refused to let up. Gwen took one of Erin's t-shirts from the bag and draped it over as much of the child as she could to keep the rain off of her.

She opened her front passenger car door to find her phone. Emergency "rules" kept flooding her brain. Don't move the victim. Don't remove piercing objects. Keep victim's warm and dry. Pfft... that won't happen. Call for help. I'm trying! I'm trying! Keep calm. Be specific. Check for signs of breathing. Oh God... please let them be breathing.

She went back to Erin to make sure her airways were clear. She gently lifted her head up and laid it on the back headrest.

She went towards the other car... Call for help. She started back to the truck to find her phone. Check for signs of breathing. She stopped to turn back around. Call for help. Stop the bleeding.

In front of both cars Gwen fell to her knees shaking. "God! Please help me!!" She was crying so hard but the rain quickly washed her tears away. She knelt there only

328

for a moment knowing that she must do something. She just couldn't sit there and cry. She raised her head and saw her cell phone under the truck. She got down on her stomach and slid under the truck. She could feel the glass digging into her skin as she reached. A little more... a little more. She grabbed the cell phone and rolled to her side keeping the phone dry. Her bare feet were scraped and torn and her stomach now had glass wounds but she tried to focus.

"911. What is your emergency?"

"This is Guinevere Collins. There has been an accident. Hwy 17 at around uh... uh... I'm not sure. The last road I passed was uh... the uh... gravel road that leads to the quarry."

"Are you injured?"

"Yes! And there are three others. Serious injuries. I, uh, think... umm..." her voice got caught in her throat. "I think one might be... dead." She squeaked the words out and a wave of sobs followed. My daughter. She is... hurt..."

"Are they responding?"

"No," Gwen sobbed. "No one is responding. Yes, I checked for a pulse, but I

329

couldn't reach Loraine. Oh, God... I don't know... I couldn't reach her. I'm sorry."

"Ma'am... Ma'am... stay calm. I am sending help your way right now. Are you in a safe place?"

Gwen looked around her and could only see the underneath of both cars and crumpled pieces of metal laying everywhere. "No. We are in the middle of the road and it's storming."

"Can you get to someplace safe?"

"No! I'm not leaving! I'm under the truck."

"Ma'am, you are trapped under the truck?"

"No, I'm fine. Please hurry."

"Ma'am... would you like me to stay on the line with you until help comes?"

"Nick..." Gwen whispered as she passed out.

"Ma'am?... Ma'am?"

"Mrs. Collins? Mrs. Guinevere Collins?"

Gwen snapped out of her trance. "Um, yes! Yes, that's me!" She raised her hand and attempted to stand up.

"Are you alright?" The nurse asked.

"Yes, yes, I'm fine," she lied. "Is my daughter… can I see her?"

"Yes, let me take you to her and the doctor will be in shortly."

"Thank you." Gwen walked through her pain and followed the nurse.

"Aw, there's my sugar pie."

Erin's eyes fluttered. She wasn't sure if she wanted to keep them open or not. They were so heavy.

"You gave us quite a scare. Don't you fret now, Mother is here."

Chapter Seventeen

Nick's jaw was trembling as he tried to keep it all together. He rested his right arm on the headrest of the hospital bed while he clasped the hand of his father with his left hand. He had dirt and leaves stuck to him but he didn't care. His father looked so frail as the tubes did the breathing for him.

The doctor came in. "I am sorry for your loss," he said, solemnly.

Nick acknowledged his sentiment but kept his eyes on his father's face.

The doctor continued, "I'm afraid... we have some decisions to make. If you would like to meet me in the hall... I could go over them with you."

Nick nodded, already knowing what the doctor was going to say. He had overheard the nurses at the nurse's station who seem to think that there is an invisible sound barrier around them. They said things like, "I don't know how he's still alive." "He's not coming out of that." "Is that Nick Penn, you know from t.v.?" "He's so cute." "And he's crying! How adorable is that?"

Nick took in a deep breath and swallowed hard. He squeezed his father's hand as if to say that he'd be right back.

But just as Nick was stepping away from the bed, Curt opened his eyes and looked directly at his son.

"Son," his voice was gravelly and he was short of breath. Nick immediately leaned back in and took his father's hand again. "Son, take care of things for me. Everything should be in order." He gasped for air.

"Don't talk, Dad. Save your breath."

Curt shook his head, "I don't have much time. For once, your mother is actually ready before me." He made a feeble attempt at laughter.

Nick could barely swallow for the lump in his throat but forced a smile for his father's sake.

"I have been blessed," Curt went on between coughs. "I am proud of my boys. It is... your mother's and my dearest wish, that you boys will continue to stay close... be a family..."

"Of course, Dad. But it would be better if you would stay."

"I can't son. My heart is with your mother. I love you boys... so much," a tear slipped from the corner of his eye, "...but your mother, is ... my light. I don't want to be here without her."

"But, Dad..."

"No son. Someday, you will find such a light and you will feel the same way. It's a good thing. I want that for you."

"I want that too, but..."

"I have to go. Take care of my barn."

Nick laughed, "That, I do know."

"I've tried to do the best I could for you boys. I know I had to work a lot, and I know that I wasn't as affectionate as your mother..."

"Dad, don't... please..."

"But I just want you to know that I love you. And I did the best I could."

"I know, Dad... We all know. We love you too."

"I have to go..." He took a deep ragged breath, and chuffed, "I can hear your mother calling me to come home..." He closed his eyes and breathed his last.

"Dad?" Nick whispered. "Dad?" Tears fell down his face. He grabbed both of Curt's hands with both of his and placed them to his forehead. "I love you, Dad. Tell Mom, that I love her too." He fell into the chair and laid his head on the edge of the bed, and cried.

"Mother?" Erin's weak, tiny voice spoke into the air.

"That's right, dah-lin', Mother is here."

"Am I dreaming?" Erin asked.

"Now don't be a goose. Of course not." Mary Ann Cavenaugh stood at the end of Erin's hospital bed. She wore turquois blue running pants with matching jacket and a light yellow v-neck underneath. She looked over her shoulder and then back to Erin.

"Where is my... my new..."

"Now listen here, don't you speak, you just rest. I'll take care of everything."

"But... you don't want me..." The drugs were heavy and Erin's speech was slurred. She still wasn't sure if she was dreaming. Was everything about Miss Gwen being her new mother a dream? She searched her brain for facts. "You left me..."

"Now suga..." the Southern, gentile accent came out. "I didn't leave you, per say, but we didn't want to make Brother and Sister uncomfortable on vacation, now did we?"

"But..."

"You know Mother cares about you. Don't you remember all those pretty dresses Mother bought for you? And don't you remember how I would read you stories?"

"You didn't read me stories."

Mary Ann Cavenaugh cocked her eyebrow and pursed her lips. "Don't be a brat. Of course I read you stories."

Erin's eyes blinked slowly. A smile crossed her face when she saw, or thought she saw Miss Gwen come into her room.

"What are you doing in here?" Gwen confronted Mary Ann. She ran over to Erin's bedside and looked everything over to see that it hadn't been tampered with. Lord only knows what this insane woman was capable of.

"You have no right to use that tone with me. We have a common interest here." She spoke coolly.

"You are mistaken. You have no business in this room at all." Gwen's blood was boiling. "Nurse, please call security."

The nurse looked back and forth between the two women before she started for the door.

"Just a moment, you can't call security on me. I'm on the board."

Gwen laid Erin's hand on the bed and walked with purpose to face Mary Ann. "You have ten seconds to get out of this room or I will have you escorted out. I don't care what board you are on. And in less than an hour, I will have a restraining order set against you and so help me, if you come within 50 yards of this child I will have you sent to jail."

"Really, Ms. Collins, is all this drama necessary."

"Eight seconds. Did I not make myself clear?"

Mary Ann, dropped her gaze. She reached up and robotically touched and tucked the hair pins back in her hair out of habit. Then with as much decorum as she had left, she cocked her eyebrow and nodded to Gwen and left the room.

The nurse pressed her lips together tight and looked down as Ms. Cavenaugh walked past her.

"I don't know who I have to talk to but that woman is not allowed in this room again," Gwen spoke sternly.

The nurse nodded. "I'll tell security and I'll let the doctor know that you are ready to speak with him."

Gwen softened her voice, knowing that the poor nurse had nothing to do with the previous events. "Thank you."

"Momma?" Erin spoke softly.

Gwen spun around and went to the side of the bed. She touched Erin's cheek and brushed her blood-matted hair away from her face. Erin's head was bandaged up all the way around the back and sides and tufts of her blonde curls sprung out from underneath and through the bandages.

Her thumb stroked her child's cheek, "I'm here, sweetie. I'm right here. Are you okay?"

Erin nodded, but then realized that was a mistake, her head hurt her. "Are you my momma or are you my dance teacher?"

Gwen giggled and said, "Well... I'm both, I guess."

Erin smiled a sleepy smile. "Oh good. I thought it was just a dream."

"Nope, sorry, honey. You're stuck with me forever."

Erin smiled again. "I'm sleepy."

"You go ahead and sleep. I'll be right here."

Gwen looked back over her shoulder to check to see if Erin was still sleeping as the doctor finished up his consult, just outside in the hallway.

"She should be able to go home in a few days. We want to make sure there is no brain swelling, but I don't think we have to worry about that. The stitches will dissolve on their own and she should be good as new. The nurse will have papers for you for her home care." He tried to sound pleasant but it just came out as mechanical.

"Thank you. Thank you very much." Gwen shook his hand. He obliged and then immediately pushed the hand sanitizer dispenser on the wall.

Gwen did her best not to feel offended. She was turning to go back in to sit with Erin when she did a double-take at the Nurse's Center.

"Mark?" she called out to the man standing there. She walked, or rather hobbled toward him.

"Gwen!" Her ex-husband came over to her and wrapped her in his arms. She did not return his affection.

"Mark, what are you doing here?"

He looked shocked that she would ask such a question. "Where else would I be? Jerry told me that you were in a car accident. I rushed over here as soon as I could."

"Jerry? How did Jerry know?"

"He's a dispatcher for the police department now."

She stared blankly at him not knowing what to say.

"Are you alright?" He embraced her again. "What's the damages?" He pulled back and saw the bright pink cast on her leg and

341

foot and the bandage on her arm. "Oh, your arm... what... your leg!"

"Mark, I'm fine. You don't need to be here."

"Baby, this is exactly where I'm supposed to be. You're hurt. I'm here to take care of you."

"You weren't too worried about me being hurt before," Gwen said under her breath. She was in no mood to fight. She was tired and her body was so sore. She just wanted to sit by her little girl and rest.

"So, uh... Jerry said you mentioned a... uh daughter... in your call? Were you... I mean, were we pregnant? Am I a father?"

Gwen took in a deep breath and let it out slowly not wanting to delay his departure. "I adopted one of my students." She kept it brief.

"Oh, I... uh... that's great. I am so happy for you."

"You are?"

"Of course I am." He reached out and took her hands in his. She flinched as he ran his thumb over the back of her tender wounds. "Now, maybe we could..." He looked up at her hoping she could finish the sentence for him.

"We could, what?"

"You know, we could pick up where we left off."

She squinted her eyes at him not sure she was hearing him correctly. But before she could respond, the elevator door opened to her left and she saw Nick stepping out and walking toward her. His eyes were red-rimmed and it looked like he had been punched in the stomach. The raw pain was written all over his face. He stopped when he saw her.

"Nick!" Gwen called out and pulled her hands away from Mark. She tried to move toward him but he had already turned and walked back to the elevator.

"Nick, wait. Please."

The elevator door didn't open in time. He looked back over his shoulder at her. His eyes were now cold and it looked like he was going to throw up.

"Don't," was all he said and he walked down the stairs.

Gwen's head dropped and her heart ached for him. A tear slipped from her eyes.

She loved him. She was coming to his house to tell him. And now...

"Was that Nick Penn?" Mark came up behind her completely unaware of the raw emotions. "He's from that *Real Lives, Real People* show! Dude, I love that show!"

Gwen turned around to look at the man who had torn her heart in pieces and suddenly realized that he was a fraction of the man who just walked away from her. "Mark, What. Do. You. Want?"

"Baby, I told you. I heard you were hurt and I wanted to come and see..."

"There is nothing between us any more. I am no longer your concern. My daughter and I have a new life and it doesn't include you. You made your choice. I made mine."

"But does it have to be either or? We could be a family, I thought that's what you wanted."

Gwen thought for a moment. She stood up tall and squared her shoulders. "It is what I want. More than anything. And I'm going to do everything I can to make that happen."

"Baby, I'm right here. We can start again."

She looked him dead in the eye. "It's not you, Mark. Go home." And she walked away.

Chapter Eighteen

After the funeral, Evelynn and Gwen sat on the back porch and drank lemonade.

"I can't believe they're gone." Evelynn said.

Gwen just looked down at the ice in her drink. She was still weighed down with guilt.

"They were such nice people. And their sons. Handsome and kind. Every last one of them."

Gwen nodded, agreeing. "All those grandkids." She attempted to be part of the conversation.

"How are you holding up?"

Gwen shrugged. She still had a light bandage on her arm. She lifted her foot to show off her hot pink cast, "It goes with everything, don't you think?"

The two women grew silent again, staring out into the back yard. Finally Gwen

347

said what was on her mind. "He couldn't even look at me at the funeral."

Evelynn let out her breath in a sigh. She reached over and put her hand on Gwen's arm. "Honey, he was kinda busy."

"I know but..."

"He is hurting so much right now."

"I know because of me! But I... but he..."

"But what? You didn't want him to love you last week."

It was Gwen's turn to sigh, "I know. And I... I don't mean to be selfish. But... I do love him. And I do want him to love me. And now it can never happen. I killed his parents!" Gwen's tears flowed freely.

"Honey, you didn't..."

Gwen shot her a look to stop her train of thought.

"It was an accident."

"That doesn't change the fact. Even if he didn't want to love me anymore, I could live with that, if only he'd forgive me."

"He will... in time. But right now he is mourning their loss." Evelynn looked over at her friend and her heart went out to her.

"You have to forgive yourself before you can expect anyone else to.

Gwen cried and shook her head. "I can't... I just can't. It was horrible. I can't get through a single night without seeing it in my mind. I see everything in slow motion. I couldn't stop. I was pushing the brake and I couldn't stop."

"Gwen..." Evelynn looked over at her. "Guinevere," she called her name her again.

Gwen looked over at her best friend and could feel the tears streak her cheeks, make-up flowing with them.

"You have to forgive yourself. It was an accident."

"I killed the man I loves parents!!" She raised her arm and let it flop back down on her lap. "I know, I know. And it's selfish of me to want him to be thinking of me, but I just can't help it. First I push him away and then I take his family from him!"

"Stop talking like that."

"But it's true!" Gwen wailed, tears spilling down her cheeks.

"The man is in love with you. You cannot convince him otherwise. He is grieving. He's not going to stop loving you."

Gwen looked up at her hopefully.

Evelynn handed her a tissue and said, "You need to go and talk to him. When things quiet down, just go and talk to him. You are the best of friends. I'm sure he needs you."

Gwen nodded and wiped her face. "Where did you get this tissue?"

Evelynn smirked, "Don't ask." Gwen looked at her suspiciously. "What? It was a funeral, I came prepared." They both laughed.

Evelynn changed the subject when she heard clamoring and laughing going on in the kitchen behind them. "How long is your mom staying in town?"

Gwen looked over her shoulder as if she could see her. "Erin gets her stitches out next week. I think at least until then. They are having the best time."

"I know she's wanted grandkids for a very long while."

"I am happy to give her such joy. It's like ten years have come off her life. She says she has purpose again." Gwen laughed at the thought.

"Grandkids are important. My mom's been after me since... I don't know, since I was eighteen, I guess."

Gwen laughed. "You'd better get on it then." She looked over at Evelynn and was surprised not to see a return smile. "Honey, I was only teasing."

Evelynn nodded and swallowed hard. "I know, and I'm ... going to make a valiant effort."

Gwen furrowed her brow. She slipped her legs off the ottoman and sat up straight to face her best friend. "What is it? Is there something... I should know?" Gwen wasn't sure if she should be worried or excited. Evelynn's face betrayed nothing.

"Well..."

"C'mon woman, out with it!"

"This is totally not the time I wanted to talk about this, but... You may have to run things at the Centre for a few weeks in December..." Evelynn said with the corners of her mouth ever so slightly turning up.

Gwen gasped. "Evie St. Lawrence! Are you pregnant?"

Evelynn burst out laughing. "No!" She turned to sit up straight so hers and Gwen's knees were touching. She leaned in conspiratorially, "No, I'll be on my honeymoon."

"Ahhhhhh!!!" Both girls screamed and stamped their feet as if they had just been asked out to prom.

"Oh! Evie!! That is so exciting! I am so happy for you!" Gwen squealed as she hugged her best friend's neck. Then suddenly, she leaned back on her lounge chair and looked at Evelynn, squinting her eyes. "Who is it, exactly that we are marrying?"

Evelynn looked away coyly. "David Ripke and I are getting married."

"What?"

"What?" Nick looked at his childhood friend with shock and surprise.

"I asked, she answered. We are." Dave shrugged.

"But, you are a womanizing maniac."

"WAS, a womanizing maniac... was."

Nick was shocked into silence. Every time he thought he was going to say something, he couldn't make the words come out. He loosened the knot on his tie and strained for his top button to be released. "But... I mean... uh... Do you love her?"

"Dude... I can't think of anybody else but her. She is the smartest, most beautiful, funniest... dang, she's just so amazing."

Nick blinked at the grown up answer that was coming out of Rip's mouth. "You barely know her."

"Right! I'd better tie the knot before she realizes she's getting the short end of the stick!"

Nick laughed and slapped his friend on the shoulder. "Well, I'm happy for you, man. Really, I am."

"Did I mention that she laughs at my jokes? She thinks I'm funny, Nick."

Nick nodded, "That pretty much says it right there. She's definitely in love with you."

"I know, right?"

"Cause your jokes aren't funny."

"I know! That's what I'm saying!"

"Really... I don't mean to doubt you, but we've known each other for a lot of years, brother. I don't want..."

Dave thought for a moment. "I have never felt like this with anyone... in my LIFE, Nick."

"So you're ready for the whole settle down and have kids kinda lifestyle? 'Cause, I'm pretty sure she's going to want kids."

"Yeah, I think I am. Being here and working around all the kids and just seeing how her face lights up to work with them... it's made me see things a lot differently."

Nick chuffed, "Gwen too. She loves those kids." He swallowed hard and shook the memory from his thoughts. "So, there's finally going to be a Mr. and Mrs. Ripke."

"And don't forget the little Rips."

"Little Rips? He wants children?" Gwen was still shocked her friend agreed to this.

"He does. It's amazing to watch him around them. He gets down on their level and plays with them and chases after them. When he sits in the classroom and watches, they actually climb up in his lap."

"That's cause they're the same age..." Gwen spoke glibly.

Evelynn laughed. "I know. I'm a little surprised, too. But, Gwen, when we are alone and he's relaxed and comfortable, he says the most endearing things. He is interested in the theatre. He wants to help. And.., and... I didn't get a chance to show you, but he made a two minute video about the Center that we can show before all of the productions and put on the website. He's just so... thoughtful and ... creative."

"Aww, that's so sweet! I... I honestly can't imagine that side of him."

"It's been there, you just haven't noticed."

Gwen heard the comment the way it was meant. "I am sorry for that. I was so lost in my own drama that I didn't even notice that my best friend was falling in love. Oh, Evie. I am so happy for you." She leaned over and hugged Evelynn around the neck. "So... we have a wedding to plan!"

Evelynn smiled. "We do. And, I was hoping you would be my maid of honor."

Gwen squealed, "Of course I would!!"

"Man, of course I would. I'd be honored. That means I'm in charge of the bachelor party too, right?" Nick smiled and rubbed his hands together.

"You know it, brother! And you know what I like."

"Yeah, well, you're not getting any of that any more. You're practically a married man. That was just a test."

"You know what? You're right. I'm okay with that."

"A wise answer."

"But no cute chicks pool party, got it?" Dave scolded.

Nick laughed. "Got it! Did you want a California send off or an Arkansas send off?

Dave shrugged. "I'm good either way."

"You are a changed man! The old Dave would have demanded Las Vegas!" Nick laughed.

"The old Dave wouldn't have gotten this far."

"So, what happens after the honeymoon?" Nick asked suddenly thinking of the Fine Arts Centre and the theatre and what's at stake.

"Well," Evelynn began, "We'll be coming back here."

Gwen breathed out a sigh of relief. "Oh, I almost had a panic attack there for a moment. Do you think Dave will be happy here?"

"I asked him that too. He thinks he will. He is going to go to the local stations to see if he can get some work there, but he says he'd be happy wherever I am."

The two girls giggled and squealed at the sweetness of that sentiment. You're never too old for romance, it turns out.

"We're having the wedding at the theatre aren't we?"

"Do you think we should?"

"Oh yes! You can make it into any thing you want!! We have Jeanne on the staff! The best artist and set designer anywhere! Oh, Evie! It's going to be wonderful! And you are going to be beautiful!"

Evelynn laughed. "I'm going to have to wear flats."

"We shall find the perfect ones!" Gwen leaned in and they put their foreheads together. "Oh, Evie! I am so happy for you."

"You know what this means, don't you?"

Gwen looked around her and thought about it..."Uh... no?"

"How many times have you told me, 'I will if you will'. Well, you have fallen waaaay behind." Evelynn teased.

Gwen smiled and pulled back to her chaise. "It helps if you have a willing partner."

Evelynn fell back into her chair dramatically, "Oh! The excuses!" Evelynn dropped the back of her hand against her forehead and laughed.

"I'll go talk to him, I promise." Gwen turned toward her best friend, "But first, do we have a color scheme yet?"

"Mom," Gwen called out as she pulled the hot casserole dish from the oven.

Judy, Gwen's mother walked in from the living room just as Gwen was turning around placing her dish on the counter.

"Oh, hey." Gwen smiled. "Do you mind if I run this over to Nick's house? Can you keep an eye on Erin?"

A smile spread across Judy's face, "It's about time."

Gwen tried not to blush and shook her head, "So, I can take that as a yes?"

"Yes, daughter, yes. Take as much time as you need." Judy kissed her grown child's head across the bar. "I guess we have to fend for ourselves for dinner since you're taking the good stuff?" Judy leaned over the casserole dish to breath in the smell.

Gwen smiled, "Ah, not so much, I made some for you too!" Gwen set the second casserole dish on the bar to cool.

"Mmmm, it smells delightful."

"I hope he thinks so too." She took in a deep breath and tucked the casserole dish into it's thermal carrying case.

Judy cocked her eyebrow, "Clever. Using the good dishes so he has to return them. That's my girl."

Gwen winked, "Learned from the best." She paused and a tiny smile tried to emerge, "Or... he might, hopefully ask me to join him."

Judy winked. "I'll keep my fingers crossed for option two."

359

"Thanks Mom." Gwen laughed. "You know, I just miss talking to him. We have so much to talk about, it's like... we never run out of things to say. I've never had that before." Gwen furrowed her brow searching for references in her brain library. "Even with Mark, it was just the surface stuff. He didn't really like to dig in and learn things, or... I don't know. And Nick actually hears what I say. To this day, I can promise you that Mark still couldn't tell you my favorite color. But Nick knows. I don't know how he remembers everything, I just ... miss talking to him. Maybe I'm thinking too much."

"Maybe, but conversation is important. When the kids grow up and go away, and the passion has dwindled, you still want to be sitting next to your best friend."

"That's the way Loraine and Curt were. They still held hands on the front porch swing. I want that."

"I want that for you too. Now just go talk to him."

Gwen had both hands full with her casserole dish when she went out her front door. She almost walked right into a man who seemed to be coming up her driveway.

He was about her height and wore a camouflage ball cap that was adorned with a large gold fishhook. He had tattoos going down one arm, peeking out from under the sleeve of his black t-shirt.

"Oh, I'm sorry. I didn't see you there." Gwen smiled. "Can I help you?"

The man, barely more than a boy, Gwen noticed, shook his head and pulled his cap down lower on his head. "Naw, just passin' by."

"Oh, well, have a nice day." Gwen continued around to the passenger side door of her rental car.

"You live here?" the boy asked.

"Yeah. I do. Do you... live in the neighborhood?"

"Just moved here."

"Oh, welcome." She scurried back around to the driver's side. "I don't mean to be rude, but I'm in an awful hurry. I guess I'll see you around?" She climbed in the tiny car and pulled the door shut. The young man touched the brim of his hat and stepped back from the car, then made his way down the street.

Gwen pulled her rental car into the paved section on the side of the house. She saw Nick's black truck and another rental car next to hers. As she walked by the garage, she saw that Curt's dark green SUV was parked in its usual space.

She took in a deep breath and hobbled up to the door. She carefully took the front steps one at a time dragging her casted foot after each step. She knocked and waited. She didn't hear any movement after about a minute, so she knocked again.

The door opened and a woman stood there in a bikini and a flowing, see-through wrap. She eyed Gwen but said nothing. Finally she turned her palm over and gave Gwen a look to let her know that she was impatiently waiting for the reason for interruption. "Yes?"

"Uh... I was... uh..." Gwen stammered. "Is Nick home?"

"He's upstairs. He's in the shower. And you are...?"

"Oh, uh... I'm Gwen, I just brought some food over... for..."

"More food? I have never seen so much food in my life! Your people just keep bringing food. Do they not know there's only one person living here? And it's all so fattening."

"I'm sorry, and *you* are?"

"I'm Christy, Nick's girlfriend." As if that was obvious.

"Oh. Well, Christy, Nick's girlfriend, I'm sorry to have bothered you. Down here, in the south, it's a tradition to bring food to those who are grieving. It shows we care."

She scrunched up her face in disgust, "Well you must not care too much, cause, I mean, all this stuff has meat and cheese in it. I can't find a Vegan restaurant anywhere. What does that tell you?" she laughed.

Gwen blinked, smiled and decided not to answer that question. In fact, she handed over the casserole dish, stepped back, away from the door so as not to say *anything* she might regret. "Um. Yeah, I... have to go... Again, sorry I bothered you. If you could just tell Nick I stopped by to clog his arteries, I'd appreciate it." She smiled her best fake smile and turned to walk back to her teeny tiny rental car, clomping along on her fractured foot, and gritting her teeth the whole way.

She slammed the door when she got in. "That is not Nick's girlfriend." She started the car and backed out of the space and headed up the long driveway. "Your people..." she fumed.

The sunshine peeking through the trees eluded her as she grumbled up the three miles to the main road. "That is NOT Nick's girlfriend. It couldn't be. He couldn't..."

Her face rested in a deep frown as she kept rehashing the last seven minutes of her life over and over again. "That is not Nick's girlfriend." She turned right on the small two-lane highway. "She is very pretty in her... artificial way. Artificial hair color... artificial tan... artificial teeth... I mean, whose teeth are naturally that white? Her artificial... bo...you know what? Who cares?" Her frown dug deeper into her face turning her outlook grey. "I can't find a Vegan restaurant anywhere. What does that tell you?" She mocked in a high-pitched, squeaky voice. "It tells you we like our bacon around here, sister!" She pinched her brows together so hard, they almost touched in the middle. She didn't even realize that she was clinching her jaw.

She sped down the narrow highway and came up to the site of the accident. She slowed down and looked beyond the grassy median to the opposite side still expecting to see debris and glass and twisted metal and… blood. But it was all gone. Clean. Like it never happened. Like two people didn't lose their life at this very spot on the road. Life went on.

Gwen pulled over onto the shoulder and burst into tears. "God, I'm so sorry! I would gladly give my own life if I could bring them back." She rested her head on the steering wheel and let her tears flow. She sobbed and heaved until her tears and prayers were spent.

She cried for the loss of her friends, Nick's parents. She cried for the pain she caused Nick and his family. She cried for all of her selfish shortcomings. She cried for not seeing the gift of second chances in front of her.

"Maybe that *is* his girlfriend. Why would he want me? She doesn't kill anything!" She wiped her face with the bottom of her tank top, feeling very sorry for herself. She waited until her breathing calmed and new tears stopped forming before accepting her fate. She alone is responsible for getting herself in this situation. Nick *was* meant to be her soul mate, and now... it was too late.

She turned the key over in the ignition and slowly drove home finding every single reason why Nick would want Christy over her.

It was late. Gwen couldn't sleep. Everyone was right. She waited too long.

Of course he should go back to his girlfriend. *I practically pushed him into her arms,* she tortured herself. She sat up in her bed and folded her legs in front of her. She tried to stick her finger down into her cast to reach the unquenchable itch she had just beyond the length of her finger. *Two more*

*days, you stupid cast... then I can scratch my
leg whenever I want!*

She leaned over and tapped the home
button on her phone. 1:47 am.

*Why am I even awake? This is what I
asked for. I asked him to leave me alone. I told
him I didn't want him. I'm glad he's happy.*

She flopped over to her side. "No I'm
not," she sighed.

Gwen thought she heard a noise and
instantly went on "Mommy-alert". She lay
perfectly still waiting to hear another sound.
And there it was. The tiniest whimper. She
sat up in her bed and pushed her legs over
the side. She paused again making sure it
wasn't a two time thing. Nope. Erin was
crying.

Erin's door was cracked, and the only
light came from the corner of her room; a
glass butterfly light that her Grandma Judy
gave her.

Gwen pushed the door open slightly.
"Erin? Honey, are you okay?"

Erin did not reply but she was
definitely crying.

"Sweetie, what's wrong?" Gwen walked in and sat down on the side of her bed and pushed her wet curls from her face.

"He's here." Erin whimpered finally.

"Who, sweetie? There's no one here."

Erin opened her eyes to look at Gwen but said nothing. She slowly turned her head toward the window and Gwen's gaze followed.

"What is it?"

Erin looked toward the window and then closed her eyes. Gwen stood and walked to the window pulling the curtain back, "See?"

Then Gwen screamed.

Chapter Nineteen

It was a dark night. There was no moon, and Nick's thoughts wandered. He drove the same back roads that he has driven his whole life. He knew them like the back of his hand.

He was still reeling from the loss of his parents but was tired of being cooped up in his house. Tired of paperwork. Tired of lawyers. Tired of people. Tired of ham. Just tired. He had to get out, even if it was just for a couple hours.

He had put his ex-girlfriend on a plane the day before. His home was finally empty. He wasn't even sure why she came. This was the first time she had ever come to Bakersfield. She said it was to offer support, but it was more like a guilt trip. She wanted him to come back to California.

"I don't even know what I ever saw in her," Nick said to no one. Gwen's face passed through his mind. He smiled thinking of her.

369

He wanted so badly to talk with Gwen. He caught himself instinctively heading in the direction of her house. He stopped and turned around just before he hit her sub-division.

"No... don't do it. First of all, it's late. I wouldn't want to scare her to death. Second, I told her I'd let her go. I have to respect her wishes. If she wants me, I told her to... Whoa!" Nick slammed on his breaks, but not before hitting something that crossed the road in front of him.

Nick threw his truck in park and jumped out. In the light from his high-beams, an animal lay on its side.

"What the hell? I think I hit a wolf."

Nick cautiously approached the animal. It lay perfectly still. He leaned in and saw that it's eyes were open and it was panting heavily.

"Hey buddy... you okay?" Nick spoke softly and reached out to touch the animal. His fur was matted and filthy. There were scratches and dried blood on his paws, and while his eyes were open there was a vacant look about them. It tried to lift its head, but just let it flop back down on the pavement.

It's tongue hung from it's mouth and lay where if fell.

He stoked it's head and his finger got tangled in a worn piece of string. He followed the string around the wolf's neck and came to a tag. MAX

"You're not a wolf at all, are you? Max. Is that your name? Max?" The dog tried to thump it's tail but whimpered at his effort.

"It's okay… I'm gonna help you, okay? Don't bite me. I'm going to pick you up."

Nick struggled under the weight. "Whoo!" Nick's eyes watered trying not to breathe in the stench of whatever Max had been through. "I think a bath is on the priority list."

He managed to get the dog/wolf in the back seat of the truck. Max whimpered and tried to feebly move toward the open truck door. "Hang on… hang on… I'm not gonna hurt you. Let's get you to my house, Max. Let's see what the damages are."

All the lights were on and Gwen held
Erin close to her on the couch. The police
department sent three officers and Susan
Carter was called. Gwen rocked Erin back
and forth as the officers inspected the outside
of the house.

Gwen's finger hovered over Nick's
name in her phone. She wanted him here.
She needed him here. *She* wouldn't feel safe
until he said everything was all right. But she
couldn't do it. She couldn't make the call.
She was afraid that when she did the
girlfriend would pick up the phone and tell
her that he was sleeping and to never call
again. Gwen threw her phone on the table
and took in a deep breath. *He respected my
wishes; the least I could do is respect his. Even
though they are wrong. I have to be brave for
Erin,* she told herself.

Susan Carter came through the front
door and was out of breath as if she had run
the whole way. "I came as soon as I could.
Are you alright?"

Gwen nodded. Susan sat on the couch
beside Gwen and leaned across her and
stroked Erin's hair.

"I'm so sorry, sweetie. You are such a brave girl." Susan tried to encourage the child.

Erin had stopped crying but simply shut down. When the police tried to talk to her she could only stare at them. She could not form words.

Susan spoke in hushed tones, while the officers buzzed around behind her. "Can you tell me what happened?" She was addressing Gwen, but was hoping that Erin would be able to give the missing details that the police were wanting.

"I... heard Erin crying so I went in to talk to her. She said, 'He's here.' I was trying to comfort her showing her no one was 'here' so I went to the window and pulled back the curtains... and ... and..." A tear fell from Gwen's eye as she relived the moments, "A man was standing there. He wasn't afraid of being caught or anything. He looked right at me. Stared at me." She looked off in the distance, seeing the man once again in her mind's eye.

"Do you know who he was?" Susan asked, placing her hand on Gwen's.

"I... I... don't know who he was."

"Could you describe him?"

"He was… he was…" Gwen blinked and looked over at Susan. "I… can't. All I remember is his eyes. So… filled with… hate."

"It's okay," Susan put her arm around Gwen. "It's okay. Is your mom still here?

Gwen shook her head, "She left yesterday."

Susan nodded, taking in the information and assessing the situation.

"We've searched the perimeter, Ma'am," Officer Baker spoke to Gwen. "We didn't see anyone, but we are continuing our search.

"Thank you, Charlie," Susan offered.

"Do you have a gun on the premises, Ma'am?"

Gwen looked up shocked at the officer, "Uh… no… no I don't"

"You should really think about getting one. We have classes…"

"Thank you, Charlie," Susan reached up and touched his wrist. "Can we talk about that later?"

"Right. We uh… we did find this…" Charlie nodded to another officer who brought a plastic bag to Officer Charlie Baker.

He opened the bag and revealed a worn teddy bear inside.

"Does this belong to you?" He asked.

Gwen shook her head, "I've never seen it before."

"We found it outside, under the girl's window."

Erin looked up and saw the bear. Tears streamed from her eyes. She cried into Gwen's side as Gwen held her tighter.

"Honey, what is it? Do you recognize that bear?"

Erin bawled harder.

"Give us a minute would you Charlie?" Susan asked and shifted her knees toward the child.

"Erin..." Susan reached over and put her finger under Erin's chin. She gently lifted the child's face to her own. "I know this is hard, but... Erin, did you know the man at your window?"

Erin swallowed hard, but said nothing.

"Is this your teddy bear?" Susan asked holding the plastic covered bear on her lap.

She pushed the blonde curls away from Erin's face and looked for unspoken answers. "My sweet girl," Susan spoke again.

"You are not in any trouble. This man frightened you and I can't have that. I want you and your Momma to feel safe. So, if you can help me..."

Erin turned her face back into Gwen's side.

"Okay... okay," Susan backed off and ran her hand over Erin's curls.

Gwen leaned down and kissed her head. "Honey... it's okay. You know you're not in trouble, right? Use your words, remember? Can you tell Miss Susan about the man? Do you know him?"

Erin looked up at Gwen's face and it almost broke Gwen's heart right there. The fear and the innocence and the loss all rolled up and battling in those beautiful blue eyes.

"I can't," she squeaked out.

"What? Why?" Gwen questioned.

"He said he will kill you," Erin's raspy, tired voice revealed.

Gwen and Susan looked at each other. Susan tried to elicit calm to Gwen without words.

Susan's voice was calm as she asked, "You know who the man is?"

Erin nodded.

Susan smiled and nodded in return. "Good girl." She ran her fingers along the edge of the child's face. "Can you tell me who he is? I promise, I won't let him hurt your Mom, okay? If I tell the police, then he can't be mad at you, right? Can you tell me? Can you tell me who the man is?"

Tears slipped from Erin's eyes, and in a voice that barely held sound, she said, "The Bogey Man."

Susan closed her eyes, and nodded. She opened her eyes again and locked eyes with the child. "I hear you. Can you tell me... has he been here before?"

Erin nodded.

Gwen swallowed hard, pleading with her own body to stop shaking.

"A lot?"

Erin nodded and looked away. "He stopped when Gramma was here."

Gwen covered her mouth and closed her eyes. Her skin prickled. Erin slept almost every night with her Gramma while she visited. Then Erin bawled when Judy left, but Gwen didn't think anything of it. Didn't think there was a deeper meaning to it. *How did I not see signs,* she chided herself looking up to the ceiling as the tears slipped down face.

"Did he... touch you?" Susan continued.

Erin shook her head but offered no more.

"Is this your teddy bear?" Susan asked again lifting the evidence bag for her to see.

Erin nodded.

Gwen squeezed her tighter and kissed her head while she prayed. She wiped the tears from her own cheeks.

"Where was it?" Susan continued.

Erin shrugged.

"You don't know?" Susan asked for clarification.

Erin shook her head.

"Can you..." Susan looked away trying to put her thoughts in the right order. "Do you... remember when you had your teddy bear?"

Erin nodded.

"Where was that?"

"At my house."

"Your house with your foster family?"

Erin shook her head.

"Your house before that?"

378

Erin nodded.

"Okay... okay..." Susan smiled at her. And cupped her jaw while stoking her cheek with her thumb. "You did great. Thank you."

Erin sat up straight and covered her face while shaking her head from side to side.

"What is it, honey? You did amazing. You are so helpful," Gwen offered.

"I'm not supposed to tell." Erin cried through her hands. "I'm not supposed to tell. I'm not supposed to tell."

"Hey... hey... listen," Susan reached out and removed Erin's hands from her face. "You didn't tell. You didn't. You're going to be okay."

"But he said he would..." she looked up at Gwen. She threw herself across Gwen's lap and started to cry again.

"No, listen, Erin. We are not going to let anything happen to Miss Gwen. Your Momma. She loves you so much and we are going to protect you both. Okay?"

Erin stayed buried in Gwen's lap.

"Honey, can you look at me?" Susan's voice was kind and soft. "Please?" She waited for Erin to lift her head and lean into

Gwen's side. "You did nothing wrong. Do you believe me?"

Erin's eyebrows clenched debating her sins.

Susan took her tiny hands into her own. "I'm here for you. I'm not going to lie to you. You did nothing wrong, okay? You were very brave. " Susan looked imploringly at her.

Erin nodded and folded herself back into Gwen's arms.

"I'm going to go talk to the policemen for a minute. Can you wait here for me?" Erin nodded again and Susan stood from the couch and walked around behind it.

The calm and gentle voice that spoke to the small child only a moment ago now changed into the hard, protective voice of the social worker. The Momma Bear protecting the young.

"I need you to put an APB on Beau Dekker. Age... approximately around sixteen... to maybe twenty. Height around five foot eleven... I can get more details for you when I get back to my computer." She nodded and sent them on their way. "I need one car out in front of this house until you hear otherwise."

"But we don't..." Charlie attempted.

Susan glared at him with a look that said more than words ever could.

"Yes, Ma'am."

Susan went back over to the couch. "Can I speak with you for a moment?"

Gwen nodded but when she attempted to move, Erin gripped her tighter.

"Erin," Susan's voice was kind but firm. "I need to talk to your Momma, just for a moment. You can see us. We'll be right over here, okay?"

Erin paused, momentarily stricken with fear, but slowly loosened her grip.

"I'll be right back, okay... right back..."

Susan and Gwen moved over beside the kitchen table within eyeshot of the couch.

"The Bogey Man, as she call him, is her brother. It was how she referred to him when we first picked her up. The moment the courthouse opens in the morning, I will be there and we'll get to the bottom of this. I believe I told you that it was her testimony that got her pulled from the home and him sent to Rehabilitation. So... you can imagine why I need to know his whereabouts. In the meantime, an officer is right outside your door. Would you like me to stay with you?"

She was so calm and Gwen couldn't stop shaking in her skin. She couldn't shake the thoughts about this man... this boy looking in the windows of her home. More than once! "I... uh... no... I think we'll be fine..." Gwen spoke barely recognizing her own voice, shaking the way it was.

"Is there anyone you want me to call?"
Nick.
"Uh... no... I... uh... I guess not..."

Max lay on the tall metal table at the vet's office. He thumped his tail in response whenever attention was directed at him, but was otherwise still.

"You say you hit this dog?" The vet asked.

"I think I did. I saw him one minute and the next, he was lying in front of my truck. There was no puddles of blood or anything..." Nick said, as he adjusted his ball cap.

"I don't see anything broken or internal damages, so..." the vet plugged his ears with his stethoscope and probed Max's sides and belly. "I think he's just worn out."

"From...?" Nick looked confused.

"This dog has been travelling. He is malnourished and dehydrated. I think he just stopped and it just so happened to be in front of your truck." The doctor shrugged. "He needs a bath and some ointment for the wounds on his paws, but, honestly, other than that, just some good old TLC should do the trick."

"I can do that, I guess."

"The only other thing I can add is, don't be upset if you wake up and find him gone one morning. This dog was on a mission and unless you were his final destination, it seems like nothing is going to stop him from getting there. He's been through a lot."

"Good to know," Nick reached out to shake the doctor's hand. "I appreciate all your help."

"No problem. Loved your show."

Nick smiled, "Thank you. It was a good time."

"I'll have the nurse set you up with the necessary meds to get him back where he belongs physically. Maybe, you can be his final stop."

"I'll do what I can."

Evelynn opened the front door of Gwen's home to see a state patrolman on the front porch.

"Ma'am." He touched the edge of his wide-brimmed hat in greeting. "May I?" He nodded his head requesting permission to enter.

"Oh, yes, of course," Evelynn blinked realizing she was staring. She stepped back and allowed him entrance.

Gwen came out from her bedroom tying her bathrobe, her hair in one long braid over her shoulder. She stopped by the couch to check on Erin who had refused to sleep in her bedroom for the last two nights.

The officer nodded at Gwen and removed his hat. His dark hair was shaved short on the sides and short on top. His eyes were kind but stern. "Good morning, ladies. I'm sorry to stop by so early..." he paused stepping to the edge of the couch. "My name is Tom LaSalle, I'm a friend of Gillian's"

"Oh! That's why you look so familiar!" Evelynn blurted out from behind him.

Gwen smiled and nodded at the missing puzzle piece of recognition.

Tom blushed slightly and continued addressing Gwen, "I'm not officially on this case, but I wanted to let you know that I'll be adding your address to my route. I'll be driving by periodically to keep an eye on things. I wish I could do more."

Gwen walked across and touched his arm. "Thank you, Tom. It means a lot to me. How did..."

"Small town, ma'am. Word travels fast."

Gwen nodded. "Do you know anything more about the case?"

Tom LaSalle tucked his thumbs into his belt and assumed the official posture for delivering police information. "They believe

385

that the boy, Beau Dekker has been staying in a house just down the street. The back door window had been broken in and we believe we found some of his belongings. It looked like he had been there for some time. He had gotten comfortable."

Gwen and Evelynn looked at each other questioning... "Mrs. Dockery?"

"The ... owner of the home is... deceased."

Gwen gasped and drew her hand to her mouth. She leaned against the arm of the couch for support. "The... boy... did.. um... it?"

Tom looked down to the floor, "We believe so, yes."

Evelynn moved in closer, "So they still haven't found him? This... Beau person?"

"Not as yet. But they haven't stopped looking. So don't think we've given up the search."

"Thank you." Gwen said quietly.

Tom relaxed his stance and looked over at the sleeping child, "Is she doing okay?"

Gwen nodded. "She is really quite resilient. I had no idea this had been going on for so long. She is afraid of him, but... it seems... only when he is around or... when someone talks about him, if that makes any sense. The time in between, she seems," Gwen shrugged, "...normal."

Tom nodded, much softer now, "It's her coping mechanism. At this stage in her life, abuse has been more a part of it than not."

"Do you work with these cases often?"

"Not officially, but Gillian has quite a few tough cases come through her. She wanted me to check in on Erin."

"Please pass along my thanks. She really is doing much better."

Tom nodded.

"The other officers suggested that she should get back into the regular flow of life, do you agree?"

Tom took in a deep breath. "It's whatever you are comfortable with. We are doing everything we can to apprehend the suspect and don't want you to feel you have to stay cooped up in your home."

"See?" Evelynn smiled at her friend. "Don't let this scare you into becoming a recluse! That's just not you. And it certainly isn't *that* child!" Evelynn laughed. "Don't cancel your doctor's appointment. We can go get your cast off today. You'll feel so much better. And, you know she still wants to do the show at the fair. There's going to be tons of people there. What could happen?"

"Famous last words," the newly ever-cautious Gwen rolled her eyes.

"She'll be fine, won't she officer? Her people need her!"

Tom laughed, "You have to do what you are comfortable with. More importantly, what she's comfortable with." He tugged his head toward Erin. "I'm not suggesting taking this lightly, but I know Gwen would go on with regular every day things. I would caution to always be in the company of someone else."

"I'll think about it. It's still four days away. Danni will be there and she can direct my class' performances if need be."

"If you'll excuse me. Again, I apologize for the early hour." Tom nodded, officially.

"No, please, don't apologize. I appreciate your extra time." Gwen shook his hand.

He looked down to Gwen's worn and tattered cast, "I wouldn't waste another minute getting *that* thing off though." He laughed. "They are not fun."

Gwen smiled in return. "No, they are not. Thank you again."

Evelynn escorted Officer LaSalle to the front door and smiled when he turned back to wave.

She locked the door behind him and turned back to Gwen, "He's a handsome man. I hope Gillian snags him." She laughed. Seeing no response, she continued, "He's no Dave, or anything... Officer Tom LaSalle is much too tall, and built and clean cut to complete with my Dave..." she giggled to herself and was pleased to see Gwen give her a sideways glance and a smirk but then it slipped away again.

Evelynn sighed and walked over to her. "Did you call him?"

She nodded. "No answer. Straight to voice mail."

"Honey... I know that..."

Gwen shrugged, "It's okay, Evie. I did it to myself. He's moved on."

"I don't think it's what you are thinking. Dave said he sent the girlfriend home."

"That doesn't mean anything..." Gwen looked at her.

"It means..." Evelynn looked around the room for an answer, "... that she's not in Bakersfield anymore...?"

Gwen went to the fridge and pulled some eggs out and set them on the counter.

"If it makes you feel any better, he isn't returning Dave's texts either."

Gwen turned around and leaned against the counter. "Isn't it obvious? If he talks to Dave then Dave will talk to you and you will talk to me."

Evelynn walked over and placed her hands on Gwen's arms, "Really? You think you are *that* important and *that* loathed that he's not going to talk to his best friend anymore?"

Gwen shrugged and raised her eyebrows, "I must be." She turned away from her friend, "How many eggs do you want?"

"Dude! Where have you been? I've been trying to get a hold of you all week!" Dave was shouting the moment he opened his door. He stepped out of his car and started walking over to the front porch of Nick's house when suddenly he froze in his tracks.

A huge wolf came running from around the corner growling and with his fur standing up. It slowed to a stalking walk but was still headed right for Dave Ripke.

"What the.... Nick!"

Nick came down off the porch and patted the dog on his head.

"Max... Max... it's okay, bud." The dog stopped immediately but kept his eyes on the unexpected visitor.

"Can... can I move? Is that thing going to eat me?"

Nick shrugged. "I don't think so, he just finished off a vacuum salesman and a girl scout. You should be safe."

"Very funny, Nick. I'm laughing on the inside." Dave scowled at his friend. "Seriously, can I move?"

"C'mere, Max. You don't want that one anyway." Max ran back to the front porch and lay down at the top of the steps and thumped happily as Nick awarded him with ear scratches.

Dave approached the house and scrunched his face when he got a closer look at his best friend. "What in the hell happened to you?"

Nick shrugged and went back to sit on the cushioned porch chair.

Dave walked up the front steps and gingerly inched his way past the dog that watched his every move. "I haven't talked to you in days. Your phone is off. You look terrible and... what is that thing?" He nodded back to Max.

"The ex girlfriend wouldn't stop texting and calling and calling and texting me so, I turned off my phone. No one needs to talk to me anyway. I'm retired, remember? I don't answer to anyone anymore."

"So not answering a few pesky texts means not talking to anyone? Not shaving and wearing the same clothes for, what... at least a couple days, judging by the smell?"

Nick turned his palms up and frowned at Dave. "What's it to you, Rip? The camera isn't on. It's just me."

Dave sat down on the chair across from Nick as he continued.

"Just me." Nick looked out to the wide-open pasture beyond a row of manicured trees. His mother's flowers and plants taunted him everywhere he turned. "I bought out my brothers' share of the house thinking that it would be the right place for me to settle down. But now... it just feels, hell, I don't know. They are everywhere. I keep waiting for them to walk back in the front door again. I feel guilty warming up food in my mother's kitchen." He pushed his fingers into his eyes attempting to force the tears back inside. "I don't know what I'm doing anymore. Maybe this was all just a mistake." Nick leaned back in his chair momentarily and flopped his hands on his knees before leaning forward resting his face in his hands again. "I love her, Rip. I just can't do this anymore."

"Whoa, before you go all Grizzly Adams on me or go running back to

Hollywood, let me tell you what you've missed out on…"

"I don't care. Save your breath. The one I don't want won't leave me alone. The one I do want can't stand the sight of me. I have this big empty house filled with memories of my parents…" Nick rubbed his face with his hands. "How did I go from having it all to having nothing?"

"Dude, will you just listen?"

He threw his palms out in front of him, exhausted with everything. "What, Dave… what."

Chapter Twenty

"Okay, everyone, eyes on me," Evelynn shouted over the cacophony of children's and parents voices. She raised her hand over the crowd signaling the need for silence. All the other teachers raised their hands and it soon spread to the parents and finally the children until one voice remained chatting away. Erin.

The entire group looked at the one voice until she finally realized she was the only one talking. Gwen rolled her eyes, "Why does it have to be my child?" The parents around her laughed. Erin shrugged her shoulders and laughed sheepishly, "What?"

Evelynn continued, "Okay everyone, thank you. I am so excited that you all took time out of your busy Saturday to perform for the fair today! Thank you for that! It's almost time for the first group to go on stage, so we need to get in our class groups please. Miss Danni's class, you're up first, so I need you all over here by the stage steps. Miss

Gwen's class, over there. Miss Gillian's class over here, Miss Jenni's class over there and all the drama kids come over here with me. You guys are going to be great! I'm already so proud of you! Just smile and have a good time. And please, please, please wait for your parent after your performance is over and don't just go running off!" Evelynn smiled at the mass of faces. She loved her job.

"Oh, oh, and one more thing. Parents, if you take pictures- and I know you will- please share them with our Facebook page or with the teachers so we can put them on the website! Thank you! Okay, everyone- places!!"

The group scattered while the teachers had their hands in the air trying to corral their students.

Danni Carrigan ushered her tiny dancers onto the stage.

Evelynn leaned over to Gwen, "You doin' okay?"

Gwen nodded. "I'm glad to be busy. It quiets the brain."

Evelynn nodded in understanding. "How's the foot?"

"A little tender, but much better without that heavy cast on!!"

"Aunt Evie..." Erin hugged her waist, "I got make-up on."

Evelynn bent down and kissed her nose. "I see. You look beautiful. Don't forget to smile pretty. That's what makes you really beautiful."

Erin giggled under the praise.

Nick pulled his truck up into a surprisingly close parking space on the field next to the fair. The rides were already humming along and human traffic was everywhere.

He checked his face in the mirror. He adjusted his hat... then took it off and fixed his hair... then put the hat back on... then took it off. He looked over his shoulder into the back seat where Max was watching the primping. "What do you think, Max? Hat or no hat?"

The dog just blinked at him.

"This is serious, Max. I want to look just right. Hat or no hat?"

Max nodded his head and wagged his tail.

"Right, me too. I should be comfortable..." The hat went back on. "Okay, boy, I won't be long. Can you wait here for me? I'll be right back. You've got all the windows down... here, "He got out of the truck and opened the back door. Max was ready to be let out until Nick held up his hand for Max to 'wait'. He poured a bottle of water into a bowl on the floor of the back seat. "Don't spill this. And don't eat anybody. I'm going to find Gwen and... and... hell, I don't know.... live happily ever after..." He laughed and closed the door. He took a few steps forward then backed up, threw the hat in the car and walked off again.

The drama kids were on stage offering up a selection of skits and songs they had practiced in the drama camps. Kids were everywhere; some getting ready to go on, some waiting for parents and some just watching the show.

Gwen and Evelynn half watched the performances and half watched the children relying a great deal on parental assistance. The more eyes the better. Evelynn both loved and hated "on location" performances. It was great press for the Centre but the logistics could be a nightmare.

Gwen turned to look at Evelynn's face as a smile crossed her lips. It was a different smile. Not a proud-of –these-kids smile, but something else. Gwen followed her stare and laughed to herself. Of course... Dave was on the other corner of the stage filming her kids as if they were his own. Gwen's heart swelled. Dave crossed in front of the stage with his camera on his shoulder. He paused in the center and made his way over to the left side where they were standing. Without missing a beat, or a shot, he turned away from the action, kissed his fiancé and was back to business. Evelynn blushed but could not stop smiling. Gwen couldn't either.

The audience applause brought Gwen back to focus. The teenagers were exiting the stage and the tech crew was rearranging for the next set of dancers.

"Hey, Miss Gillian, is Shurita going to be here today? I left my cell phone at home," Danni asked, breathless from her last performance.

"I'm sorry, no honey. She's babysitting for the Browns today. But I can have her call you tonight, if you'd like."

"It's okay. I'm good. I'll text her when I get back home."

"Hey, how's your mom?"

"She's fine. She's over at the Library Booth, I think." Danni looked past Gillian, "Hey, Aaron, wait up!"

Gillian smiled at her student. "Tell her I said 'hi'."

Gwen moved over by Gillian. "They grow up fast, don't they?" she asked.

Gillian nodded. "You'd think after all my foster kids and all these amazing students we are blessed with that I would get used to it. Them growing up and moving on... but, I don't."

"It's my favorite when they come back and visit." Gwen smiled in reverie.

Gillian joined in her thoughts, "It is. It lets you know that you've really touched their lives and that makes it all worthwhile."

Gwen breathed in deep and smiled.

"You'll see," Gillian continued. "Now that you have one of your own, your entire perspective changes even more."

"You got that right. Oh, and I never got to thank you for sending Tom over. It was such a comfort. I really do appreciate it."

Gillian touched her arm. "Of course. I have known fear... believe me..."

Gwen nodded. "Speaking of which..." Gwen's eyes scanned the crowd in front of the stage. She looked to her left documenting every little face. She looked to her right zeroing in on every small blonde-headed child. "Do you see Erin?"

Gillian stood a little straighter and examined the faces of the crowd. She glanced back at Gwen and furrowed her brow.

Pricks of fear and heat slid up Gwen's neck. *Don't panic... she's an eight year old child... at a fair... in a sea of children. I'm sure she's close by...*

Gwen causally, but with purpose walked closer to the edge of the stage so she could have a better look at the audience. *Erin loves to watch the other Centre performers, she must be here... She knows not to run off...*

401

Gwen swallowed hard as she looked back at Gillian. Gillian shook her head and raised her shoulders.

"Evie," Gwen's breath quickened. "I don't see Erin."

"Relax, honey. She was over with Tereza helping her pack her bag after she came off stage. She's probably still there."

Gwen took in a deep breath and blew it out. "Oh... this is so hard." Gwen looked up and felt silly for worrying. "I'm going to go check on her." Gwen shook her head. She made her way toward the side steps of the stage through kids and musicians making their way to the platform. She looked up and noticed dark clouds forming overhead and hoped all the mini shows would be able to get through before it decided to rain.

She walked past the steps to the flimsy partition that hid the dancers from the audience and saw Tereza, Emily and Shelbi sitting around their dance bags. "Hey girls, is Erin back here with you?" Gwen asked.

The girls looked around each other as if the answer was obvious.

"She was," Tereza said, "but not now."

Shelbi looked up with her big eyes and spoke with her quiet, shy voice, "I think she went back that way." She added a shrug just in case her information was wrong.

"Thank you," Gwen said smiling trying not to panic again. "Be sure you get all of your belongings."

A chorus of "okays" and "we wills" followed her as she ventured around toward the back of the stage.

The stage was just a raised concrete platform with stairs on either side. Only during fairs or concerts do they hang the black canvas drape along the back creating a wall.

Gwen walked along the edge of the stage peeking under the curtain for little feet or ... anything out of place. She saw the usual cords and instruments waiting to be utilized. She looked to her left and saw nothing but the woods. She dismissed that option, because Erin would never go there. She reached the other side of the stage and looked at the crowds of people. *Erin... please, please be here.* Every child with glasses. Every child with curls. Every child. She must be here...

Gwen breath stopped short. The woods... She wouldn't go in there but....

Gwen walked back along the edge of the woods and looked into the shadows for anything... anything at all. "Erin!" she called out. "Erin, can you hear me?"

She ran back to the side of the stage to Evelynn and Gillian. "She's gone. I'm not just panicking... I can't find her. There's woods..." Gwen was just short of hyperventilating.

Evelynn took charge, "Gwen, come and sit down... for just a second."

"I can't! Evie, I can't!! I've been a mother for twelve minutes and I've lost my child!"

Gillian took her hand and encouraged her to sit on the stage steps. "Okay, okay... let's figure this out. We're at a fair. Let's not think the worst."

"Shouldn't we start with the worst and work back from there? He took her! I know he did!"

The ladies all felt the shiver go through them, praying that it wasn't the case.

"It's been a whole week, honey. The police haven't seen or heard anything of him.

I'm sure they scared him off." Gillian commented.

"Now, we know your child is the one who doesn't listen," Evelynn attempted humor. "I'd be willing to bet she has followed the music to another stage. You know how she loves music."

"And lights! All the rides are probably pretty enticing to her." Gillian added.

Gwen tried to imagine the scenarios and they did seem quite logical, but her gut was telling her otherwise.

"Okay, so let's do this," Gillian crouched down beside Gwen and had her hand on her knee, "Jenni and I will stay here and wait for the other kids to get picked up. Why don't you go to the security tent and we can get some more eyes out there. And I'll text Tom and give him a heads up to let us know if he hears anything, okay?"

Gwen nodded. Her breath was short and she was anxious to get moving, but her friends were trying to get her to relax. *Won't happen... I need to go...*

Just then, Miss Jenni, one of the ballet teachers of the preschoolers came up holding a little girl's hand.

"Hey, Miss Gwen, I think you should hear this," Jenni said nudging Sharon forward.

"What is it, honey? Are you alright?" Gwen spoke calmly to the child who was one of her own students.

Sharon brought her light brown fingers to her mouth. Her hair was pulled up into a tight ball of brown curls on top of her head. She looked at her ballet teacher and looked away.

"Honey, you're not in trouble. What do you need to tell me?" Gwen tried to keep the panic from her voice.

Jenni helped get things started. "Sharon told me that Erin left with her brother."

The three woman collectively gasped and reached out for one another.

"Tell me, sweetie. Tell me what you saw."

Sharon twisted her body back and forth and Gwen took in a deep breath. "Sharon, Erin may be hurt..."

"But he said he was her brother, she finally spoke around the fingers in her mouth.

Evelynn tried. "Tell us what you saw, honey. Where was he?" Gwen was slapping her hands against her knees willing the child to speak faster.

She pointed to the opposite corner of the stage.

"Did he say anything?"

Sharon nodded. "He said that he was going to surprise Erin. It's a secret."

Jenni interrupted. "He picked her up and took her off."

"Oh my sweet Jesus," Gillian uttered under her breath.

"Where? Which way?" Gwen stood.

Sharon pointed along the wooded edge of the fairgrounds.

Gwen didn't wait to hear the rest, she took off in a dead run in that direction.

Max lay in the back seat of Nick's truck trying to behave. He would lift his nose up and take in the smells that wafted along on the breeze. He could smell the various food truck offerings as well as the human scents.

Every once in a while an interesting sound or smell would prompt him to stand up and stick his head out of the window for further investigation, but would eventually amount to nothing important. He crouched down on his front paws to reach the water bowl and lapped at it a few times, more out of boredom than actual thirst. He turned around, and around and around before flopping back down on the seat. He yawned and rested his big head on his front paws... slowly tuning out the sounds and the smells for some much needed sleep. It's been at least seven minutes since his last nap.

Max heard something and opened his eyes, trying to decide if it was worth lifting his head for... maybe just a quick peek. He sat up and checked out the scene from the front window, once again disappointed. He took in a deep breath, filling his nostrils with the smell of hot dogs and funnel cakes and let out a long, verbal groan.

As he was just getting ready to slip into that deep sleep he heard the tiniest voice. Her voice.

He perked his ears up and lifted his head waiting for his eyes to focus. He scanned the horizon out of the front window of the truck. He saw nothing, but wasn't satisfied.

He stood up listening to every little sound. He stuck his head out the window sniffing the air for confirmation. And there it was. He didn't hesitate. Didn't think. Max jumped from the window of the back seat of the truck. She's here. He had to find her.

Chapter Twenty- One

Nick casually walked the fair grounds nodding at people who waved or caught his eye. Sometimes a random person would ask for his autograph or just want to come up and shake his hand, but it seemed like the little town was getting used to having a celebrity in their midst, and they were okay with that.

He stopped to grab a Pepsi from a vendor and continued his search for Gwen amongst the mass of people.

There were rides of every shape and size, jutting up from the landscape. The sun would shine off the glittery metals and blinking lights beckoning the next group of riders.

Music filled his senses. He could hear bands and singers trying their hand at karaoke. And of course the canned carnival music that you'd expect to hear accompanied the rides and game booths.

Nick saw Gwen hurriedly rushing in his direction. "Gwen!"

She looked at him and ran straight to him. She bumped into him so hard that his drink flew from his hands, but he didn't even care. He wrapped his arms around her and kissed the top of her head. "Oh Gwen, I'm so sorry I wasn't there for you. I missed you so much."

Gwen pulled away from the grip she had on him and Nick saw that her face was draped in sheer panic. The dust and make-up along with her tears made streaks down her otherwise beautiful face.

"Gwen, what... what's happened?"

She looked at him and hugged him again. She buried her face into his neck and held him like he would disappear any moment.

"I'm here. I'm here. I've got you. Why are you crying?"

She pulled back from his embrace again. "It's Erin! He took her! He.... He... "

Just then, screams were heard at the other side of the fairgrounds.

Nick looked down at Gwen and they both thought the same thing. He grabbed her hand, "Come on!"

They both ran toward the noise as people started pushing against them trying to run in the opposite direction.

Screams continued. Nick blocked Gwen from being hit by people as he forced panicked guests to let him through.

Like a flock of frightened birds, the swarm of people suddenly changed direction.

Nick tried to look over the crowd confused. His eyes widened when he saw the cause of the panic.

Max had run into the crowd of people and was sniffing the ground. He didn't pay attention to any of the people screaming and running away from him. He did sidestep a man who tried to reach out and grab his fragile yarn collar that hung next to his new leather one.

It had just started to rain, which only made the crowd scatter more.

"Max!" Nick yelled at the very intense, very scary, wolf-looking dog. His voice was lost in the crowd. Nick pushed to get closer before he bolted off again. "Max!"

413

The dog responded and made eye contact with Nick but sniffed the ground once more and took off past them, in the direction that Nick and Gwen had just come.

Gwen looked up at Nick blinking at the raindrops hitting her face, "Max?"

Nick was obviously frazzled but took a moment to answer her. "Yeah, uh, long story short," Nick, still holding her hand, turned back to follow the dog. "He showed up and literally passed out in front of my truck from exhaustion and hunger, apparently and ... yeah... so he's kinda with me."

"Max. How do you know his name is Max?"

Nick was trying to be patient when he really wanted to take off in a run to leash the dog that was causing all kinds of havoc. "He had a homemade name tag that said Max."

"Erin!" Gwen gasped. She stopped. She tugged Nick's arm causing him to stop and looked up at him. "Erin's Max! It's Erin's Max!!"

Nick slapped his forehead with the palm of his hand. "I didn't even think of that!"

414

"It's *her* Max!! He knows where she is!! We have to follow him!!"

They both took off running, following the parted masses of screaming fair-goers, more than the dog. He was silent but was easy to trail if they just kept in close range of the aftermath.

The rain was coming down harder and making the dirt paths muddy and slippery.

They came to the edge of the fair and looked out over a field of neatly lined parked cars. They stopped breathless wondering which way to go. They looked back at the crowd of people for clues and a clump of boys pointed them in the direction of a row of vehicles. They started walking slowly down the aisle.

"I don't see anything." Gwen shouted over the sound of rain hitting the cars.

I don't either." Nick leaned over and put his hands on his knees fighting for air. He stood back up and stepped up on the running board of a nearby truck to get a better view. "I... I don't know."

"She's got to be here somewhere. Erin!" Gwen called out.

415

"Max! Where are ya, boy?" Nick added a whistle. "Erin!"

Gwen started to cry. "She's here, Nick... I just know it. That dog..."

And before she could finish her sentence, they heard Max bark.

"C'mon!" Nick took off toward the sound. He paused long enough to let Gwen catch up and then grabbed her hand before taking off again.

They walked quickly searching for signs of Max and Erin. Nick and Gwen were drenched from the rain. Nick wiped his face trying to see in front of him.

They heard Max bark once again and heard a loud cry following. Nick turned sharply to his right to locate the origin of the sounds.

A car door slammed and Nick looked over to see Max trying to jump into the window. Now Max was barking wildly. He was up on his hind legs bouncing outside the window and barking at whoever was inside.

Nick and Gwen cautiously crept up to the car but couldn't see who was inside, just that Max was determined to get at them.

"Erin! Erin are you in there?"

No response.

"Erin," Nick tried. "Are you alright?"

Just then a voice from the car shouted back. "Go away! She's mine."

Nick and Gwen looked at each other and came closer to the car.

"Listen, son, I need you to come out of the car. I need to know that Erin is okay." Nick spoke sternly.

"She's fine. And she's staying with me. I am her family."

Gwen tried to push past Nick to get to the car but Nick held her back. "Wait... just wait a second, we don't want him to hurt her. Max isn't going to let him get anywhere." Gwen nodded, terrified.

There was movement in the car, but Nick and Gwen held their ground. Max moved to the front window. He barked and tried to bite his way through it.

They heard the clicking of the motor trying to turn over.

"He's trying to jumpstart the car," Nick said.

"Beau!" Gwen called out. "Please! Please let me have Erin back. I love her! I can take care of her."

417

"You don't love her!" Came the voice from the car. "You don't even know her!"

"Beau, please!" Gwen cried.

"She loves ME! She's the only one on this whole planet that loves me. You can't have her." His Southern drawl dripped from every word.

"That's not love, Beau." Gwen walked closer to the car, pleading with the boy. "Beau, she's afraid of you. That is not love."

"You don't know what you're talking about!"

"Beau," Nick called out. The police are on their way. Let us have Erin and we'll tell the police that you worked with us."

The car was silent, but they could see movement. The thunder clapped loudly overhead.

Just then the passenger side door opened and Beau took off running down the row of cars. In a flash, Max was around the car and chasing after him.

Nick looked in the car and saw a small still body pressed against the opposite door. "Gwen!" Nick called over his shoulder, "She's here!" Then he quickly followed after the dog.

Gwen ran to open the door and crawled inside. "Erin? Erin? Sweetie, are you okay?"

Erin uncurled herself to look back at the familiar voice. "Momma?"

"Yes," Gwen burst into tears and scooted in closer. "Yes, baby, it's me" She pulled Erin onto her lap and kissed her face and head.

"I lost my glasses..." Erin looked up at her mother.

"It's okay..." Gwen covered her in kisses again. "Are you alright? Are you hurt?"

Erin shook her head and allowed Gwen to push her wet hair back from her face. "Nick! I've got Erin! She's okay!"

Max caught up with Beau and grabbed a hold of his pant legs causing him to trip and fall forward. He kicked and screamed at the dog, but Max had no intention of letting go.

Nick picked the boy up from the ground and punched him in the face. Max stepped back waiting for instructions.

Beau stumbled back a few steps. "Is that all you got?" The boy spit his words out like venom. His mouth was bloody, but he

419

stayed standing. "Go ahead, hit me again. Everyone else has. You think you can do any worse?"

Beau pulled out a knife from his waistband and waved it at Nick, who paused. Beau shook his head to remove the drops of water impairing his vision and hanging from his hair.

Nick wiped his face with the inside of his elbow which didn't do much.

Max was crouched low, his shoulders bobbing back and forth waiting for permission to pounce.

Nick was so filled with rage and knew that if he laid hands on the boy he was afraid of what he might be capable of.

"You think you're so much better than me? Who decided that you get to come in and break up my family? They's all I got!"

Nick's heart softened, "Son, come on, let's get you out of this rain. It's over."

Beau laughed in a twisted way, "It ain't over. You got what's mine. I been lookin' for her. An I ain't afraid of you." Beau spit blood to the ground and lunged at Nick.

Nick clenched his jaw and grabbed at his arm that held the knife. His arm slid off

Nick's wrist knocking it away before making contact. Beau quickly brought the knife back around and attempted to slice upward.

Max jumped between them just as the knife made contact. The dog yelped but as he landed on his feet, he turned on Beau biting his leg just above the knee.

Beau cried out as he fell forward. Nick kicked the knife from his hand. It flew a few feet and landed in a muddy puddle.

"You will never touch my little girl again." Nick pulled back and hit him across his jaw. He fell back to the muddy earth and lay still. Nick's chest heaved as he looked at the boy laying with his legs under his body. The rain slowed. The thunder rolled off in a distance letting the earth know that the storm was over.

Nick picked up Beau off the ground and drug him to the back of an empty truck next to the vandalized car that held the women he loved.

He took in a deep breath and wiped the rain from his face and stuck his head in the car. "Hey beautiful. You okay?"

Erin nodded. "I'm glad you came for me."

"Of course, I told you I would protect you."

Nick was so overwhelmed with emotion that he was either going to smother the two girls with affection or beat the unconscious assailant to death. "Your Momma's got you sweet girl. No one is going to ever hurt you again."

And just then, Max decided that his prey was close enough to dead that he could climb into the seat with everyone else. He pushed his way under Nick's arms to reach Erin. So, both Max and Nick were half in and half out of the car.

"Oh! Max!" Erin squealed, "You found me! Oh, I just knew you would. I've missed you so much!"

"He's bleeding," Gwen noticed.

Nick nodded, "He saved my life too. That's one amazing dog you've got there, sweetie."

"Thanks, Max," Gwen whispered to the dog. Her eyes filled with tears as she looked up to Nick. No words could possible express her gratitude to this man. He looked down at her and ran his hands over her wet, slicked back hair. No words were necessary.

The police eventually came and gathered everyone's statements and put Beau Dekker in handcuffs. They stuffed him in the backseat of one of the police vehicles and walked over to talk to Nick.

"Would you mind coming down to the station to answer a few more questions, Mr. Penn? Just a formality."

Nick stood with one arm around Gwen as she held Erin's hand. The other hand was being bandaged by an EMT. Nick flinched at the prodding and wrapping.

Max was at his feet getting the same EMT treatment; bandage wrapping around the armpit of his front leg.

"Right. Of course. No problem." Nick said but not wanting to leave Gwen's side.

"And Ma'am" the officer continued directing his comment toward Gwen. "Officer Guthry is going to take you and the child to the hospital to make sure everything is okay. She has to wait for DFS to arrive before she can complete her questions."

Gwen nodded but looked at Nick wishing he were coming too.

Gwen stood a moment longer clinging to Nick's hand lost in prayer. *Lord, I am so sorry for thinking my ways are better than yours. You were trying so hard to speak to me, but I was so hyper-focused, that I didn't... couldn't hear you. Thank you, God for being a God of second chances and forgiveness. I can promise that I won't let it happen again, but You know me, Lord... I am grateful to know that You will forgive me again and again. I love these to people... so very much. Thank you, Lord... thank you...*

Tears filled Gwen's eyes as she looked up into Nick's eyes. He questioned her expression with his eyes, but before she could speak, the officer's began to separate them.

The officer held open the door to his patrol car and indicated that Erin should climb in the back. Erin slid in the back seat and Max jumped right in before the officer could shut the door.

Officer Guthry bent down to attempt to remove the dog, but at Max's low deep guttural warning, she thought better of it. She closed the door and opened the passenger side door for Gwen.

"If you could come this way, Mr. Penn..." The other officer needed Nick to move to the car in the opposite direction.

As Nick and Gwen were being pulled apart, they lingered until the last touch of each other's fingertips slipped away. Their eyes stayed on one another until they slipped into their escort's cars.

Gwen sat in a cushioned chair and kept her eye on the curtained room that held a girl and her dog. She couldn't help but smile and shake her head every time a new nurse or orderly would open the curtain and was greeted by Max, who refused to leave Erin's side.

She could only half listen to the officer asking her the same questions for the third time. Susan Carter was sitting in the chair behind her. When Gwen could sense the fourth round of the same questions posed in a different way was about to begin, she interrupted the officer and looked back at Susan Carter.

"I don't understand. He kept saying that he loved her. The officer at the fairgrounds said that he had escalated his behavior with other victims. So why? Why go backwards? Was he going to do those same things to her? How could he think that is love?" She didn't wait for an answer before turning back to watch the curtain "protecting" her child.

Susan raised her hand to the interrogating officer signaling a pause in the interview and thought about her response to Gwen's question. "Sometimes," she cleared her throat, "abusers return to prior victims because..." she paused taking in a breath, "they... are familiar. He knew exactly how she would respond, and that gives him a sense of power. He knows that she doesn't realize that she can fight back. She doesn't fight, means... she doesn't object." Gwen's stomach turned over.

"She is... special to him," Susan continued gently to offer some understanding, "in his mind... To him, she is not a victim. Perhaps, that's why he does what he does, because it gives him the feeling that he equates with love. Maybe that's all the love he has ever known."

Gwen's lip curled in disgust.

"But the child was also the reason Beau Dekker was caught and punished, so he could have easily been after vengeance," the officer added.

Gwen frowned but shook her head non-committedly, "No, he wasn't after vengeance." But then a thought came to her and she again turned to the authorities. "Where is he now? If he came after her once, he can do it again."

"We have him in custody, ma'am."

"But what happens next?" Gwen had a shadow of fear cross her face.

Susan rested her hand on Gwen's knee, "He is still a minor, but his charges will be more severe this time." Susan decided to change the subject, "Let's have someone take a look at your leg. I'm sure the doctor wasn't expecting you to run a marathon when he cut you out of that cast." Susan smiled at her.

"But..."

"He's not getting out from behind those bars any time soon," Susan reassured her. A smile spread across Susan's face, "

427

Besides, you have more important things to deal with." She nodded toward the corridor.

"Nick!"

Nick walked toward the nurse's station and was about to ask about Erin when Gwen ran up to him and threw her arms around his neck. "Thank you, Nick. Thank you," she whispered into his neck.

He wrapped his arms around her and they felt so perfect to her. She looked into his eyes and reached up to kiss his lips. "Oh Nick, I'm so..." He responded to her kiss then began to smother her face with kisses.

"...happy to" Kisses... "...see you." Kisses...

"I'm so sorry. I've been so stupid." She sputtered between kisses.

He held both sides of her face gently and looked at her. He shook his head, "Shhhh"

"But I..."

He silenced her with a deep, passionate kiss that she could feel all the way to her core. Her stomach flip-flopped and when the fear tried to bubble up inside her, she held on to him tighter.

She pulled back to smile at him, vowing right then and there to give him her heart, all of it. She loved this man. She knew it. And she wasn't going to waste another moment.

She pulled back and looked at his face. Her hand lifted off his ball cap. Her words couldn't come out, so she just looked into his eyes. Those eyes that she wanted to see every morning for the rest of her life.

"I... I love you, Nick. I know that I love you with every fiber of my being."

He smiled down at her and resisted the urge to kiss her for just a moment more. "It's because I'm amazing. I tried to tell you." He winked at her and leaned in to kiss her.

"Where's the child?" he asked.

Before Gwen could answer, she heard someone walk up to the desk behind her.

"What room does this go to?" they heard an orderly say at the desk.

"Exam room five," one of the nurses responded and then giggled.

Gwen made eye-contact and smiled at the nurse but did not betray her.

She held her finger up in front of Nick, mouthing, "One sec, watch this."

She turned around still wrapped in Nick's arm pressing her back into his chest. Gwen winked at the nurse who covered her mouth with another laugh.

The orderly took the cart over to exam room five and threw back the curtain. There, Max was waiting to be the judge and jury of who could approach the bed.

The young man screeched like a teenaged boy and tripped over the cart attempting to get as much distance between him and that wolf.

The entire nursing station exploded with laughter.

Nick shook his head. "That's just wrong." But couldn't help a chuckle of his own. Even Erin was giggling at the young man trying to regain his composure and right the toppled cart.

"There's my brave girl," Nick walked over to the bed Erin was laying in.

"Mr. Nick!" She climbed up on the bed and launched herself at Nick's body. He caught her with ease as she wrapped her arms and legs around his neck and torso like a sloth. Nick hugged her tight, thankful that she was safe.

"Uuughh!! You're squishing me!" Erin squeezed out the words.

Nick laughed and pulled Gwen into the hug and buried his face between the two. "My girls..." Max stood up and nudged against Nick's leg, not to be left out.

Nick glanced down at the furry beast whose head came up to his hand, "I'm sorry, buddy.... *OUR* girls..."

The End

Epilogue

The theatre was dark and the audience was still, completely drawn in to Act Three of Lerner and Loewe's *Camelot* that played out on the Bakersfield Fine Art Centre's stage.

Judy sat third row center with a tissue clutched in her hand at the ready. Erin, who was leaning against her, had fallen asleep shortly after the jousting scene, leaving her glasses askew on her face. She was dressed in her prettiest blue dress and was even allowed to wear lipstick, but the dramatic scenes were not enough to hold her attention.

The scene was in the castle. The ladies in waiting had just been dismissed, leaving the Queen, Guinevere and the King's most trusted Knight of the Round Table ,Lancelot alone.

Nick as Lancelot was crooning to his Lady Guinevere, "*If ever I would leave you... how could it be in springtime....*" Their

433

forbidden love served as the climactic scenes in the dramatic musical.

Judy's eyes darted back and forth as if this were the first time she had seen the story. She felt the agony of betrayal along with King Arthur played surprisingly well by their local Roy Rosenberger.

"Mordred, go back and tell my people that I shall be out hunting all the night and won't return until mid-morning," Roy shouted from center stage as Arthur.

But when her child, her own Guinevere sung to Nick as Lancelot, the tears poured from her eyes and her tissue was not wasted.

"The silence, at last was broken, we flung wide our prison doors..."

Judy did not have a dry eye for the remainder of the production.

From the moment they confessed their love to one another until the final moments where King Arthur sang the memories of a splendid and magical *Camelot*, Judy was enthralled.

At long last, Judy saw her daughter portray the character she was named after.

On stage and off, Gwen and Nick would be a starring couple for their many, many years ahead.

Acknowledgements

Barbara Bourgeret. My mother, my biggest supporter. She keeps me chugging along always making sure I'm working on my next book! I love you, my Momma...

Steve Frank, my photographer. I took Steve out of his comfort zone and he took it on like a champ! The photo found in this book hardly does his work credit. He has become widely known for his bright colors and scenic photography that "pops". He has a brilliant eye and loves to play with light sources. He is best known for his scene-scapes, flora and fauna, but I made him point the camera at a human. They are completely different from my other photo shoots, and I love how they turned out! He is truly a great talent!

Patricia Lambert- Lead Editor. We made it through another one! Thank you, as always for your time and patience and helping to make me not look too much like an idiot!

The Department of Family Services of Arkansas. I am not permitted to mention names, but there were a few key people who helped me with some tricky subject matter and to those people, I am deeply grateful. I can't imagine the strength you must have to do your jobs and fight for these children every single day.

My very own Man in Blue, Don Muschany. Our friendship goes back almost twenty years and we have been Facebook friends for many years, so when I needed an insider view of the role of the police force, he was my go-to. And of course, he didn't disappoint! Thank you for allowing me to interrupt your sleep (he was working nights at the time) with questions and for your patience in explaining details.

Katherynn Bourgeret- Caldwell. My daughter. You always find time to entertain my quirky questions and it makes my heart sing when we can hash out scenes together. I love you more and more every day.

And I am so very grateful to God for allowing me to continue to produce books. It was a tough year and I was worried that I wasn't meant to write any more. He showed me that not only am I meant to write, but I am meant to flourish with it. So, I keep moving forward and hopefully am listening when He guides my hand, because He is the Master Story-teller.

About the Author

Elizabeth Bourgeret is the creator of the Leading With Love movement, a teen workshop and several works of fiction.

A beach girl at heart, she is constantly trying to out run cold weather as she is happily living out her dream of traveling and writing- stopping in the state of choice to discover all that it has to offer.

She loves teaching workshops, working with kids, helping other authors reach their dreams and creating new stories with vibrant characters that will touch your heart.

She still believes that love conquers all and is on the mission to give away as much as possible as she moves about and interacts with others.

When she's not behind the computer or in front of an audience, you can usually find her out of doors, near the ocean or some form of water, or embracing her full-on inner tourist-nerd; visiting any and all tourist traps that catch her attention. A "forever student", she is always seeking and learning from each and every adventure put in front of her.

Connect with her on Facebook, (www.facebook.com/EBourgeret)

or on Instagram (@ebourgeret)

www.elizabethbourgeret.com

www.ingramcontent.com/pod-product-compliance
Lightning Source LLC
Chambersburg PA
CBHW022239020726
47496CB00004B/979